Mallory Goes to Therapy

Chasing a Cure in His Own Way

Book 2 of the Kevin Mallory Series

Thomas Keech

Real
Nice Books
Baltimore, Maryland

Copyright © 2023 Thomas W. Keech
All rights reserved.

No part of this publication may be reproduced, stored in, or introduced into a retrieval system, or transmitted, in any form or by any means (electronic, mechanical, photocopying, recording, or otherwise), without the proper written permission of the copyright owner, except that a reviewer may quote brief passages in a review.

ISBN 979-8-9856670-6-6 Hardback
ISBN 979-8-9856670-7-3 Paperback
ISBN 979-8-9856670-8-0 Ebook
ISBN 979-8-9856670-9-7 Audiobook

Library of Congress Control Number
2023932474

Published by

Real
Nice Books
11 Dutton Court, Suite 606
Baltimore, Maryland 21228
www.realnicebooks.com

Publisher's note: This is a work of fiction. Names, characters, places, institutions, and incidents are entirely the product of the author's imagination or are used fictitiously, and any resemblance to actual persons, living or dead, or to events, incidents, institutions, or places is entirely coincidental.

Cover photo by Shutterstock.
Set in Minion Pro.

For Brenda

Also by Thomas Keech:

The Crawlspace Conspiracy
Prey for Love
Hot Box in the Pizza District
Doc Doc Zeus: A Novel of White Coat Crime
Stacey in the Hands of an Angry God
A New God in Town
Mallory's Manly Methods

Chapter 1: The New Deal

Kevin Mallory was employed as a Customer Service Representative at the UniCast Cable Company. He was supposed to answer cable customers' calls about glitches in their reception, walk them through some simple steps to see if they could get their systems going again and, if all else failed, order a technician to drive to the home to try to fix the problem. But Mallory had decided long ago that that was too boring and simplistic a task for a man of his caliber. For over a year, he had ignored, misled, insulted, and cut off customers according to whatever mood struck him. Mallory never gave his real name to his customers on the phone, and UniCast Cable kept no track of customer complaints anyway. Mallory spent much of the time thus freed up gorging on cinnamon buns from the Dough and Go or devising ways to get even with his co-worker, Nell.

Mallory had no formal training in representing employees against management, but he had gained a lot of personnel experience from having been fired from eight jobs in the last fifteen years. In the last six months, a series of interim managers at UniCast, intimidated by his threats of lawsuits and his reputation for having derailed the career of his previous boss, had pretty much let him do whatever he wanted. People in the building were getting used to him cruising the corridors between the cubicles, wearing his worn suit and clip-on bow tie, bragging to anyone who asked that he was on his way to represent a fellow employee who was in trouble. His duties as an unofficial employee representative allowed him to ignore his customers' calls, to roam UniCast's building at will, and to visit the break room whenever he felt that all this exertion was leaving him short of breath.

He was now annoyed that his two current clients were both located all the way on the other side of the building. The week before, he had received an email from Adele, another Customer

Service Representative like himself, complaining that the company was getting ready to fire her. He didn't know any of the details of her case, but he had heard that she was old and ugly, and so he had been putting off making the long trip. He also heard a rumor that Charles "Chub" Pierce was being fired for missing fourteen days of work in a row without calling in. He decided he'd take on Chub's case first. As he finally worked his way slowly down three corridors and past twenty-six other cubicles to Chub's, he knew this case would be tougher than usual – not because of the fourteen days Chub had missed, but because of Harrison.

Harrison was the new permanent manager. Mallory had heard that Harrison was questioning his role as employee representative, though he had not yet gone so far as to suggest that Mallory do any work. As Mallory trundled his bulbous stomach past cubicle after cubicle, he pondered the path of his career. Even though he had graduated from Community Technical College twelve years before, he had never progressed past an entry level job in any field. For the past year, he had stayed on at this particular entry level job and held out against UniCast's Cable's many efforts to fire him because he enjoyed the fights – but even more because he'd been in love. But he wasn't in love anymore, and he was now feeling unappreciated even in his new occupation of harassing management.

He reached Chub's cubicle and stood in the doorway while absentmindedly rubbing his belly against the edge of the partition. Chub caught sight of him in his peripheral vision and jumped. Chub's nickname was accurate, but his excess weight was distributed more evenly and softly than Mallory's. A broad shaft of his blonde hair was combed over to cover his advancing baldness. Mallory had recently been cutting his own hair himself. Between his suits and his cleaning bills and his cognac bills and the lease payments on his Escalade, he had maxed out two credit cards and was rapidly using up a third. There was no way he could pay for regular haircuts.

"You're in big trouble," Mallory began. "Harrison told me he's having Ms. Marcie prepare the paperwork to fire you." Mallory hadn't talked to either Harrison or Ms. Marcie.

Chub put his face in his hands, causing his combover to flip forward until it was covering half his face. "Can't you do anything?" he quietly whined from behind this hanging curtain of hair. "I lost my wife. I lost my daughter. I can't lose my job, too."

Mallory held up his hand to signal Chub to stop talking. He had no interest in hearing Chub's sob story. His gaze drifted away from Chub as he idly glanced over the other contents of the cubicle. A picture on the bookcase immediately grabbed his attention. It was a photo of a young, pretty woman with brown eyes set in a clear oval face, her dark hair set in a dramatic French twist, who was looking into the camera with a conspiratorial grin. "Is that your daughter?"

"What? You think I'm seventy-five years old or something? That's my sister, my little sister, Lilly."

"Oh. She's like, how old?"

"Twenty-five. Her birthday was last week. No, my daughter Stephanie is only eight years old. Here's my daughter's picture."

Mallory glanced briefly at the picture of the little blonde girl that Chub showed him on his phone.

"Why did you miss work?"

"I'm an alcoholic. So, when all this happened …."

"You know I've never lost a legal case?" Mallory interrupted.

"That's what everybody says. But they also say you're not a lawyer. Is that true?"

Mallory hesitated. "That's true." Then he thought he'd balance that out with a lie. "But I have a whole crowd of lawyers who can do all the court work on your case for me."

"Oh."

Mallory stared blankly at Chub with a thoughtful look. But he was actually thinking about Lilly. There didn't seem to be room in his mind for anything else at that moment.

"I have to admit," Chub interrupted his reverie. "I didn't show up for work or call in for fourteen days. Harrison is right about that."

"Yeah." Mallory lowered himself onto the tiny chair facing Chub that was crammed into the cubicle. He nodded and looked off into the middle distance as if he were thinking. "You need professional representation for sure. I'll need to do a lot of research about alcoholism. You might have some kind of claim under the All Americans for Disabilities Act."

"You think I might have a chance?"

"Possibly. But I'd have to do a lot of research. Research takes a lot of time. I'd need $500 just for starters."

"I don't have any money." Chub spoke in a low whine. "I was already in debt when it happened. Now I just maxed out my credit card on booze."

Mallory stared at the photograph on Chub's desk. The combination of that devious grin and that glorious hair set off a surge of feeling in his chest that he hadn't felt for a long time. "Has your sister got any brains?"

"She's a college graduate, working on her masters, if that's what you're asking."

"Does she like you?"

"She loves me."

"Do you think she'd help me research your case? Maybe with her help, I could waive my fee."

*** ***

Mallory didn't know whether he loved or hated Nell now. It was agonizing that she worked only six feet away from him, separated only by a fabric-covered cubicle wall. For months they had tortured and used each other without ever becoming lovers. Mallory had never even touched that sleek, dark brown hair, cut in a style he once thought she wore just for him. He had found out in the hardest possible way that she loved only Kathie, their co-worker. But after everything blew up, they had reached an uneasy truce, if only so they could both keep their jobs.

Now he entered the break room and saw her sitting alone at a table, staring intently at the arched entryway as he came through. Their eyes met. He turned to go, but he couldn't bring himself to act like such a coward in front of her.

"How's Koko?" he managed. He mentioned the cat first to make sure Nell wouldn't think it was her he was pining for.

"Koko ... is fine." She quickly cut her eyes up to his. "It was obvious that you took good care of him – after you stole him."

"Of course I took good care of him. He belongs to me – morally."

"Morally? Ha! Since when did you take the slightest interest in morality?"

Mallory ignored her comment. In his opinion, morals were something people made up just to justify their fear of reaching for what they really wanted. "Seriously, is Koko healthy? Does he still have that beautiful black and white fur?" Mallory had treated Koko like a king in the few weeks he had the cat in his apartment. Koko had reciprocated, allowing Mallory to pet him, slowly walking through Mallory's hand caress from his nose to the tip of his long tail. Koko was currently the only creature on earth that would put up with Mallory's touch. "I'd love to visit Koko sometime."

"Forget it. I'll show you a picture once in a while. But listen. I need to warn you about the Cheer Committee."

"Is the committee having its holiday party at the Pirate Bar again?"

"No, they won't allow us in there. Not even after you paid for all the damages last year." Nell allowed herself a smile as she flicked back her precisely cut, dark bob. Mallory tried not to be distracted by that one feminine thing about her. He forced himself to notice that, as always, she wore no makeup, no bright colors, no clothes that would reveal her shape, no jewelry, nothing that a real woman would wear to attract a man. The only decent thing about her was her hair. What an idiot he had been to be seduced by just that! But she kept talking, almost as if she couldn't appreciate all the turmoil she'd put him through. "This is what I need to tell you. Supervisor Harrison has asked for a list of all the Cheer Committee members. Should I tell him you're still a member, coming to all the meetings?"

For almost a year, the Employee Cheer Committee had been Mallory's excuse for not being available to answer customers' calls. It seemed he would need at least that excuse and possibly more under the new regime at UniCast Cable. "Yes. Harrison's a tougher nut than Teitelbaum ever was. Put me down as present for every meeting."

*** ***

Mallory had hung onto his job at UniCast ever since his old nemesis, Teitelbaum, had been fired. The old manager had been replaced so far only by temporary, acting managers. Mallory had intimidated every one of these interim bosses by threatening lawsuits against them personally, telling them truthfully that he had never lost a legal case and falsely that he could take all their assets, including their IRAs and 401(k)s, when he won. The interim managers quickly found out that he had actually filed court cases pretending to be a lawyer and had somehow gotten away with it. They learned to leave him alone.

Harrison, the new, permanent supervisor, had been recently questioning Mallory's employee representation activities. He had told Mallory more than once to spend more time on the phone, answering customers' calls. On those rare occasions when Harrison walked by, Mallory had to pretend he was on the phone. He hadn't come up with an overall strategy to counter his new boss until Chub fell into his hands.

Mallory didn't have an appointment to meet with his supervisor. He simply stood in front of Ms. Marcie's desk and pointed to the open door to Harrison's office. Ms. Marcie, Harrison's assistant, looked puzzled for a second, but then she hesitantly ushered him in. She seemed to think, probably based on her empirical observations of what had been going on in the workplace for months, that Mallory had some kind of authority to represent employees who were in trouble. Harrison at first looked taken aback when Mallory appeared at his office door, but then he found himself going along with Ms. Marcie's theory also, gesturing Mallory toward a chair.

"Don't waste your time, or my time, on Chub, Mr. Mallory. He's being fired." Harrison spoke with the assurance of a manager whose authority had never been seriously challenged.

"You can't fire Chub for his disability."

"What disability? I don't see anything in Chub's file about a disability."

"That would show up only in his confidential personnel health file," Mallory confidently asserted, making up the story as he went along.

"What is his disability?"

"You have no right to know. And managers who have intruded into employees' confidential health personnel files have successfully been sued, sometimes for hundreds of thousands of dollars," Mallory continued.

"Listen, Mr. Mallory. I can't believe that a disability that causes you to not show up for work for fourteen days in a row, and not even to call in, needs to be accommodated. Forget it."

"Okay. Okay. I'll give you some of the details, if that's what it takes to convince you. Chub is an alcoholic." Mallory ventured briefly into the truth with that statement, but then quickly turned to the much more vibrant and prolific world of his imagination for the rest. "Chub has been sober for fifteen years. Goes to AA meetings regularly. You can't discriminate against him because he's an alcoholic."

"But what about his not showing up for work for fourteen days?"

"Relapse is part of the process. Ask any alcoholic counselor. If you fire him, you'll be firing him for one of the features of his disability."

"I don't think I'm buying this. I have to think about this. I'll check with human resources. Get out of my office."

*** ***

"Yeah, Chub's a lot older," Lilly told him over the phone. "But he's the only relative I have. He took care of me when my parents died. He's always been good to me."

Mallory could not figure out why she was telling him these things. But he didn't ask her why. He didn't want to press his luck. He had told Chub that if he really wanted to get a handle on his disability defense, he would need to do a deep study of his family dynamics, starting with a long talk with his little sister, Lilly. Chub had set up the phone call with her and explained that Mallory was his last hope. Lilly had promised she'd do "anything at all" to help her brother keep his job. Mallory remembered those words.

"We need to meet in person," he insisted.

They met at a casual restaurant not far from the Dough and Go, the source of most of Mallory's meals and all of his knowledge of the world. She had arrived first and quickly sized him up as he approached the table – and without the usual double take at his suit and tie. "Kevin? Kevin Mallory?" She raised her eyebrows in a kind of restrained curiosity as she pronounced his name. He glanced down at her long legs first, but he couldn't keep his eyes off that glorious, dark French twist that seemed to crown her long, pretty face. Her solemn brown eyes seemed to contradict her almost mischievous smile. She had a fine spray of freckles across her cheekbones. The last hint of any desire he had for Nell instantly disappeared.

"I want to thank you for meeting me," she began as soon as he said hello. "I know Chub is at fault, but he's had a really tough time the past few months, and he can't afford to lose his job on top of all this."

Mallory was more interested in her long legs than her sob story. They were tantalizing him by peeking out from under her short print skirt, but he lost sight of them when he had to sit down himself. She wore a white business-type blouse, but she was not trying to hide her shape like Nell did. And she wore a bracelet, earrings and a necklace – all good signs of a woman accepting her instinct to display herself for men. He was a little disappointed that she didn't seem to be wearing any makeup.

He thought he should at least pretend to care about the Chub situation. "Lilly, I'm going to take all the time I need to learn all about your situation – I mean Chub's situation. Let's order a drink and relax, and you can tell me your story any way you want to tell it. Most of all, I want you to know one thing: I care."

She ordered a glass of white wine and began to tell the story. She seemed relaxed, breathing slowly, but glancing at his eyes to assure herself he was really listening. He couldn't keep his eyes off that French twist, and he marveled now at her tiny sapphire earrings contrasting with the smooth, white skin of her neck. He was sure she had dressed up for him.

"It's been awful for us," she started. "Chub has a long history of drinking. He met his wife in rehab, and they both did great for at least ten years. Then his wife started taking tranquilizers for her nerves; then she started taking harder drugs. Chub seemed to be pretending it wasn't happening – until she disappeared three weeks ago, taking their daughter, little Stephanie. So, what does Chub do? He goes out and gets drunk himself." She gave him a grim smile. "That sounds so stupid of him, I know. I've learned how insidious alcoholism can be. But I guess you don't want to hear the whole sad family story."

"I most certainly do," Mallory insisted. What had he gotten himself into? Did she think Chub had hired him as some kind of social worker? Mallory had convinced Chub that, because he was an alcoholic, he was therefore in denial and incapable of being objective, and that Mallory needed information from a family member who could objectively tell him the facts of his case so that he could adequately represent him.

Lilly took a big gulp of her wine, sat up straight and shook off the wariness in her eyes. "I'll give you the worst-case scenario. Chub's hiring a lawyer to get a court order giving him custody, but he can't even afford that. He put the lawyer's initial fee on his credit card. But if he loses his job, he'll lose his lawyer, his daughter, and probably his apartment, too. He could be out on the street, and I'm afraid he'll start drinking again."

Mallory hadn't expected to have to listen to all these facts. But as she told her story, Mallory tried to concentrate and focus on those facts that were most likely to get Lilly into his bed. But he couldn't help noticing the catch in her voice and the tears she was trying to hide. "Chub's the only family I have. And I think I love little Stephanie as much as he does." Before he could figure out a way to take advantage of her emotions, she seemed to shake off her sadness. She gave him a tiny, embarrassed smile.

Mallory noticed that she held herself with a certain kind of dignity that he had never noticed in a woman before. He was really attracted to that. And he couldn't help imagining what it would be like to watch that dignity melt away under the power of his passion. He figured Chub would lose his apartment if he was fired. He would probably move in with Lilly, sleep on her couch while he drank himself to death, making it awkward for Mallory to make any time with his sister. He wondered if he could prevent that from happening.

"My brother says you're an employee representative or something." Lilly switched subjects, checking him out now, her wry smile and slightly raised eyebrows hinting at doubts about even this aspect of her brother's judgment. "He says you're somebody who knows how to keep the company honest."

"Honest?" Mallory had never thought of that concept in relation to his job. "There's nothing honest about UniCast Cable."

She pulled back a fraction of an inch and leveled her eyes at him. "So, why do you work there, then?"

Mallory was flummoxed by the naivete of this girl. "Do I have a choice? Does anybody in America have any choice but to work for Algonquin J. Tycoon?" He explained that Algonquin J. Tycoon was his term for those billionaires and hedge fund managers who spent all their time searching the corporate world for a merger that would throw as many workers as possible out into the street.

"There are other places to work," she responded, leveling her eyes on him in a way that made him uncomfortable, "besides in corporate America."

She didn't seem like the kind of woman he could get into bed the first night. He was glad he didn't have to pay for her food. As it was, he was barely making the minimum payments on his credit cards. He was still leasing the Escalade that he couldn't afford, and the cleaning and alterations bills for the suits he wore all day, every day, had increased his clothing bills by a factor of ten. Still, the car and the suit were the only things that set him apart from the rest of the drones at UniCast Cable. That and the fact that his bosses were half afraid of him.

"I do want to thank you for trying to help my brother." She seemed very confident, and she acted as if she were totally in control of the situation. He wondered how this twenty-five-year-old girl managed that.

"I know how to handle management." He felt he needed to prove himself to her. "I'm also handling another case right now, at the same time. They're terrified of dealing with me on both."

"Honestly, I can see why UniCast is angry with him. People have to show up for work. Chub has a real drinking problem."

Mallory had never given Chub's personal life a second's thought. He had never asked Chub why he drank. He was starting to resent the effort he was undertaking to get him out of trouble at work – when all he was getting in return was some sister's sob story he couldn't care less about. His mind wandered to all the expensive alcohol, mostly cognac, he had purchased in his attempts to get Nell into his bed. If he wasn't getting any sex now, at least those cognac bills weren't still piling up. He did have half a bottle of Hennessy left over from those days. He wondered if he could use its magic on Lilly.

"Everybody drinks sometimes."

Lilly's sharp glance cut him short, and her words were even sharper. "Chub is one person who cannot drink. Now he's lost his daughter, my niece, maybe forever."

Mallory forgot about the tycoons, and Chub, and even Lilly, for a moment. *Daughter. Niece.* Mallory had never even thought about these concepts. He was an only child himself, and he had never been married or had any children.

Lilly seemed to really care about her brother. He wondered if that was how sisters were. He thought maybe he should respond to what she was saying. But she beat him to the punch.

"Do you really think you can help him?"

"I know I can."

*** ***

Mallory had no idea whether he could help Chub. He wasn't used to going all out for anybody but himself. But now he thought he had his own skin in the game. He wanted Lilly in his bed. He needed that, and he suspected she was falling under his spell. As he looked at his porn site that night, he tried to imagine she was the woman on the screen, screaming in ecstasy. But that substitution didn't work so well. Lilly didn't seem like a woman who would lose all control under his manly touch. But he knew she was a real woman anyway. He wanted her to be grateful to him. He wanted to share a cup of cognac with her in his apartment. He wanted to feel those skeptical lips pressing against his.

He insisted she come over to his apartment the next evening to do computer research on Chub's case. He first deleted all the shortcuts to his two porn sites and to Manly Man, the internet guru whom he still visited occasionally, despite the disastrous advice he had been given on his relationship with Nell. He typed "disability" and "alcohol" into Google and bookmarked fifteen or twenty of the sites he came to. He couldn't bring himself to actually read anything. He had sprung for a fresh new bottle of Hennessy for his kitchen counter.

She came over bringing her own tiny laptop. It was a good thing it was small. Mallory's computer and screen and their tangle of wires took up half the room in his tiny efficiency apartment, and a creaky wicker bench was the only other furniture in the room, except for his sofa bed at the far end. Mallory was not unhappy that the two of them would not fit on the computer bench at the same time. He was sure they would eventually retreat to the sofa, which was also his bed.

Mallory had laid the groundwork for Chub's case so that it would be a win-win-win for everybody. He was also handling a case for Adele, the elderly lady whose phone manner had become so erratic there was a complaint about her almost every day. Customers said they couldn't understand what she was saying. When Mallory finally got up the energy to talk to her, she had acted fine for about five minutes. Normally, Mallory wouldn't spend more time than that with any woman over forty, but he stayed an extra minute just out of curiosity about what was supposed to be the problem. Then Adele started babbling about her grandchildren, one of whom was Abraham Lincoln.

Harrison had been much more sympathetic to Adele than he had been toward Chub. "The poor old lady is obviously losing it. It's too bad we don't have a disability plan, or extended sick leave."

"Or health insurance," Mallory contributed. "Or anything else."

Harrison bristled as if he were the only one who could criticize the company. "So, what do you want me to do? We can't leave her on those phones."

"You have to accommodate her disability. Pay somebody to sit there with her and take over the phone when she goes off the deep end."

"No. I don't think so."

"You have to. It's the law," Mallory asserted. Without any knowledge of the subject. As he always did. But it was a tactic that Harrison already seemed to be figuring out.

Mallory had no real faith in the legal disability arguments he was making for either Adele or Chub. But he also knew it would take weeks, if not months, for Harrison to get any answer from corporate personnel, and even more time to get a legal opinion from company counsel. And Mallory would be a hero to the two employees, even if all he accomplished was keeping them on the job for a few more months. In short, Mallory had snowballed these two cases into a huge headache for Harrison and an easy advantage for himself.

As Mallory explained to Lilly in his apartment that night, all this talk about the employees and their misconduct and their rights was only half of the story. They had been searching for answers about alcoholism and disability on their computers for over an hour. Neither of them had found anything definitive. Mallory gave a big sigh and stood up from the rickety computer bench. Lilly was sitting on the sofa with her elbows on her knees, her lips pursed in frustration. Mallory sat down next to her.

"Chub is getting so depressed. I know they're going to fire him soon." She snapped shut her laptop and leaned back into the cushions.

"Let's take a break. I'll get you something to drink."

"Maybe a glass of water?"

He brought her a large glass full of cognac. He believed this special drink was an aphrodisiac for women.

"Wow. I don't usually drink anything except beer and wine."

"Taste it."

"Oh. It's good. But I don't think I can drink this whole glass."

"You don't have to. Take little sips. I guarantee you'll feel better. And I'll explain to you how the system at UniCast Cable really works."

He decided he'd go into a long, slow explanation as she drank. He didn't go into exactly how he had learned so much about a company's firing practices. Over the course of his own many rancorous personnel campaigns, Mallory had learned that searching for weakness in management, and attacking those weaknesses, was usually more effective that trying to prove that he deserved to keep his job. He hadn't won all of his battles, but the damage he had wrought was legendary in the small circle of employers who had ever heard his name.

"Are you liking that cognac?" He interrupted his own story, carefully noting that she had already consumed two inches of the drink.

"Whew! This stuff is strong. But it's good. How does this *attack-the-management* theory work?"

"Let me just tell you this much. The people who fire line workers, drones like me and Chub, are the middle managers. The young middle managers are keeping an eye out for any chance to advance their careers. The rest of them just want to hold onto their jobs with the least amount of aggravation. The last thing any of them want is for their unit to get a reputation for any kind of dysfunction or chaos."

"Let me guess." Lilly smiled, then took another sip of her drink before she went on. "You're Mr. Chaos. You have some way to convince this Harrison guy that firing Chub would make him look like an inept manager."

"I'm working on it."

"Ha ha." She relaxed, resting her head against the top sofa cushion and looking at Mallory from this new angle. "You're kind of a rogue, aren't you?"

Mallory pretended to take another sip of his drink. He set his hand next to hers so they were just barely touching. When she didn't recoil, he told himself this was going better than he had hoped. She had worn a skirt this time, a reddish knit skirt short enough that, when he watched her fold one leg under herself on the sofa, he remembered again what life was all about. She did that little maneuver on purpose for him, he was sure. Her female instinct was telling her to show herself to the dominant male. He suppressed his disappointment that she wasn't wearing stockings. His old girlfriend had worn stockings, garters, straps of every kind underneath, just like the girls in the porno sites he visited every night. But Lilly was obviously a different kind of woman. She dressed attractively, and in a feminine if somewhat girlish way, but her clothes weren't screaming out for male attention. She worked at a nonprofit, and it was obvious she took her work seriously. Way too seriously, he thought. But she was still a real woman, and a different woman than any he had had before. And now it was obvious she could drink a little, loosen up. She seemed to have a slight smile on her face as she followed him curiously with those dark eyes.

"I'm sure I can get your brother off the hook," he said, as he took her hand.

*** ***

Even though his heart raced at the memory of Lilly's touch, Mallory was bored with both personnel cases he had taken up against Harrison. In Chub's case, he quickly realized that researching a disability claim would be incredibly tedious. Lilly began emailing him pdfs of laws and regulations and articles about the subject. Realizing how old-fashioned he was, she also printed each item out and had Chub put it on Mallory's desk every morning. Mallory could not bear to read all that legalistic prose. He barely had time to shove the latest batch of papers into his lower desk drawer before Chub would arrive with another one. He never asked Chub where he had gone, or what he had been doing during the fourteen days he had missed work. And he didn't want to hear any more of the sob story about his daughter.

Adele was even worse. The old hag simply forgot who she was half the time. Harrison put a monitor on her phone. She would handle six or seven customers in a row politely and efficiently, even throwing in a few little-old-lady endearments – then suddenly decide that the next caller was her granddaughter, who had called to ask what dress she should wear to the prom.

"What do you expect me to do with her?" Harrison insisted, brushing off his half-rim reading glasses with an irritated flourish. "God knows what she's going to say next."

"The only thing you can do," Mallory began, leaning forward with his elbows on the edge of the desk, "consistent with the All Americans for Disabilities Act, is to promote her to a job where she doesn't have to talk to people. At least, somewhere where she doesn't have to make sense."

"And where do we have a job like that?"

"I hear you have a vacancy in human resources."

Harrison scoffed. "Very funny. But really, Mr. Mallory, the poor woman has lost it. She can't function in any job here at UniCast. She probably should have some type of guardian even in her home."

"I see you're giving medical opinions now. Do you have a medical license?" When Harrison ignored this attack, Mallory thought of a better one. In fact, it was his favorite new tactic. "You have a duty under the law to accommodate her disability. She could sue the company, and you personally, for hundreds of thousands of dollars."

"Mallory, I've talked to human resources." Harrison abruptly leaned forward, his face tightening. "We're not violating any disabilities laws. Not in Adele's case, and not in Chub's case either. You're wasting my time in both cases. Unless you have any realistic defenses – and I haven't heard any yet – both of these people are out the door."

"You underestimate me. I haven't even begun to fight."

"Ha. I don't think so. And from now on your phone will be monitored more closely to make sure you are spending your time helping customers instead of threatening me."

Mallory leaned back in his chair and folded his arms behind his head. "You obviously don't know how UniCast's upper management really works. And you haven't heard what happened to Teitelbaum."

*** ***

Lilly agreed to meet him again at his apartment to further discuss her brother's case. "No booze this time," she implored. "We didn't get much done last time."

Mallory silently agreed they hadn't got much done, neither on Chub's case nor in his own quest to get her into his bed. Lilly had gripped his fingers, but hard, in a buddy gesture more suitable to two football linemen preparing for kickoff than to a man and a woman testing out a budding mutual passion. He decided he had moved too soon, before she had drunk the minimum required amount of cognac. He wondered how he could draw out their next session without having to discuss her pathetic brother, or those tedious disability issues.

He was disappointed that she wore jeans to his apartment this time. Even more disappointing was that, when he arrived at the steps leading to the landing outside his apartment, he found her engaged in a conversation with Thomas, his Black friend who lived across the landing. He was not as close to Thomas as he used to be, but they had a long history.

Mallory was sure that most regular people were just as skeptical of Blacks as he was. He believed that no good could come from messing with them. They were aggressive and dangerous and probably carried guns in the pockets of their hoodies. The only exceptions to these rules were the three Black people he actually knew, Ava and Edison and their son, Thomas. They had lived right across the areaway from his apartment. He had taken an instant liking to gregarious young Thomas; and, throughout the course of their misadventures, Ava and Edison had repeatedly stunned Mallory with their demonstrations of how parents who actually loved their son were supposed to act.

Thomas's parents were out of the picture now, and Mallory still hoped to take the twenty-year-old under his wing. He didn't like the curiosity he saw in Lilly's eyes as she acquainted herself with this athletic, handsome young man. He didn't like the idea that she was closer in age to Thomas than to himself.

"We have work to do," he announced as he heaved himself onto the last step to the landing.

"Hello, Mr. Mallory." Thomas's voice was a shade cooler than in the old days.

"Hi." Lilly's greeting also was matter-of-fact.

Didn't these two appreciate what he had done for them? Mallory despaired of the lack of gratitude being shown him by the younger generation. He stepped between them. "We don't have much time. They're having a big personnel meeting about your brother tomorrow," he lied. "We have to get prepared."

Young Thomas stared at him, shaking his head almost imperceptibly. Mallory had apologized to him for some of the more hurtful lies he had told him in the past, but he had never claimed he wouldn't lie to get a woman in his bed.

Lilly turned fully toward Mallory. Her eyes startled wide for a second, but her mouth seemed suddenly tight and a little skeptical. "I didn't realize it was coming to a head so fast."

"I'll explain it to you inside."

Inside, he told Lilly his theory of economics. "To begin with, the Algonquin J. Tycoons who own UniCast don't care about anything but making a killing by breaking the company up and selling it to someone else as soon as they can. They don't care what's happening to employees or customers."

"So?"

"Let me get you a drink and I'll explain it in detail."

"You know, Mr. Mallory, I really loved that stuff you gave me last time, but … maybe not again on a weeknight." She moved an inch away from him on the sofa. He watched her cross her long legs in those jeans. He was really disappointed that her dark hair was pulled back into a ponytail now, and she was wearing black-framed glasses he had never seen before. He suddenly realized she was smarter and more together – and less wary of him – than any woman he had ever tried to seduce before. He went into the kitchen and poured two glasses of cognac and came back and handed her one. There wasn't any place near the sofa to put down a glass, so she had to keep holding hers in her hand. He clinked his glass against hers and took a sip. She sighed and rolled her eyes, but then took a tiny sip.

Mallory understood she was just trying to be nice, and he knew that a little alcohol probably wouldn't get her drunk enough to shimmy out of those jeans. But Manly Man always preached that no man should ever be intimidated, that all women, even those who appear book-smart, confident and successful, are just holding back that hidden craving for the male domination that is built into their genes. Boldness, craft, and power would always trump book learning and superficial female confidence. And he had a long range plan that would eventually fire up all of Lilly's repressed desires – and satisfy his own raging lust for this woman he was sure would soon submit to him and give him satisfaction like no other.

*** ***

He had prepared well, starting with Harrison. Harrison was the first permanent supervisor since Teitelbaum, but he had never met or had a chance to talk to Teitelbaum about anything at all, much less about Mallory. Advantage Mallory.

"A manager who fires one deadbeat employee is efficient, a go-getter," Mallory had told Harrison the week before. "But if a manager fires two employees, that means there's a problem in his department. He's the manager, and he's responsible for this malfunctioning department. Therefore, in the minds of the owners of the company, he's a bad manager."

"What does this have to do with Chub missing fourteen days in a row?"

"It has to do with you. Look at the records. Teitelbaum tried to fire me and Nell at the same time. That made it look like his Customer Service Department was dysfunctional. He was gone before they ever got around to looking into the cases against me or Nell."

"So, you're saying …." Harrison sighed. This was the first time Mallory saw even a sliver of doubt reflected in his new manager's face. Harrison slowly waved his head from side to side. His dark hair was going grey around the edges. He probably hadn't gone very far up the corporate ladder for his age. Mallory guessed that his aggressive stance against the two malfunctioning employees was fueled by his desperation not to stumble again in his too-slow journey to the top.

"I'm saying you're fighting two employees, Chub and Adele. They both have legitimate disability claims. At least, they both have enough of a case to tie the company up in court for years. And every time corporate counsel mentions this to the bigwigs, they'll be reminded that you caused both of these headaches. Bigger headaches than Teitelbaum ever caused."

Harrison seemed interested. "Let me think about this. Come see me tomorrow."

Mallory smiled. "While you're thinking about this, remember that I can offer you a solution." Mallory paused until Harrison looked up over his reading glasses. "Here's what it is. I'll let you fire one of them. I won't raise any defense. They'll be out the door, without any personnel or legal hassles. The other one stays employed. No hassles there, either."

A smile slowly crept across Harrison's face. "No hassles, huh? So, under your proposal, I'd get to fire only one. To tell the truth, it'd be hard to figure out which one of these employees is worse. But you're saying that's all I have to do?"

"No, I'm not saying that. The other part of this deal is, I get to pick who stays and who goes."

*** ***

Mallory found Chub in his cubicle and kicked at his chair to get his attention. Chub looked over at him expectantly. Mallory couldn't help but smirk. "Harrison is ready to let you go. Your job is hanging by a thread, and that thread is me."

"Isn't there something you can do? Anything?"

Mallory's lips curled in a grimace. "His mind is pretty much made up. I'm the only thing stopping him. If I drop your case, you'll be out of here in 24 hours. No job, no income. No place to live."

Mallory tightened his features even more. For the first time in his life, he felt the adrenaline rush of a man exercising real power over lesser humans. "Or, Chub, there could be another result. I can guarantee you can keep your job. You won't be out on the street. You won't have to be sleeping on your sister's sofa." He felt intoxicated by a new feeling of manly power. He paused for effect. "But your sister will have to be sleeping on mine."

Chapter 2: Delusions

Mallory had checked to make sure the tape he had put over the lens of the surveillance camera in the break room was still intact; but he couldn't be sure that UniCast hadn't also bugged the break room, so he spoke to Nell in a low voice, practically mumbling. Nell still wore her hair in that sleek style that had once so captured his imagination. Day after day, night after night, he had imagined running his fingers through that precise brunette bob, stoking her urges even as his manly powers grew. But as the months went by, she had trained him, excruciatingly slowly, to hope for less and less, meanwhile pressing him for more and more favors.

"I got something going with a girl," he confessed proudly. "A real girl this time. I'm not having those fantasies about you anymore."

"Oh, that's good. Good for you, Kevin." Nell's voice was also hushed. He had thought she would ask more questions – at least the name of the girl. After he and Nell had suffered through their own degrading relationship months ago, and after they had now reached a sort of truce, he thought she would at least be a little interested in his new, non-deviant, sexual adventure. But Nell's inward stare signaled to him that she was thinking of something else.

"I have something going on, too," Nell mumbled this as if she were in a trance. Mallory thought he knew, but he was going to wait her out, make her say it. She finally cut her eyes up to him, but then took a deep breath like she was still trying to keep the story from coming out. But she couldn't. "I didn't know what real love was until now." Her voice was really small, and she was avoiding his eyes now. "It's Kathie." She still couldn't stop. "I never thought there could be a human being so beautiful."

"Yeah, she's not bad." Mallory had always appreciated Kathie's tall, thin build and massive blonde curls. "Good hair. Nice green eyes."

"No. I mean spiritually beautiful. She's so great." Nell put so much feeling into those last few words they both looked around to make sure no one else had heard.

Mallory knew she expected him to be happy for her, but even though their own debased relationship had long since ended, it still hurt to see her eyes glow with such passion for someone else. But it wouldn't be manly to show jealousy.

"Are you two going to get married? It's legal now, you know."

"Oh! We don't talk about that. We're just enjoying every day, every magical day."

"You see each other every day?"

Nell steepled her eyebrows, changed her tone. "You don't have to interrogate me." When Mallory remained silent, she admitted, "Only Friday nights, so far. Kathie's got her own life, her own family, but she's working me into it." Nell's face flushed as she went on. "I think that's the right way, to go slowly, because of our *situation*. Her family's very traditional. But I know this is the real thing."

Nell sounded like she was talking herself into something, blaming Kathie's family for the slow progress of their relationship. Mallory had never had much of a family, but he remembered thinking he would throw it all over, quit his job, get a better apartment, a better job, a new life, instantly, if he could live his life with Nell. It didn't seem like Kathie felt that same kind of passion for Nell. He decided that some lesbians had a strong sexual drive, and some didn't. He patted himself on the back for so quickly attaining such an acute psychological insight. He felt no need to gloat over Nell's situation. In fact, it bothered him a little that Nell might be sinking too deeply into some kind of lesbian quicksand.

Looking embarrassed, Nell quickly changed the subject. "You have a girlfriend now?"

"You could say that. We've been out on a few dates. She comes back to my apartment almost all the time."

"Are you plying her with your famous cognac?" She raised her eyebrows comically. It seemed she was finally in the mood to forgive his many, crude, failed attempts to seduce her.

He hadn't thought there was anything funny about their former degrading relationship until that instant. He felt a movement in his chest almost like laughter. It seemed his body was agreeing with her that their thing was finally over. Surprisingly, he didn't feel the need to exaggerate his current progress in the field of love. "Yes. Well, she drank some cognac once or twice, but not enough to …."

"You didn't pass out yourself, did you?"

"Very funny." It was just like her, he thought now, to never let him forget what happened the first time he tried to get her drunk.

"You didn't steal her panties?"

He guessed she was now fishing for a confession about that other night, the night she passed out herself in his apartment. Mallory had never admitted he stole Nell's panties. He was sure Nell was dying to know what happened after she blacked out and later found her panties in her purse, but he wasn't going to give her the satisfaction. He tried to smile enigmatically.

"Just kidding. We should forget all that," she quickly added, not very convincingly. "At least, I hope you're smart enough not to pull stunts like that again."

"Her name is Lilly." He stopped, then realized there was really no reason to hide any part of his present life from Nell. "She's actually Chub's sister."

"Oh! I know who she is. She came to the Cheer Committee once, trying to raise money for daycare for kids in subsidized housing projects. She seemed nice. Way too cool for you, though."

"You're so gay, Nell, you don't even know what a real woman wants in a man."

"I just can't picture her with you."

"You underestimate me, Nell. I have a plan. A foolproof plan. This woman, this gorgeous, *very heterosexual* woman, will be mine by the end of the week."

✳✳✳ ✳✳✳

Mallory prepared himself to be the man he needed to be for Lilly that night. He opened the bookmark for his porn site fifteen minutes before she was due to arrive. He was a little sorry he had only bought the $13.99 economy version of the site, as the videos were always a little dark and sometimes out of focus. But the audio was always great. He watched it a little longer than he intended to. He was waiting for his favorite ensemble, Bed Rock and the Rockettes, to appear; but the scene on the monitor was enough to keep him aroused – and so distracted he didn't even hear Lilly's first knock at the door.

Her second, louder rap on the door shook him out of his erotic trance. He jerked himself up so quickly he knocked over the wicker bench he had been sitting on. He quickly grabbed for the monitor and shoved it around so that the screen was facing the wall. Her third knock sent him into a panic. He lunged for the doorknob and flung it open before she could change her mind and leave.

"Did I come too early? Is this a bad time?"

"No. No." He knew he was breathing heavily, and his suit was disheveled. He wasn't making a very manly impression right then, he knew. But it still wasn't a bad time. There was no such thing as a bad time for sex.

"Chub told me not to come," were Lilly's first words as she stepped across the threshold and brushed by him. "He's my older brother. But he doesn't control me."

She was carrying a worn leather bag stuffed with her laptop and a lot of files and papers. As he focused on catching his breath, she explained she had just come from giving a presentation to some government housing officials. She was wearing stockings and heels. A short slit in her bright green skirt had already caught Mallory's attention – that and the fact that she obviously wasn't listening to her older brother.

"I'm glad you're not listening to Chub. He isn't the smartest on tactics and strategy. I don't think he understands all that's at stake."

She walked directly to the sofa and sat down, even kicking off her heels. She pulled her laptop out of her bag. "I was talking to a lawyer who was at the meeting. He thinks we might have a case, but we have to pare down our research. Pick one theory and go with it, he said."

"Of course. First, relax. Something to drink?"

"Yes. Just a glass of water, please."

"You don't mind if I take some cognac?"

She let out a short laugh. "No. Drink whatever you want. I have an idea for simplifying our case, like the lawyer said."

Mallory took a deep drink from his glass as he returned from the kitchen. He was miffed that Lilly was consulting an outside expert of any kind. Didn't she understand the whole case was in his hands anyway? Wasn't she here to seal the deal with him?

Mallory appreciated that Chub didn't know his sister that well. Chub was just a mealy-mouthed IT guy who sat in his cubicle all day, unable to help himself and afraid to let his sister help. But Mallory realized that his sister was a player. She met lawyers and government officials every day. She knew how to make a deal. And she obviously recognized a good deal when she saw one. She was gladly submitting to one night of erotic love with him in return for securing her brother's future.

"Are you sure you don't want at least a small hit of cognac before we begin?" he pleaded now.

"No, I want to get this done. Let's get started now."

She was anxious to get started! His heart pounded even faster. It was really going to happen. He sat down so close to her their legs were touching. He knew a manly man would start with a compliment. "First, I want to say how wonderful it is that you have saved your brother's job."

"What do you mean? I haven't done anything yet."

"What you're going to do right now is going to save his job. I guarantee it."

"You mean research?" She shrugged in her seat a little. "Would you mind not sitting so close to me?"

"There's no need to be coy, Lilly. It's a simple deal. Chub's out on the street tomorrow – unless you sleep with me tonight."

Lilly snapped her laptop shut. "You're kidding, right? I don't think that's funny."

"No, can't you see? It's a great deal It's a win-win-win, for everybody."

Oh! Oh! Please! Oh! Faster! Please! Oh! Oh!

"What the hell is that?"

"Um, something to get you in the mood."

Faster! Faster! Harder! Oh! Oh-oh-oh-oh-oh-oh-ooooo....

"Oh my God! You mean it." Lilly slammed her laptop into her bag and ran for the door.

As the door slammed shut behind her, Mallory picked up his wicker bench from the floor, sat down, and turned the screen around, figuring he might as well get something out of the evening.

O MY GOD! OH MY GOD! OH! OH! DON'T STOP! OH-OH-OH-OH! OH-OH-OH!

*** ***

The joy was short-lived. After it was over for him, he noticed the woman on the screen was not really very good looking. Bed Rock and the Rockettes came on next, but he turned off the computer in disgust. Then his phone rang. He checked the screen and was surprised to see Lilly's name.

"You've changed your mind?" he guessed. "Well, it might be too late, for tonight anyway."

"Of course I haven't changed my mind. Do you watch that stuff all the time?"

"Doesn't everybody?"

"And you thought I would sleep with you to save Chub's job?"

"That was the deal."

"And you thought that porno tape would get me in the mood?"

"Of course."

"Mr. Mallory, I know you have been trying to help Chub. But I think you might have a serious problem."

"Why don't you come to my apartment so we can explore deeper into my problem ... um, no, right now wouldn't be good. Maybe in a couple of hours."

"You seem to have a one-track mind. I think you might have a sex problem, Mr. Mallory. It doesn't mean you're an evil person. It means you have a problem. A lot of people have similar problems. You can get help for that kind of problem."

Mallory couldn't have felt more humiliated. He was used to women turning down his advances, but this was worse. She was acting as if she liked him – and at the same time telling him he was some kind of pervert. He was struck dumb. He waited on the line for her to hang up, but she didn't.

"Mr. Mallory, Chub really likes you. And you do want to help him, I believe. I have faith that there must be some good in you. Maybe Chub and I together could find some therapy group or something that might help you."

Mallory was struck speechless. To seduce this beautiful woman, he had played his ace in the hole, but still lost. She thought his idea of trading sex for her brother's job was disgusting. But she didn't think *he* was disgusting, or she wouldn't be still trying to help him. And, strangely enough, he still liked her. But, to be her friend, he might have to change just a little bit his ideas about what women were like.

*** ***

Harrison called him into his office the next morning. "I accepted your deal," he began. "Both of those employees deserve to be fired, but I'll fire only one, the one you pick. The other one gets to stay. So – pick."

"I haven't decided."
"Both of them are out the door if you don't pick soon."

Chapter 3: A Manly Necessity

Seeing Officer Selby standing there with his badge and his gun roiled the considerable contents of Mallory's stomach. They hadn't spoken in months, ever since that memorable incident when Selby had negotiated his peaceful surrender to the SWAT team and Mallory had gotten off with nothing more than an $85 ticket for parking in a handicapped spot. Selby's calm, masterful presence had always calmed Mallory's suspicions about authority – yet Selby was now staring him down like he had lost all respect.

"I have the right to get my rifle back." But Mallory felt the hesitation in his own voice. He had lately become aware that the truth sometimes existed somewhere other than in his imagination. All he really knew about his gun rights was that Spike, his waiter at the Dough and Go, had told him the police had to give him back his gun.

"What you did to that woman at the courthouse was awful."

Mallory had hoped Selby wouldn't bring this up. It was old, past history as far as Mallory was concerned. Everyone back then had seemed to be appalled that he had made Nell falsely confess over the public address system at the courthouse that she had been abusing Koko. But he was on speaking terms with Nell now. So how bad could it have been?

"Can't you just give me my rifle back?"

Mallory had first met Officer Selby the night he arrested him for the attempted illegal disposal of a ferret. He had imagined they had formed an unusual but manly sort of bond that night. But some of the little things that had happened since then – the stolen cat, the lies, the Chinese bullets, his exercise of his right to display his rifle at the courthouse – could have possibly changed Selby's opinion of him for the worse.

Selby's ruddy face was immobile, his dark eyebrows pinched together in disapproval. Mallory wanted to be this man's friend more than he could explain. To Mallory, Selby was a man's man, facing down the bad guys day after day, dealing out justice in the face of ever-present danger. Selby's life seemed to have nothing in common with the timid hopes and pathetic dreams of the employees of UniCast Cable, where Mallory pretended to work along with two hundred other drones.

"I was desperate." Mallory felt he could be candid. "Desperate people do desperate things."

"So, now you're saying I should give a gun to a desperate man?"

"I know you have to give me the gun back. I know the law."

Selby's mobile features drooped. He sighed like a father trying not to act totally disgusted by his idiot child. It was true that Mallory had successfully defended his friend Thomas from a bogus criminal charge, but that had happened only after he had blundered his way around the courthouse frantically for weeks like a child who couldn't find the men's room. It was Selby who had shown him the way. And he knew he would probably be in jail himself if Selby hadn't intervened.

"Actually, you're right. You have the right to get it back," Selby admitted. "There are no IQ standards for who gets to carry a gun." He turned around from the counter and disappeared quickly through a doorway. He came back in two minutes with the rifle and laid it on the counter. He made Mallory sign a sheaf of papers, shoving one after another at him without a word. Finally, he handed the gun back to Mallory. Mallory held it out in front of himself in both hands, pivoting around in the stationhouse lobby for everyone to see. The barrel almost touched the wrinkled face of an old woman slouched in one of the plastic chairs, but she didn't flinch at all. She simply sighed deeply, almost as if she expected the death penalty for whatever infraction had brought her to the station.

"You point that gun at people, and I'll immediately arrest you for assault."

Selby's loud command startled Mallory, but then his practiced verbal counterpunching technique kicked in. "Oh, like *I'm* the criminal element."

Mallory felt a surge of power as he turned and walked out of the station with the rifle in his hands, kicking the door open with his foot. A middle-aged man in a suit, probably a lawyer, stepped back off the sidewalk to give him a wide berth. But Mallory hadn't gone ten steps farther when he heard Selby calling his name as the officer ran up beside him.

"Always assume the gun is loaded! Don't swing it around like that. Here." He showed Mallory how to carry it pointed at the ground.

"Okay. Thanks."

"You don't know anything at all about guns, do you?" Selby's voice was suddenly soft now, more like a teacher than a cop.

Mallory turned around and rested the end of the barrel on his shoe. Outside of the intimidating atmosphere of the police station, and with his rifle in his possession, Mallory felt like he and Selby were part of the same manly breed. But he was surprised when this brotherly feeling led him immediately to make a confession. "My Dad promised to teach me how to shoot. I kept waiting for him. For years. He never did."

Selby seemed uncomfortable with this personal revelation. "Maybe you should focus on the here and now. What if I teach you how to shoot?"

"You would? You would teach me? That would be great!"

But the offer turned out to be another disappointment in the long line of disappointments that had taught Mallory not to expect anything from the world except what he could wheedle out of it with his lies. Selby offered to teach him at a gun range nearby. It didn't cost that much, and Selby said he could take him free, as a guest, for the first two times. But Selby added one condition. Mallory would have to keep his gun locked up at the gun range between lessons. He wouldn't be able to carry his rifle in his car or have it in his apartment.

"No way." Mallory turned and walked off across the parking lot, wobbling a bit until he figured out how he could use his rifle as a sort of cane.

Chapter 4: Dufus Ex Machina

One thing Mallory was learning in his modified relationship with Nell was the value of editing his revelations. He hadn't mentioned to her his ultimatum to Chub. And after Lilly told him his scheme was disgusting, he decided never to mention it again. Unfortunately, however, Nell now seemed to want to talk. They were not sitting in their usual spot in the break room. This time, she had come into his cubicle, very quietly.

"How's it going with Lilly?" she asked.

"I'm not saying a word until you show me a picture of Koko."

She complied. He grabbed her hand and stared at the picture of that beautiful black and white cat until she wrenched her phone back out of his hands. "You are a true sickie. You know that?"

"Yeah. Everybody says that."

"Including Lilly?"

"We're over."

"I'm not surprised."

"Tell me something, Nell." He lurched forward in his chair, stopping close to her and whispering so he wouldn't be heard over the cubicle walls. "She says women don't scream when they have sex like they do in the porn movies. Is that true?" Mallory had a suspicion that Nell might know. He guessed she had made love to more women than he ever had.

"How would I know what they do in porn movies?"

Mallory shrugged and settled back in his chair, but he noticed there was a look on her face like she was holding back something, something she was dying to say. He waited.

"Oh, Kevin. I do think some women … um …."

"Kathie! Kathie screams, right?"

He watched as her blush rose. She opened her mouth, but then stopped. There was a story inside her that was fighting its way out. He waited for it.

39

"Oh, Kevin. It's so, so great. Kathie is so, so great."

Nell's revelation that Kathie was a screamer brought back Mallory's earlier fantasies of a threesome with the two lesbians, and the scenario now also included an audio of Kathie's screams overlaid on top of the visuals. But he was disappointed that Nell wouldn't give him any details about how she and Kathie did it. In his fantasies, he had to extrapolate from what he experienced watching his computer at night. At the same time, Nell over the next few days seemed to want to share every non-sexual detail about her relationship with Kathie, all in breathless, hushed tones in the break room or in his cubicle. Mallory was jealous of her happiness, of her sex life with Kathie, of the screaming.

Mallory now had proof that Lilly didn't know everything about sex. No matter how much Lilly had supposedly been disgusted by the audio from his porn video, the truth was that some women did make ecstatic noises like that. Maybe Lilly was wrong about therapy, too. "Lilly told me to go to therapy," he blurted out to Nell one afternoon, interrupting her detailed description of her latest Friday night dinner-and-drinks date with Kathie. "She says I might have a problem."

"Maybe you do have a problem." She stared at him. She said this in the same dull, matter-of-fact voice she might use to make an announcement that there was going to be a change of date for a meeting of the Cheer Committee. "Frankly, the way I see it, nothing seems to be working out for you. Maybe *you* are the problem."

Mallory hunkered down in his cubicle for the next few days, answering customers' calls in the dispirited voice of all the other drones who had completely given up and were slaving their lives away for Algonquin J. Tycoon. Harrison stopped by his cubicle and told him he wanted a name by Friday, or he was going to fire both Chub and Adele. He seemed disgusted with Mallory's indecision. Mallory now wondered why he had ever wasted his time dealing with those two losers.

He wasn't happy. Lilly had rejected him. Nell just wanted him as a sounding board for her tales of her fascinating affair with Kathie. Officer Selby treated him like a nut case who needed instruction on so simple a thing as pulling the trigger on a gun. Further back, his old hetero girlfriend had told him he made her sick. He didn't have any other friends. His bill for his last personalized computer advice from Manly Man had put him close to his credit limit on his third card. He hated his job. The only good things in his life were his Escalade and his .30-.30, and he hadn't even managed to get the bullets for that rifle out of their box yet.

Harrison popped his head into his cubicle early Friday morning. His half glasses had slid halfway down his nose. He looked worried, distracted. "Decision time."

"Can you give me an hour?"

"You started this game, and I'm sick of it. Make up your mind."

"I'll be in your office in fifteen minutes."

Mallory was frustrated. The only reason he'd made this deal with Harrison was to get Lilly under his total control, but Lilly turned out to be too snotty and self-righteous to get into bed for her brother's sake. All he got from Lilly was a recommendation that he go into therapy. He didn't need therapy. He felt that both Lilly and Chub had cheated him.

He took the long way through the corridors of cubicles toward Harrison's office. He glanced quickly into each cubicle as he passed, wondering if every occupant was as unhappy and unfulfilled as he was. As he rounded the corner and came to the last row of cubicles leading to his supervisor's office, he was surprised to see Adele staring at him through her oversized, shocking pink glasses. He knew Adele was a customer service representative like he was, knew she was supposed to be facing the computer screen and wearing her headphones. "Do I know you?" she suddenly called out. "Aren't you my lawyer?"

Mallory stepped into her cubicle, brandishing his belly to make her roll back her chair a foot or two. But she kept talking. "Customer service. You know what it's like. I've been doing it for 17 years.

And now they want to kick me out." She punctuated her sentence by screwing up her lips, a maneuver that rearranged the map of wrinkles on her face. "Seventeen years, and now they want to pull the plug on me."

"They say you're not talking sense to the customers."

Her look couldn't have been angrier if he had been a member of management confronting her. "Ninety-two percent! Ninety-two percent of my customers said they were very satisfied with my service."

Mallory was stunned. He had never gotten over 35% approval from his customers. Judging by the percentages, Adele was more than twice as good as him at the job. What was worse was he had to make a choice now between Adele and Chub. And no matter which way he went, there was no advantage to him. He had to make a choice, but he had lost his usual moral compass. He had always made all his choices based on whatever would make him feel good in that moment. That method had always made every decision easy – up until now.

Adele put a finger to her face as if she'd forgotten something. "Oh dear. Oh honey, something new has come up that I need to talk to you about. I'd like your opinion on this. Mr. Trump has called me and asked me to be his First Lady the next time around."

*** ***

Mallory strode into Harrison's office, proud that he had made up his mind. Harrison was on his desk phone. He motioned for Mallory to sit down. "Okay, okay, fine," he murmured into the receiver. "But I want you to remember this was not my recommendation." He hung up and sighed, stared at Mallory.

"The deal's off," Harrison began. The words seemed to stick in his throat.

"Oh yeah? Let me tell you. You're going to regret this." Mallory at this point couldn't care less whether Harrison fired Adele, or

Mallory Goes to Therapy

Chub, or both of them. But his long-honed instincts for bureaucratic infighting kicked in, telling him to act angry and offended. "We're going to sue. We're going to make your life miserable."

Harrison held up his hand to make Mallory stop talking. Then he let his hand sink slowly to the desk, following its path down with his eyes. "No, it's not what you think. I just got word from the Director of Operations upstairs. Adele is being promoted to the position of Training Supervisor on the second floor. She'll be getting a big raise."

Mallory was dumbstruck. "She just told me that Trump has asked her to be his First Lady."

Harrison leaned forward, both hands flat on his desk, shaking his head. "I guess I'm learning how this company operates. Management has always said their decisions are objective, data driven. Well, can you guess who, of all the customer service representatives on the first floor, has the highest percentage of customer satisfaction?"

It took Mallory a few seconds to connect the dots. "But she's still batshit crazy."

"I know. But that decision was taken out of my hands." Harrison allowed himself a little smile. "And so, Adele is no longer my problem." He paused, waiting for Mallory to say something, but Mallory stayed mute. "So, the only personnel problem I have now is Chub." Still, Mallory said nothing. The mention of Chub's name just reminded him of Lilly, and of Lilly's opinion that he was psycho, and of Nell agreeing with that opinion. He couldn't pretend he had any interest at all in what Harrison did to Chub.

"This whole company is a batshit crazy," Harrison went on. "Chub's a good guy. I think he's getting some help. I'm not going to fire him."

*** ***

Chub and Lilly insisted on taking him out to dinner, and Mallory insisted on the Dough and Go. The Dough and Go was where Mallory got his doughnuts to eat at work every morning as well as his carryout dinner meals, usually pizza or tuna salad subs. They sat in one of the plastic booths across from the long counter. Mallory rarely sat at the stools at the counter because he didn't want to hear any snide comments about his size. Spike, the young kid who usually waited on him, was the owner's son. He was a community college student and, aside from Manly Man, he was the sole source of Mallory's knowledge of the world around him. Spike raised his eyebrows on seeing Mallory's unexpected companions. His glance lingered a little longer on Lilly.

"We can't thank you enough," Chub began. Lilly had come directly from work and was wearing a short white skirt over patterned stockings. She smiled at him as she shifted in her seat to cross her legs under the table. Mallory was disappointed that he didn't have a better view of that maneuver. He had to fight off his manly urges and try to focus instead on what she was saying. But it was nothing he didn't already know.

"It was so sudden." Lilly seemed to relax. Her eyes softened and sought out Mallory's. "Harrison just called Chub into his office this afternoon and said he won't be fired. I guess he really was afraid of that disability claim you filed."

"I told you I could do it." Mallory darted his eyes to brother, then sister, then back.

"I guess we can drop that claim now?" Chub suggested.

"Yes, that was part of the deal." Mallory had never actually filed a claim.

There was an awkward silence in the booth. Lilly swallowed hard. "The deal …. You saved Chub, even though we didn't meet your, um, … *terms*." She nodded at him as if to make sure he understood. Her smile was grateful, but her eyes were stern.

"What I wanted from you – I'm not asking that now." He knew he was never going to get it anyway.

"What we mean to say," Chub interjected, "is that maybe we

can repay you in another way, a way that ...."

"Therapy," Lilly interrupted quickly, as if she wanted to get to the point before Mallory's imagination ran wild over all the possibilities of what she might do for him. "I wanted to have this meeting with you in a public place, with Chub here. Otherwise, frankly, I'd be afraid to meet you. I'm not a psychologist, but I think you might be a sex addict. That's nothing to be ashamed of. If you went to therapy, you would soon learn that you're not alone in having this problem. That's what we can do for you, in return for all you've done for us. Help you get to therapy."

Therapy. The word didn't seem so humiliating to Mallory as it would have a few months before. Before Nell scorned him and began satisfying her own deviant needs while he sat alone staring at his computer screen every night. Before he learned that the only way he could get any respect at work was to drive himself into credit card hell. Before Officer Selby implied he wasn't competent to carry the type of gun that twelve-year-old boys regularly went hunting with. Before batshit crazy Adele got a 92% customer approval rating.

Chapter 5: God-Given *What*?

"Show me the law that says I can't bring my rifle to therapy." Mallory was convinced these do-gooders were trying to strip him of his manhood. The guy at the door of the church basement was dressed in jeans and a plaid flannel shirt. Mallory was sure he was one of those ministers who disguised themselves as normal people.

"It's one of the church's rules. No guns on the property. One lady, a member of my group, a very nice lady. She turned and ran around the corner of the building when she saw that gun. I have to go get her back." The man switched his glance from Mallory to Chub and Lilly, who were accompanying Mallory to his first therapy session for his supposed sexual addiction.

"That rule seems reasonable," Lilly spoke for both herself and Chub. "I mean, people go to therapy to confront their emotional problems, meeting others who are having their own emotional difficulties. The last thing you need is a gun in the room."

"I have a God-given, constitutional right to bring my gun anywhere I want!" Mallory insisted. He had no idea what his constitutional rights were. He hadn't thought of the constitution since civics class in seventh grade, a class he had passed with a D-minus. And he wasn't sure he believed in God, though he somehow hoped the minister did. Mallory had been wrongfully deprived of his gun for months after his confrontation with the SWAT team in the courthouse parking lot. He had gotten out of that imbroglio only because Officer Selby came out and faced down the trigger-happy SWAT team, and because he didn't have any bullets for the gun with him. Mallory was not now going to admit to the minister, or to Chub or Lilly, that he had never managed to open the box of bullets. But he was sure that his rights were his rights, and that was all there was to it.

"Sebastian." Lilly addressed the minister so casually Mallory immediately suspected they were lovers. Maybe she went for the older type, bald with just an inch-wide circle of white hair left to prove he once was a man. "Sorry about this glitch. We didn't anticipate this. But, like you said, nobody would be here if they didn't have problems. Let's see if Chub and I and Mr. Mallory can work this out."

They didn't have a chance to work it out themselves, as a police squad car, lights flashing but without a siren, rounded the corner and almost ran into them. Braking sharply, the officer then jumped out and quickly scanned the group.

"Kevin Mallory? Again?" The group froze. Lilly's mouth dropped open in surprise. "Mr. Mallory, I'm glad you've at least learned how to safely carry that gun." Officer Selby moved toward them, in such a slow, casual way that all the civilians seemed to relax. "Lady called from the parking lot on the other side of the church. Man with a gun. I guess that's you, Mr. Mallory. Reverend, you want to tell me what's going on?"

"I'm not a minister. I'm Sebastian, the group therapy facilitator. But this church has a rule: no guns anywhere on the premises. I've told this man that we welcome him with open arms to begin the healing process. We just can't have the gun."

"Is this rifle loaded, Mr. Mallory?"

"No."

"Still haven't gotten that box of bullets open?"

Selby was only a little taller than Mallory. Dark, wavy hair, thick black eyebrows, a ruddy complexion and a no-nonsense if not quite handsome face. Mallory squirmed at his question about bullets, but he didn't answer it.

Lilly spoke up. "Officer, we, my brother here and I, are just escorting Mr. Mallory here for his first visit to Healing Hearts Therapy. We had no idea he would bring a gun. But we think it's important that he begin this therapy. What if Mr. Mallory gives us the gun, and we'll return it to him after the therapy session is over?"

"Therapy, huh?" Selby stared at him. Mallory cringed. "Very good, Mr. Mallory. This lady has given you good advice," Selby

God-Given What?

went on. Mallory scoffed. Then Selby's tone turned authoritative. "I need this gun off the property, now. I'll take the gun, and I'll return it to Mr. Mallory's apartment tonight."

Mallory felt helpless in the face of all the police and religious power lined up against him. He handed the gun to Selby.

"You all are helping this man, I can tell." Selby's seemed relieved, and suddenly cheerful. "And thank you for speaking up, Miss, uh …."

"Lilly. Lilly Pierce." She gave Selby a wide smile Mallory had never seen on her before. Selby nodded in response. "And, Mr. Mallory, I'll see you tonight." Selby carefully put the gun in the trunk of his cruiser, got in, and started the engine.

"Well, that's more excitement than we usually have at these sessions," Sebastian the facilitator commented. "Mr. Mallory, maybe you should go right in. The group meetings are supposed to start at eight. It might be best to get there at the beginning so you can introduce yourself and give them an idea why you're here."

"Why? So all the sickos can think I'm just as bad off as them?"

Facilitator Sebastian traded quick glances with Lilly and Chub, but he was not the kind of man who was easily discouraged. "Oh, there's no requirement that you reveal your prob… the reasons you are coming to the group. There's no requirement that you talk at all, other than to say hello to the group and tell them your name. And you can even use a pseudonym – we call it a therapy name – if you wish."

Lilly gently put her hand on Mallory's arm and guided him toward the church basement. Mallory felt like he was descending those dull concrete steps into a special kind of churchly hell. But he couldn't turn around and brave Lilly's disappointment. He walked down a dim corridor until he came to an open door on the left. He peeked in, then immediately regretted it. A motley crew of twelve losers was seated in a semicircle of folding metal chairs. All of them turned to look at him. He felt like he had been brought there to explain his sins. He turned to go, but then suddenly felt a hand on his shoulder. Facilitator Sebastian guided him to an empty chair.

Chapter 6: Approaches to Therapy

Lilly was neither surprised nor discouraged by Mallory's clumsy initiation into the world of therapy. She had been in enough of these groups to know that the newcomers often denied that they needed to be there at all. She hadn't denied her problems when she was first referred to a group for teenagers who'd lost their parents. She'd had to go alone. Chub was all she had, and he was five years older and already working and going to community college. To his credit, he had always pretended he didn't mind having his bachelor independence diminished by having to take care of his baby sister. Because of her, Social Services didn't want him drinking in the home; but he *was* drinking in the home, and she had to pretend she didn't know where he stored his booze. They had each other's backs. She left her last therapy group to take a part-time job. Looking back, she thought the groups might have helped her, but she preferred to deal with the world she could see rather than the things inside her head.

She had two jobs by the time she graduated from high school, and she moved out to her own apartment when she was eighteen. Chub was already a heavy drinker by then. He couldn't blame it on his parents' sudden deaths. He had been drinking since he was fourteen. It took years for Lilly to figure out that all teenage boys weren't like that. When she lived alone with him, Chub often got sloppy drunk on weekends. She thought some of his friends were taking advantage of him. They did not take advantage of her. Chub warned them to stay away from his little sister, but her sour smirk probably did the job on its own. She grew into a woman who wasn't the least bit afraid of drunks, or impressed by drinking.

Although she didn't have much time for dating in high school, she had no trouble attracting boys – and not just Chub's old boozehound friends. But she rarely dated. She and her dates often ended the night professing they both had fun, but she wasn't the type to moon over anybody. None of the boys she dated seemed quite as mature as she expected them to be. Once a guy got too serious about her, she started noticing flaws. She didn't have time for flaws, or for working on relationships. She had been excruciatingly aware from the time she was fifteen that she didn't have the love and support other kids had and she'd have to focus to make a life for herself. And she did.

Her little niece's disappearance, and Chub's relapse, ended the period in her life when she thought her family was catching up with everybody else's. She tracked down her brother and got him back into AA and helped him make a plan to get little Stephanie back. It hurt to see Chub back at square one again while she was doing so well, loving her job, her co-workers, her clients, her boyfriend. Why was she always the lucky one?

Chub was only now taking the first steps toward finding his daughter. The process of finding her and getting her back was going to take weeks, at least. He needed something in the meantime to keep him busy, keep him from falling again into a drunken morass of despair. Mallory, she decided, was a challenging project that she and Chub could work on together. Helping Mallory in this way would give her a chance to keep an eye on her brother. And, although she was not a trained therapist, she felt she could not possibly do any more psychological harm to Mallory than he had already done to himself.

"I admit it. He's disgusting," she told Chub as they walked away from the incident in the church parking lot. "But I don't think he's dangerous at all."

"Our work here is done. We got him into therapy. We even got him into the building," Chub chuckled as he navigated his car through the church parking lot. "Wait a minute. Is that *his* car there? That guy is a customer service representative? And he drives an Escalade?"

"That's his. I'm sure. He talks about it all the time."

"He must have *family money*." She sighed to hear Chub bring up the subject of family money. It annoyed her that he mentioned this so often, as if that were the main thing that had been missing from their lives.

"Don't obsess over it, Chub. Any idiot with a credit card can lease any car they want."

"Yeah, but can he keep paying for it?"

"I know that kind of guy. They don't think two seconds ahead." They pulled out of the parking lot.

"Let's forget about Mallory for now," Chub sighed. "I still have to work with him every day. And I'm still not sure I trust him, even after what he did for me."

"Yeah, let's forget about Mallory," Lilly agreed. She waited until he stopped at a stoplight, then turned to catch her brother's eye. "Tell me, Chub. What did you think about that cop?"

*** ***

Mallory recognized Officer Selby's authoritative knock, but he hesitated to answer. As he cracked his apartment door open, he felt himself shrinking down in the presence of this better man. Selby held the rifle by its stock, business side down, and waited for Mallory to open the door wider. Mallory felt he had opened too many doors too wide recently, but he took a deep breath and let the officer in.

"I noticed it's still unloaded," Selby began abruptly. "You still don't have bullets for it?"

"You're wrong. I do so have bullets." Mallory's tone was defensive. When Selby raised those thick, expressive eyebrows, Mallory decided there was no sense in trying to fool him. The man was a streetwise cop, after all. "Okay, I only have those Chinese bullets."

Trying to get bullets for his rifle had been one of the most difficult challenges Mallory had ever faced. When he originally bought the gun, Gus, the owner of Guns-R-Us, told him he was totally out of bullets for that Winchester .30-.30 rifle. And Gus never seemed to have them in stock after that. Mallory, desperate to protect himself from the criminals he believed were running rampant in the streets, bought a box of cheap .30-.30 ammunition on the internet. But everybody, including Gus and Selby, told him he might blow himself up with "those cheap Chinese bullets."

He had never had the chance to blow himself up, simply because he hadn't yet been able to open the container they were shipped in. Mallory was not good at long-range planning, and he didn't own as much as a razor knife or a pair of pliers; and so those bullets had sat on his kitchen counter for months, gleaming with deadly power through the thick transparent plastic, mocking him every time he glanced their way. "They're still in the box," he admitted now.

Selby scanned the room, which was all there was of Mallory's efficiency apartment besides the tiny kitchen and bathroom. He located the leather carrying case for the gun in a corner of the room behind a tangle of computer and video wires. He grabbed the case, zipped the rifle inside, then knelt down and put it on the floor underneath Mallory's sofa bed – all without asking Mallory's permission. Mallory didn't mind. He was flattered to be treated with such familiarity by such a manly man.

"So?" Selby straightened up. "You're in therapy now? I guess that's good."

Mallory didn't answer, instead offered him a drink.

"No. Oh. Yeah. Okay. I'm off duty."

Mallory brought him the same glass with the same cognac left over from his attempts to seduce Lilly.

"Whew! I don't usually drink this stuff. I'm a beer man myself. But – not bad!"

Mallory made a mental note to buy some beer. He thought he might have embarrassed himself just now. Was beer for men and cognac for women?

"I did let those two do-gooders talk me into going into therapy," he admitted. He could barely look Selby in the eye.

"They say a lot of people have been helped by therapy."

Was Selby just spouting modern day, social-worker-cop talk? Or did he really believe that therapy was good, even for men? Mallory waited, hoping to hear what Selby felt about this from a real man's point of view. He couldn't shake his fear that therapy was just a crutch for pitiful losers.

But then he had an idea. "Sex addiction therapy. I might be a sex addict," Mallory added, feeling this was a problem most men could understand.

"Oh. Yeah. Maybe I could use a little of that, too." Selby flashed him a knowing smile.

Mallory was ecstatic. "Maybe you could come and join the group, too?"

"Um, no. I'm kinda busy. I'm on my own time now. I gotta get going."

"No. Wait. Maybe not therapy. Um. You know, maybe I should take those lessons. I mean, you said you'd teach me how to shoot."

*** ***

Welcome to the UniCast Cable's Customer Assistance Line. All of our representatives are currently in the bathroom. Your wait time will be approximately 94 minutes.

*** ***

Mallory decided that Chub owed him for saving his job. Even so, the employee representation business had not been worth all the hassle it caused him. He was annoyed that Chub now smiled at him whenever they passed in the corridors and sometimes even stopped by his cubicle as if they were friends. At least he could go back to his old habit of annoying customers. After batshit crazy Adele had been promoted rather than fired, Harrison had given up on cracking down on inefficient employees, and so Mallory now felt free to revert to his old philosophy of letting the customers solve their own problems.

He sometimes still fantasized about making it with Lilly. He'd have to move much more slowly than he usually did when on the track of a woman. He told Chub that, although Harrison hadn't fired him, he considered him to be on probation, and that Mallory was responsible for keeping him on track. He told Chub they should meet after work every once in a while to discuss his progress and to keep one step ahead of Harrison. "And bring Lilly. I appreciate Lilly's insight in getting me into therapy, but I'm a little intimidated by the other members of the group. I really need her encouragement."

"I don't mind you meeting with her, Kevin, as long as I'm there too, every time."

Mallory had only been to two therapy sessions so far. At the first meeting, Sebastian the Facilitator had guided him toward the chair at the end of the semicircle, which was the only chair not occupied. Mallory bent his knees a little but hesitated to sit all the way down. As soon as he did, he would become one of those losers. But Sebastian the Facilitator kept his hand on his shoulder and gently pushed him onto the seat.

"I'm here under protest," Mallory found himself shouting. "You all have deprived me of my God-given right to bring my rifle into this meeting."

The semicircle of losers did not act as surprised as he'd expected. Some of them just looked thoughtfully at him and nodded their heads. Some of the women just looked aside. He decided he couldn't continue with his speech and check out the women at the same time, so he stopped talking. There was an old, thin, frail woman who looked like she was ready to fall right off her chair. She wore large glasses with orange plastic rims that seemed ready to fall off her face. Mallory could hardly imagine doing the sex addict thing with her. There was a middle-aged woman with puffy cheeks and a little too much meat on her bones, but with pretty blue eyes. He focused on the youngest one, a girl in her early twenties, short blonde hair, short black skirt, one leg bent under herself on the chair. Mallory knew all the other sex addict men were salivating over her, and he wondered if it were possible that any of this nebulous group of sad-looking men were actually doing her. Probably not. What a waste. He was sure he could solve that problem.

Sebastian simply ignored Mallory's complaint about his gun. "Why don't you introduce yourself and tell us a little about why you are here?"

"Oh. Okay. Call me Ramsteel. A friend of mine, a gorgeous young woman, she said I was too much for her. She said therapy might help. I think she wants me to, like, *spread around the joy*, if you know what I mean."

"Welcome, Mr. Ramsteel. Let's all introduce ourselves to Mr. Ramsteel. Names only for now. No need to go into anyone's unique outlook yet." Sebastian turned to Mallory. "We don't talk about *problems* here. We believe that some people just have a different *perspective* on life. We're here to celebrate those perspectives as we each share our own."

Mallory had blanked out as soon as Sebastian started talking, and he didn't remember any names except that of Grace, the hot young blonde, and Michaela, the brunette with the blue eyes. But another loser, a man in late middle age with a wispy grey fringe of hair around a mostly bald head, and a beard that he was way too proud of, insisted on repeating his name. "Peter. You got that? *Peter.*"

Chapter 7: Misfire

Lilly was thirteen when her mother, a medical researcher who had prided herself on her active, healthy lifestyle, was diagnosed with cancer. Her bright, cheerful but confrontational personality changed almost instantly, and her whole family felt the burden of trying to pretend she was the same person underneath. Over the next few months, Lilly watched in horror as her mother's body was slowly shrunken by the cancer and its treatment. Teenage Lilly was shocked, stunned, even nauseated. She had been bickering with her mother for most of the previous year, but now the growing disdain she had felt for her mother over that time seemed to have taken root and blossomed into real disfigurement. She could not entirely convince herself that it was not her fault.

Her father would not let her visit her mother in the intensive care room on her last day. He told her that her mother had so many tubes in her she couldn't talk, she couldn't see, and it was unlikely that she could even hear. "She wouldn't want you to see her like this. She knows you love her." Lilly allowed herself to be turned away. She sat in the hospital waiting room and wracked her brain in vain for a memory of anything nice she had said to her mother in the last year.

During their constant, prickly, mother-daughter battles over the previous year, she had always felt herself trying to shrink away from her mother, and now it was as if her mother had called her bluff and was literally shrinking away herself. Lilly told herself this wasn't true. Her father assured her she hadn't hurt her mother. But in the months after her mother's death, Lilly's grief was edged with feelings of guilt that wouldn't go away.

Chub had always been a sullen teenager to his parents, exempting Lilly from his moods only because he didn't see his little sister as important enough to be worthy of his disdain. The observant little sister had been aware of his drinking since he was fifteen, but he seemed to lose all control after their mother died. She watched as her father, a mild-mannered, soft-spoken researcher like her mother, limited the discipline of his wayward son to a series of sad-eyed lectures, lectures which Chub seemed to pay less and less attention to as time passed. Chub had some obvious talent in math but, ignoring his father's advice that he would better spend his time studying, he insisted on working at any part-time jobs he could get while spending all his money on partying with friends, or on drinking by himself.

And her father seemed less patient with Chub after their mother died. The arguments between father and son grew more frequent, sometimes penetrating the fog that seemed to numb her whenever she was in the house. Lilly tried to avoid the arguing between the two males in her house. She would run to the library or to a girlfriend's house to focus on her schoolwork instead. When her father died of a heart attack six months later, she regretted all that time she had missed at home.

She had always known parts of her life would be hard, and she worked hard to make them work. After high school, she lived by herself and spent the last bit of her parents' insurance money and a small charitable grant to attend Community Tech. She had a few offers to move in with some girls she knew from high school, but she knew they would be partying all the time and she wouldn't have the time for that. She didn't want to cramp their style. She did sometimes go out with them on weekends, and she went out on some dates, but she had never felt lost or lonely on those rare weekends when neither girlfriend nor boyfriend appeared.

While in community college, she achieved genuine satisfaction from her work as an intern at Roofs Over Our Heads, a small, non-profit community housing agency. She was really good at math. Her first accounting class had seemed so obvious to her she hardly had to look at the book. The agency was glad to have her, but she did not take that job to exercise her computational skills. She wanted to deal with real people in a context that she could understand.

What she understood was isolation, scraping by. She knew she had always had Chub, and together they had at least always had enough money to get by without too much begging from the charities or the government. She knew her life had not been as tough as many of her clients' lives. But she wasn't trying to heroically save anybody. She just had an idea she could talk to these people.

She interned as a financial counselor to the tenants. Her only qualification was that she had finished Accounting I, but that fact made her the most financially knowledgeable person at Roofs Over Our Heads. The financial advice part wasn't too hard. She studied the federal and local housing subsidy rules and managed to keep a few tenants from falling into the cracks. She used her own experience to show them what bills to pay first. She begged them not to fall into the trap of payday loans. Most of her clients were women. Her job gave her the excuse she needed to wend her way into their lives, to talk to these women who had the same problems as anybody else but who didn't have anybody else to talk to. Middle aged women with children, some with epic histories of illness, abandonment, and abuse, talked to her like they knew she would understand. And she felt like she could. She experienced their lives with them for hours at a time in their cluttered kitchens and dim hallways and ratty old cars. They were the first people she had ever met who, like her, admitted they wouldn't have made it without help.

But she'd had to pull away from this direct human contact with the clients, and there was logic to this change. She needed to help more than the 25 or so people she could handle as a counselor. She needed to straighten out Roofs from the financial chaos that always seemed to be looming. And she needed a decent income herself. Her boss, Executive Director Rory McFadden, had insisted she enroll in State after she finished community college, and in truth she'd let Roofs pay for part of her tuition. She did another internship with Roofs and two more with other community organizations. She graduated *magna cum laude* in business administration and was immediately offered a job by McFadden to be the head of the new, two-person, Division of Finance at Roofs. "It's a new position, and one that's really needed." He met her eyes. "Mary's a solid bookkeeper, but we've grown, and we need someone who really understands budgets."

She felt comfortable working with grants and invoices and expense reports, financial projections and audits, light and heat and maintenance bills – so comfortable, in fact, that she began a master's degree program at night in Government and Not-for-Profit Accounting at State. But she missed spending afternoons bonding with the clients. Meanwhile, her girlfriends were dipping in and out of relationships with men. At every girls' night out, there was talk of who was getting serious with whom, and two of her friends had already paired off, maybe permanently, with the men they would probably marry. Even Chub got sober, got married, had a child, and seemed to settle into a normal life. Lilly sometimes fantasized about finding a man she could share everything with. Between work and graduate school, she hadn't had much time for a serious relationship. And she kept telling herself that, even after she first met Zach.

*** ***

"You don't have anything better to do than drive me to these therapy meetings?" Mallory was annoyed that these two do-gooders were practically forcing him to continue to undergo that humiliating experience. What he really wanted was to be alone with Lilly and convince her how much he'd changed. Or at least talk to her and get to know her. The hurt Nell put on him had once seemed like it would never heal, but maybe that was just some kind of weird lesbian witchery. He was close to finding a cure for that. But he was more aware now of the danger of stumbling forward into inappropriate relationships.

"These therapy meetings," Lilly now began. She was driving.

Chub was sitting in the front seat with her. Mallory was sitting in the back, feeling like a load of luggage. "It sometimes takes a while to realize it, but the others really aren't there to judge you."

"There's nobody in that group qualified to judge me," Mallory insisted. Even as he said these words, however, an image of group member Peter, with his bald head circled by a pathetic fringe of grey hair, his ridiculously pointy beard indicating like a laser pointer the person he was going to sneer at next, intruded on his consciousness. He worried that Peter was a defective who went to the meetings just to drag people with spirit, people like Mallory, down to his own level.

"No, there's not," Lilly surprisingly agreed. "There's nobody there entitled to judge you."

"Selby said the same thing."

"What?" Lilly suddenly dropped her patronizing, quasi-parental voice. "You mean that policeman, Officer Selby?" Mallory thought he heard a kind of flutter in her voice.

"Yeah. We're friends. Been friends for a long time."

*** ***

At his second therapy session, Michaela, the middle-aged woman with the pretty blue eyes, was tearfully telling the group why she was starting to believe her husband was having an affair. "I don't want to believe it's true. But now he's out late three or four nights a week. I want to confront him, but part of me doesn't want to know. Part of me just wants to wait and hope whatever it is just blows over. I don't …."

Mallory decided Michaela needed nothing more than a shot of courage. He interrupted her stammering narrative. "You think your husband's having an affair? Well, stick a GPS on his car and follow him. If he is, kick him out. Then lose ten pounds and find a new guy."

"Jesus!" Bald-headed Peter rolled his eyes while fingering his beard. "A simple solution from a simpleton."

"She's got a problem, she should solve it. Not whine about it."

Peter kept his gaze on the ceiling as if Mallory's opinion wasn't even worth his making eye contact. "If you believe every problem is so easily solved, what are you doing here?" he said, shifting back in his chair and waving his hand in the air as if brushing off an annoying fly.

"You want to know why I'm here? I'll tell you. People are telling me I'm a sex addict. I don't know why they think that's a problem." Mallory checked out the women's reactions. He thought he saw that hot young thing, Grace, smirk. He figured she was young enough to understand what sex addiction really felt like. "Sex addiction, that's just too much of a good thing, as far as I'm concerned."

Sebastian the Facilitator then immediately ruined Mallory's train of thought. "Maybe *too much* are the important words here. When an obsessive interest in sex damages one's relationships or otherwise interferes with one's life, then we might have a sexual addiction problem."

"You're wrong." Mallory's voice came out louder than he wanted. "I don't have a problem with sex relationships. My oldest friend's a lesbian. And I have a girl accountant friend who I don't have sex with, and I have an IT friend who's a guy."

"Then why did you say people were calling you a sex addict?"

"You tell me. You're the expert."

"In order to help you, I'd have to know a lot more about your life, and your *habits*."

"My habits are none of your business. I have the same habits as all real men. Why don't you get off me and let one of these girls talk about her sex life? What do you say, Grace?"

"I say" – Little Grace sat forward, then brushed the ends of her short blonde hair out of her eyes – "I say I don't have a sex problem at all."

"So that means you have a lot of sex?"

"Sex isn't the issue. You're new here. I guess you haven't heard enough yet about what each of us is trying to accomplish here. My mother is dying of cancer. I'm trying to face it and, you know, keep a good attitude toward … life."

Mallory shrank down in his chair and spoke not a word during the rest of the meeting. He didn't listen to anything else that was said. No one spoke to him as the group broke up. But out in the parking lot, looking for Chub's car, he started to wonder why Grace was even in this group if she didn't have a sex problem. And if she didn't have a sex problem, he wondered if that meant she was one of those liberated women who had learned the joys of submission to the powers of many manly men.

"So, how was the meeting?" Lilly questioned him as Chub started his car.

"This bunch of losers might need me."

*** ***

They had promised to take him out to a restaurant if he made it through the second therapy meeting. He insisted again on the Dough and Go. They sat again in one of the booths against the wall parallel to the counter. Spike waited on them again.

He almost hoped Lilly was gay, like Nell. He still had hope she would eventually come around and fall in love with him – unless she was gay, like Nell. Meanwhile, Lilly was chattering on about some financial issues at her housing agency, and Chub was doing a good impersonation of an interested listener. Mallory decided that he absolutely had to know if she was gay. If she was gay, that would explain why he had failed yet again to get the woman he yearned after into his bed.

The Dough and Go didn't serve alcohol, so he had not much hope of prying her out of Chub's hands and getting her into his bed that night. Mallory normally would have ignored the fact that Lilly found him psychologically defective. His belief system, now developed into an almost sacred doctrine by his long devotion to his Manly Man website, taught him that a woman's expressed opinions are only a surface camouflage covering up their deepest needs, needs which only a real man could fulfill.

Mallory, however, was having trouble applying this theory to Lilly. She seemed to have a lot more going on than these instinctive female urges. She had an important job. She helped people. She figured out regulations. She handled large amounts of money and supervised workers. She was a sister. He'd never had a sister. As he thought about all the layers of complications in her life, he realized she had buried her natural female urges so deeply that even the most manly of men could not bring them out. Therefore, he reasoned, she was probably gay. He didn't know for sure, but he did know one person who could really tell him if a woman was gay.

Selby was a streetwise cop who could size up people in an instant. He had told Mallory – too late, of course – that it was obvious that Nell was gay. Selby could tell him if Lilly was gay, too. He knew he would feel much better about his recent failures at romance if Lilly was as gay as Nell. He came up with a plan to find out.

"I'm going shooting with Selby," he announced out of the blue to Lilly and Chub.

"Oh. You mean that cop?" Again, Mallory heard that little trill in her voice. "I didn't know you knew him that well."

"Yeah, we go way back." He didn't mention that he first met Selby when the policeman arrested him for carrying a ferret down the street at night while wearing a white plastic bag over his head. Or that Selby had then nicknamed him "Mr. Plastic-Bag-Head Man." Or that Selby had intervened to save the day when the Tactical Squad had misinterpreted his statement that he was going to blow himself up.

"Oh," she said brightly. "Well, if you're going to keep that gun in your apartment, it might be a good idea to learn how to shoot it." Lilly had obviously noticed the rifle propped in the corner behind Mallory's sofa bed.

"You should come, too." Mallory imagined Lilly popping off rounds, slipping new clips in, demolishing the target, wiping the sweat off her brow with her sleeve like a real she-man. It would be such a relief to know she was gay, his failure with her was not his fault, he had just mistakenly aimed his manly pointer at the wrong target.

"You know, maybe I'd like to do that," Lilly said suddenly, cocking her head and taking a sudden breath. She met Mallory's smile with a challenging grin. "I need to try something new. When are you going?"

"Thursday, after work." He and Selby had never actually discussed a date or time. But he knew he had to say something definite or lose the moment.

"What kind of clothes should I wear?"

*** ***

Standing casually before the range master at the firing range, Selby demonstrated that the magazine was out of the rifle and the bolt was open. Without a word, he signed the book and passed it to Mallory.

"Wait a minute, Officer Selby. Are these two law enforcement?"

Mallory immediately sensed that Selby wouldn't lie, so he jumped in. "Mallory and Pierce. FBI."

"Huh. You feds wear suits even to the firing range?"

"Yes, we do." Mallory answered in a clipped voice. He tried to keep the range master's attention on himself because he was sure Lilly wouldn't lie either. In fact, he was fairly sure she was avoiding all eye contact and looking down at her black mid-calf boots. She had also worn a short black skirt that showed off her legs. It seemed to Mallory that she was toying with him. All he wanted to know was if she was hetero or lezzie, but the clues she was dropping weren't helping him settle the issue one way or the other. He hated that she would soon find out how inexperienced he was with guns. But she had insisted, even rearranging her schedule twice after he finally contacted Selby and they went back and forth over a time and date. The only good thing about her presence at the gun range was that Selby was there. Selby would later tell him which way she rolled.

"You all only got one gun? We got plenty of room today. I can get you some Department rifles if you want to speed things up."

"No, thanks." Selby's voice was strained. "For some reason, my friends both want to shoot this one particular rifle." He shrugged. "Apparently, this one has a history."

They quickly walked across the gravel surface to the last shooting enclosure. There was no one anywhere near them. This was fortunate, since Mallory hadn't brought the required safety glasses or earplugs and Selby had to scrounge them from a neighboring enclosure. Lilly had brought everything she needed.

"Let's start with how to load the gun. You have the cartridges?"

"Yeah." Mallory pulled the bullets out of his pocket, happy to relieve the internal strain in his pants caused by the rectangular box.

Selby stared at him, his voice suddenly testy. "You still haven't gotten this box open yet? You've had it for months now."

"I don't have any tools."

Selby set his feet apart and faced Mallory with squared shoulders. This awakened a memory buried deeply in Mallory's subconscious, and he cringed. But Selby just looked him in the eye and spoke softly to him, like he was talking to a child. "Let me ask you this, Mr. Mallory. When you have a problem, do you ever stop and ask yourself, 'what steps do I need to take to solve this problem?'"

"I solve problems all the time at work. That's what I do for a living."

"Okay." Selby relaxed his stance. "And I guess you tell the customers what to do, step by step. Right?"

"Yeah."

"So, what would you tell them if they needed to open a thick plastic box?"

"They never have to do that."

"But what if they did?"

"I guess ... get a big knife? Or a giant pair of scissors?"

"Well, those suggestions seem reasonable. So, if you could solve this problem for your customers, why couldn't you solve the same problem for yourself?"

Mallory didn't know the answer to that question. He knew he didn't really solve that many problems for customers. He was often unsure of what steps the customers should take. Selby's argument seemed a little off base, like it didn't apply to him. But he started to wonder if that was exactly his problem – that nothing applied to him, that he wasn't even man enough to fit into Selby's logic.

"I think he's just saying ...." Lilly's voice came from somewhere behind him. "I think he's just saying you might give up too easily sometimes."

Selby approached him and pulled the box of bullets out of his hand. He put it on the ammo shelf, took out a pocket knife and started systematically sawing through the heavy plastic container. He was making progress, but very slowly. Mallory was happy that Selby didn't say anything else. That's why he liked cops. That's why he liked Selby. He turned to Lilly, but she was looking past him. "Oh, look. I think he's got it open!"

Selby was now prying the bullets out of the box with his fingers, one by one. "Hey, look. These aren't Chinese bullets after all. They're *Serbian* bullets. They won't blow us up."

"Good!" Lilly's voice sounded behind him. "Can I help you load them in?" She quickly crunched through the gravel and edged around Mallory so she could be face to face with Selby. Mallory could tell Lilly was more interested in Selby than the gun. Lilly was hetero. She was hetero, but she had still thrown him over. Now he couldn't use the excuse that she was from Planet Deviant. He had to admit to himself he'd struck out with a real woman this time. Manly Man would tell him to avoid her from now on.

At least he would soon know how to shoot a rifle. Mallory paid no attention to the almost 30 minutes of safety instructions Selby rattled on about. He saw Lilly repeating his words soundlessly, staring at the bullets, then the gun, then back at Selby's eyes. He wasn't resentful of Lilly's fascination with Selby. He knew he was not yet half the man that Selby was. When Selby demonstrated the proper stance for shooting, Lilly stood up with him and studied his posture.

Mallory stood up himself. "I want to go first." Before Lilly could even object, he brushed by her, picked up the rifle and began to stagger around, hugging it like a drunken bar patron who had just grabbed some random woman off a barstool. But Selby quickly crushed Mallory and the gun in a manly caress, then slowly force-walked him in a half circle until the barrel of the gun was pointing downrange.

"Never! *Never* point that gun anywhere you don't want to shoot."

Mallory nodded blindly.

"Open your eyes." Selby's voice dramatically softened as he loosened his grip on Mallory's shoulders. "Never point that gun at anything you don't want to kill."

"Okay. What'll I shoot?"

"Do you know how to load it, chamber it, sight it in? It didn't seem like you were listening."

"Yeah-yeah. Sure. Show me again. This way, right? Is that the target over there?"

"We haven't even rolled it out yet."

"Why can't I shoot the target right where it is?"

"Because you might kill somebody."

"Oh." Mallory watched in dismay as the target, which was just a bunch of black concentric circles on a white background, was slowly reeled out so far into the field that he could hardly even see it. "I'm supposed to hit that?"

"Yeah. You know how to use the sight, right?"

"Yeah-yeah." Mallory had no idea. He quickly lined the rifle barrel up in the general direction of the target area and pulled the trigger. The powerful blast exploded in his ears just as the rifle stock slammed hard into his shoulder. He dropped the gun and fell to the ground, his ears ringing. He tried to put his hands over his ears, but his right shoulder hurt too much to move. He was vaguely aware of Selby approaching, then picking up the rifle and carrying it away. It was Lilly who came and spoke to him first. She helped him sit up, but his ears were ringing so loudly he couldn't hear what she was saying. With a hand on either side of her head, she pointed to her own ear protection. He maneuvered his legs under his body and stood up shakily. His hearing seemed to be coming back. Selby came over and asked if he was okay. He nodded, though he really wasn't sure. They led him to an observer's bench set up well behind the firing line. Selby and Lilly kept asking if he was okay. Annoyingly, Selby kept pantomiming his sentences, even though Mallory could hear him now.

Mallory interrupted. "Those damn Chinese bullets! Everybody said they'd blow up."

"They didn't blow up." Selby dropped the pantomime. "You didn't listen to anything I said. You have to wear ear protection. You have to hold the butt firmly against your shoulder. You have to aim with the sight."

"The bullets didn't blow up?"

"No. The bullets were fine. Why don't you listen to anything anybody says?"

Mallory went silent. He was thoroughly ashamed of his decidedly unmanly display with the firearm. Lilly had been leaning toward him, hands on hips, during Selby's speech, but now she backed up, hands still on hips, and her eyes were wandering from him to Selby to the firing line.

"My turn?" She moved slowly down toward the firing line.

Mallory grabbed Selby's sleeve. Selby turned back to him. Mallory shook his head no.

"Why?" Selby pantomimed.

"It's my rifle. My bullets."

"I'll make her buy her own bullets. They sell them here."

"It's not that," Mallory admitted. He gestured for Selby to come closer. "I just don't want to be shown up. You know what I mean, right?"

Selby's jaw dropped a fraction, but then he nodded. His eyes crinkled into a smile. "I wouldn't want to be shown up by that nice lady, either."

Lilly seemed miffed when Selby told her that they had better quit for the day. Hands on hips again, she complained that she hadn't even gotten to fire a single shot.

"Maybe I'll bring you up here some other time. Mallory just told me we can leave the gun in my locker here. You've had all the instruction today. Next time you can get right down to shooting."

Lilly opened her eyes wide and smiled. "Okay," she said. "It's a date."

Chapter 8: Daring to Ask

Mallory's ears were still ringing when he arrived back at his apartment. He was furious with himself for ignoring Selby's instructions about handling the rifle. He knew he had no chance with Lilly now that he had made a fool of himself. And she was obviously much more interested in Selby anyway. Even with his new suits and his Escalade, he had once again failed in love. And even in therapy, Peter had made him feel like an imbecile. He turned on his computer, searching for solace, but the images on the flat screen, even with audio enhancement, did nothing to assuage his feelings of ineptitude and loneliness. He collapsed back on the sofa and stared at the ceiling and entertained the kind of thoughts he had never allowed into his head before.

Lilly was never going to fall for a man like him. Nor was any other good woman. Selby was the closest thing he had now to a male friend, but the policeman was disgusted with him now. At work, Chub visited his cubicle once in a while, but Mallory knew he didn't really deserve Chub's gratitude. He hadn't actually done anything for Chub. He had simply lucked out in Chub's case due to the ineptitude of UniCast's management. He had never gone out of his way to do any good for anyone. Every friendship he had ever started had been for his own convenience.

Echoes of the low points of his childhood always flooded his brain when he was in a down mood like this. On his good days he could convince himself that he had been a worthy son. On his down days he admitted to himself that neither his mother nor his father had ever been satisfied with him. His mother noticed every one of his little mistakes, making him constantly uneasy in her presence. He had sometimes felt like a dog cowering in the corner, waiting to be hit again. His father sometimes told him not to worry too much about her "female picking, picking, and picking." In fact, his father told him not to worry about anything anybody said. "Be your own man. That's all that matters."

When his father left, when Mallory was ten, his father promised he would teach him "the straight dope, not watered down and prissified like your mother would like the world to be." For years young Mallory held onto the belief that he would learn this straight dope. But on the two or three occasions when he was alone with his father after the divorce, his father did nothing but complain about his mother. This made young Mallory feel like he was on the wrong side, because he was living with his mother. Was he supposed to have spoken up, insisted that he live with his father when they split up? He must have let his father down in that way. But he couldn't even bring himself to ask his father if that were true. Then he felt it was too late to ask. He had always been a couple of steps short of being an adequate son. When his father stopped coming around entirely a few years later, Mallory felt that he couldn't blame him.

The afternoon slowly faded into a late June dusk, but Mallory lay still without turning on a light. The creeping darkness was almost comforting. But then he heard voices on the landing outside his apartment door. He decided to go out and talk to his neighbor. He had no specific plan. Thomas, the twenty-year-old college student, lived there with another Black roommate. Mallory had had extensive dealings with Thomas and his parents the year before, but Mallory was now *persona non grata* with the parents. It was because of all the lies he had told them, especially his pretending to be a lawyer and representing Thomas in court. The parents had moved on to their newly-built house, and Thomas had collected a roommate and was now busy attending State and running track. They didn't speak much anymore.

"Hey, Thomas. Nice to see you."

Thomas turned, but his smile was wary. He introduced Mallory to his new roommate. Mallory simply nodded and mumbled hello. He still didn't understand why people were supposed to be happy to meet complete strangers, but he thought maybe Thomas would like it if he pretended to be interested in meeting his friend. After that, he had nothing to say. "Well, um, goodbye." Thomas and his friend said goodbye also, and Mallory turned and went back into his apartment. Thomas had forgiven him a lot. Thomas was a good person, with great parents. That family was living proof that not every family was dysfunctional. He closed the door to his apartment and turned the lights on.

He lay down on his sofa bed and stared at the walls. If good people really existed, what made them that way? But his mind soon wandered away from this philosophical thought to the question of what he would have for dinner. He was just about to dial the phone to call the Dough and Go when it rang, vibrating in his hand.

"Kevin, I'm just calling to see if you are alright." It was Lilly's comforting, resonant voice. When he said nothing, she added, "You seemed pretty shaken up at the range today."

"Yeah. Yeah, I was." This woman seemed to inspire honesty in him. He didn't mind her knowing his faults. "I was kind of shocked. But my ears have finally stopped ringing," he laughed.

"So, you are okay now? Do you need anything?"

"Nothing that you would ever give me."

"Oh, shame on you!" She laughed and clicked off.

The next day, at UniCast, he let himself relax and talk to the customers in a leisurely way, as if he had all the time in the world. But he could do this for only a few hours at a time, and he soon found himself in the break room. Nell followed him there eagerly, bursting with enthusiasm.

"Kathie has her own condo. Fifth floor apartment. View of the lake!"

"You've been there?"

"Yes, once. It's beautiful!"

"You guys go out every weekend?"

"Yes. Well, Friday nights, drinking, like, you know … before."

Before was all the Friday nights he had been cat sitting for her. *Before* ended with the night she returned from drinking with Kathie and ushered him quickly out the door. *Before* was when he looked back in the window and watched as Nell seduced a trembling Kathie, step by step, into her cesspool of lascivious lesbian pleasures.

"You guys don't seem too lovey-dovey around the office."

"Well, you know, if we admitted it around here, we'd probably have to register our relationship with personnel or something. We just don't want to do that."

Mallory was stunned that Kathie and Nell had not made their relationship official yet. Why was the normally up-front Nell debasing herself with this secrecy?

"What does Kathie do on *Saturday* nights?" he challenged her.

"She has family obligations." Nell momentarily broke eye contact as she said this, but then quickly met Mallory's eyes with her usual assertive stare. "And anyway, I can't afford a cat sitter two nights a week."

*** ***

Mallory had lost all interest in hot, young Grace at his therapy group the minute he found out her mother was dying of cancer. But then he wondered if that was really being fair to Grace. Should Grace be deprived of his attention just because her mother was sick? Mallory wasn't sure of how this moral dilemma should work out. But Grace said hardly anything at all at the next meeting, and Mallory's attention focused on Michaela.

Sebastian the facilitator had pulled Mallory aside after the last meeting. "Mr. Mallory …."

"Call me Ramsteel in this building."

"Okay, Mr. Ramsteel, I think you were a little harsh with Michaela at the last meeting – you know, telling her to get a GPS, kick her husband out, lose weight. The therapy group is not here to tell people what to do. We're here to help them figure out for themselves what they need to do. If they knew for sure what to do, they wouldn't need therapy."

"Why do I need therapy, then?"

"I can't answer that question. Only you can answer that question."

Mallory thought about that question. Half of his reason for coming to therapy in the first place had been to find a way into Lilly's heart. That hope was gone. But Lilly had also convinced him that there might be something less than desirable in his pornographic approach to love. He had been disappointed so far in the lack of sex talk in the group. If he wanted this group to help him get on a higher plane, they needed to at least acknowledge that part of their lives that had been spent in the gutter.

"Michaela," he said now. "You say your husband's out screwing someone else four times a week. How many times a week does he screw you?"

Peter clapped his hand to his forehead and stared at the ceiling.

"Mr. Ramsteel," Sebastian the facilitator intervened before Mallory could react. "Please try not to be so blunt. We don't want to make people uncomfortable here."

"Okay. Sorry. Michaela. Do you still have sex with your husband?"

"Yes. Maybe two or three times a month. I have to start it, though. Otherwise, he hardly even looks at me when he's home." Her wide blue eyes seemed open to the group, vulnerable. "To tell the truth, he hardly even looks at me even when we're doing it."

"I guess that's not all the sex you want?" Mallory persisted.

"I … I guess not. Mostly I just want …."

"I can do you every night if you'll give me your address."

Pointy Beard stared at the ceiling again. "For the love of God, shut up!"

"What's the point of having a sex addiction therapy group," Mallory countered, "if we can't talk about sex?"

"This isn't the sexual addiction therapy group, you moron," Peter sneered. "The sexual addiction therapy group is down the hall in Room 3."

"Oh. Oh." Sebastian the facilitator was so perturbed he almost rose off his chair. "Maybe this is my mistake. There was some, um, *difficulty*, in arranging Mr. Ramsteel's admittance to the church basement the first night. When that was all cleared up, and I came downstairs, Mr. Ramsteel was already seated here in the Healing Hearts Therapy group."

"I wanted the sex group," Mallory confirmed.

"Oh. Well, they don't meet on Tuesdays anymore." Sebastian had dropped his apologetic tone. "They meet on Thursdays now. I'll contact them and arrange for Mr. Ramsteel here to attend the very next one. My apologies to everyone."

"But I kind of like this group," Mallory suddenly objected. "Except for the bald guy with the beard. You can still talk about sex here, at least a little bit, right?"

"Please, no porno chasers here," Peter talked to the ceiling as if praying.

"I never said I was," Mallory insisted. "But, you know, I'm going to admit it. I was into porn. I am into it. But I like everybody here, except Pointy Beard here." He turned toward Sebastian. "Can I stay?"

*** ***

Selby's tone was much more hesitant than his normal police voice. "Um, Mr. Mallory …."

"Call me Kevin, please."

"Okay, Kevin. I set a date and time to go back to the shooting range. A week from Thursday at 6 o'clock. Lilly can go at that time. Are you interested in coming?"

"Where's my rifle?"

"In my locker at the range. Don't you remember? You said I could put it there. You refused to touch it."

"Oh. Yeah. But I want it back."

"No problem. You can take it back next Thursday."

"I'm not coming."

"Should we set another date?"

"That's what she called it, right? A *date*." Mallory's tone was mocking.

"She just meant a time and place."

"She called me, you know, just to see how I was doing."

"You got a nice girlfriend, Mr. Mallory."

"She's not my girlfriend."

There was a pause on the line. "Oh. Well, then, I guess you wouldn't mind if I kept this *date* with Lilly, and you and I go to the range some other time."

"Just don't use my Chinese bullets. You saw how they explode."

"Mr. Mallory, don't you remember …? I just don't know what to say to you."

"Don't let Lilly blow herself up."

*** ***

Chub appeared in Mallory's office, a guilty grin on his face. "Did you hear about Adele? She's been fired."

"Ha!" Mallory laughed out loud. "Harrison knew she was crazy, but they forced him to promote her. Now she's been fired?"

"Yeah. I was in his office when he heard the news. Apparently, Adele barged into a meeting the regional manager was holding and told him she was there to change his diaper."

"How's Harrison taking the news?"

"He was laughing so hard I thought he'd bust a gut."

"Oh. But …." Mallory gestured for Chub to come closer. Chub leaned a hand on Mallory's desk, his long combover hanging down one side of his head. "This might not be good news for us," Mallory warned. "The last thing we want is for Harrison to be energized. Try to keep out of his sight for the next few weeks."

"Huh?"

Mallory thought it was quite possible that Harrison would

again consider firing Chub now that Adele was out of the way. There never had been an official personnel investigation, much less an official act clearing Chub's personnel record, despite what Mallory had told Chub and Lilly a few weeks ago. But the longer Chub stayed out of sight, the less likely it would be that Harrison would take up the sword again – and the less likely Chub and Lilly would find out what really had happened.

Mallory noticed that Chub didn't look good. He didn't slur his words or smell of alcohol, but he had dark circles under his eyes like he hadn't been sleeping well. He denied that he had been drinking. "But I haven't been sleeping."

It occurred to Mallory that Chub might be sad because he had lost all contact with his daughter. Five weeks had passed, and Chub apparently hadn't gotten over it yet. Mallory now guessed that some people had family ties that strong. He had always assumed those people were faking it, and that in truth everybody was alone and would always remain that way. But he had seen that Chub loved his sister, Lilly, and so he figured Chub might be really missing his daughter.

"It's Stephanie, right? You're sad that she's gone."

"She's not *gone!*" Chub's eyes glittered with tears. Or maybe with anger. Mallory couldn't tell which. Mallory wondered what to do. He thought about offering Chub the rest of his half-eaten éclair, though he hoped Chub didn't really want it. He racked his brain for something that would help. He considered offering Chub his chair, but there was no way those two portly men could accomplish a switch in that tiny cubicle. Chub was breathing heavily, almost sobbing. Some kind of liquid was dribbling onto Mallory's desk.

"I'm calling Lilly." Mallory said decisively. "Give me her number."

Lilly was in the middle of a conference call. "Get off that call right now," Mallory ordered. "We're in a bar, and Chub's about to order a Scotch and soda."

Lilly obeyed. Mallory handed the phone to Chub. He didn't

want to listen to all of Chub's whining, so he exited his chair and walked down the long corridor of cubicles to the break room. He had seen some new bear claws in the vending machine that morning. Life was becoming a little more interesting.

He found Nell in the break room, brewing a cup of her Cheer Committee coffee. She raised her eyebrows and motioned with her head toward the machine. He said he'd take a cup, too. They watched silently as the last of the coffee dripped through the grounds. She grabbed two cups and poured his. They mixed their respective cups separately and sat down before either of them said a word.

"I actually came here to be alone," she started. He didn't say anything, but he didn't move away. She raised the cup to her lips and gently blew on it for longer than was necessary. He still didn't move. He thought it would be better if he stayed. He saw her shoulders gradually relax. She seemed to accept his presence then. He could tell she wanted to talk.

"Kathie told me she doesn't want to go out with me this Friday." She whispered the words slowly, like a confession.

"Why?"

"I don't know, Kevin. I just don't know. There could be a million reasons she doesn't want to go." Nell's attitude was suddenly testy.

"Of course."

But then Nell's voice suddenly dipped almost to a whimper. Mallory had to nod toward her to hear it. "But when she said it, she just looked at me with, you know, those eyes, those green eyes, and …. I mean, I knew something was wrong."

Mallory was puzzled. Would it have been okay if Kathie had brown eyes?

"I think she *wanted* me to ask her why. I felt like she was almost daring me to ask her why."

"What'd she say when you asked her?"

"Don't you get it? I was afraid to ask. I was terrified of what the answer might be. Up until now, I thought I wasn't afraid of anything in life, Kevin, but I was so scared she was going to break up with me. I was thinking, *as long as she doesn't say it, I can still have hope*. I know that's so, so pathetic."

Mallory stayed silent himself. He didn't get this at all.

"Being with her … it was everything I ever wanted." Nell's eyes filled with tears. "But now I'm afraid to be alone with her. It's all so awful!"

Mallory had never seen Nell so defeated. He had no idea what to say to her.

"Could I get you a bear claw?"

Chapter 9: A Harmonious Couple and a Gun

When she first met this blonde, handsome guy at a party, she brushed him off, believing that such an outgoing, gregarious Adonis would not have more than one night's interest in her. She went out with him three times without letting him past her apartment door, just to see if he'd keep coming back. Every time he came back, she got more excited. Even though their lives were very different, he seemed to take her seriously. When she finally decided to let this handsome, virtual stranger softly ply his way into her secrets, she was more than satisfied. She woke up the next morning convinced she had made a find.

But it wasn't like her to move in with a man. Sometimes she thought she now stayed in their apartment because she had never really awakened from that first night with him. Actually living with him, of course, hadn't been exactly the same as those first dreamy nights. She hadn't expected anything different. Nobody was perfect. He worked in sales for a firm selling mortgages over the internet. His company, he said, was trying to progress from selling mortgage loans to individual homebuyers, an industry that was tightly regulated, to the "wild west" of construction and development financing. He told her he was being trained to underwrite these loans.

"Oh. Evaluate their finances? That sounds a little bit like my job, accounting."

"Eh. We have people who do that," he explained. "I couldn't stand doing that. No, my job is to meet with the contractors in person and convince them we'd be a better choice for financing their project."

"So, you're a salesman?"

He smiled. "You could say that. But I have a much fancier title.

And I make a lot more money than most salesmen when a deal works out."

"Is that what's important to you?"

"Isn't that what's important to everybody?"

His outlook on life didn't exactly match hers, but she told herself she hadn't been looking for a clone. He was great looking, smart, and personable. She noticed how easy life seemed to be for him. He was always the first man in the room the women noticed. From the way he talked, he seemed to really enjoy his job, especially meeting with potential clients. He drank with his clients regularly, but he could do so without the slightest hint of the kind of addiction that had devastated Chub. He'd had so many girlfriends in the past that it was weeks before she dared to flatter herself that he might really want her to stay with him long term.

She was sure that Zach was going to float up somewhere high in his company over the years. But he didn't seem to have that drive to make a difference that Lilly felt. But even if all of Lilly's energy and drive was "wasted," as Zach sometimes joked, on her non-profit work, they both seemed confident in their roles. He would make the money, and she would save the souls.

One evening, as they were clearing the plates after dinner, he mentioned almost casually that they should probably make their "situation" permanent.

She froze. "I … I …. We don't know each other well enough."

"We've been living together for almost six months. I know you enough to know you're good for me."

"Oh."

Later that night, when she thought about this conversation, she realized she had been expecting more from him. She didn't mind the casual way he first expressed himself. He had soon after said he loved her, and that was enough. But as she lay in bed that night, she found herself wishing he were more curious about her. He didn't seem interested in Roofs once he found out their total budget was less than two million. He didn't want to hear her complaints about

McFadden, her boss, who left most of his work for her to do while he constantly traveled around the country. And she hadn't been able to convey to him the pride she still felt for holding out against the social worker who wanted to put her in a foster home when she was fourteen – and for convincing everyone, against all the evidence, that nineteen-year-old Chub was mature enough to take care of her. But were these just little childish points of pride?

"I love you, Zach." She touched his face to make sure that he heard. She meant those words, but they were also words of compromise, to buy time.

*** ***

"I don't see anything wrong with our life as it is," she murmured to him one night in bed a few months later. They were lying in each other's arms, relaxed after making love. She still warmed to his touch at night, but she didn't think about him in the daytime as much as she had at first.

"I want us to get married. I want to have kids. We need to start a family. Don't you ever think about that?" He had never mentioned children before. But he was always more direct, less guarded and polite, when her head was resting contentedly on his chest and she couldn't meet his eyes. She sensed he wanted to state his position without having to read the reaction on her face.

"I love you, Zach." She didn't raise her head. She stroked his stomach instead. Sometimes that got him going again. "But I don't want to think about all the rest of that right now."

"When do you want to think about it?"

She slid her fingers further down in a circular motion, still enjoying the license she had to play with a man like that. He still had that same muscular body that had attracted her to him on the beach that hot summer day they met. He still had that amazing mop of curly blonde hair. She'd been attracted to him from the beginning, and he had convinced her over time that he was a good man. What was she waiting for? She had learned in therapy that waiting for miracles was just another way of avoiding real life. Her dealings with Mallory had helped her to realize what a prince of a man Zach was, comparatively speaking. Her girlfriends often challenged her to tell them one thing that was wrong with Zach. She always said he worked too long hours. Their replies were always the same: *Look who's talking.*

Well, there was one thing, she had told one of her girlfriends once. Zach made friends almost too easily, in every situation he found himself in. He got along so well and so quickly with everyone that Lilly worried about that. "There's a million girls who would go out with him."

"So? What's wrong with that? You're the lucky one."

"I know *I'm* the lucky one. But I don't know if he thinks *he's* the lucky one."

"Oh, come on. I know he wants to marry you. I mean, he's told everybody."

"What!"

Zach's telling everyone didn't help Lilly to feel special at all. It seemed like his affection for her was diluted among all his friends, half of them strangers to her. She began to harbor a nagging fear that her status with Zach depended on their opinions. As far as she knew, Zach's friends thought she was okay. She was happy she had been found acceptable, but she still didn't like the feeling of being shopped around.

"I guess it's just me," she had told her friend. "I grew up in a tiny family. I mean, I always knew they all loved me, always. Even Chub when he was an obnoxious teenager. I mean, nobody else's opinion would ever change their opinions of me."

"People's opinions do count. They should."

"I know. You're right. I have to keep reminding myself that I don't come from a normal family."

In bed now, Zach turned and grabbed her circling hand, gripped it in his. "We've been living together for almost six months. I've asked you to marry me too many times. Don't you think I deserve an answer?"

She raised herself off his chest, looked in his eyes, dark against the faint luminescence of his blonde hair. He was not the same as her. He didn't love her in the way she had always dreamed of being loved. But that dream had just been a fantasy. And he was a good man.

"Okay. I'll marry you," she found herself whispering.

"You mean it? We're engaged!" He jumped up to a sitting position so fast her head slid into his lap. "I'll have to run out and get a ring!"

"But, one thing. No ring, yet. I don't want anybody to know it until I get used to the idea myself."

"Uh, that's kind of the point of being engaged. You wear the ring so everybody will know it."

"Yeah, but … I need to get used to the idea myself first. Help me, Zach. You know I'm not a completely normal woman. Let me do it my way."

He laughed so hard he shook the bed. "Yes. Not completely normal. I do agree with that."

She asked for and obtained an exception from her own rule to tell Chub, and Chub only. Chub did seem a little intimidated by Zach's engaging, apparently effortless way of connecting, but he seemed to like him. Lilly knew that Chub would throw his whole heart into any family that she and Zach would create. Her secret engagement to Zach had been going on for about a month when she first met Selby.

*** ***

Zach had been outraged when she told him about Mallory's crude behavior toward her in his apartment. "I'll kill him."

"Don't be silly. He didn't touch me. I think he's afraid of women, really. And Chub's been with me every time I've seen him since."

But then she remembered she had been with Mallory at the gun range – and with Selby, not Chub, as chaperone. Well, that was not worth mentioning. There had been a chaperone there, so Mallory posed no danger to her there. That was the point of their conversation. There was no point in mentioning that a different person was the chaperone. She would never be alone with Mallory again, and Zach didn't have to worry about him molesting her. That was the point of their conversation.

It also wouldn't make any sense to tell Zach that she was going back to the gun range alone with Selby. It wasn't a date, though she had accidentally used that word. She had just meant they were going to the gun range on a specific day.

Selby called and asked if she needed him to pick her up. That sounded way too much like a date, and she said she'd meet him there. She arrived early and sat in her car on the small, tree-lined parking lot facing the low, brown administration building of the gun range. She didn't see Selby, and she wasn't going to go in early and introduce herself as the woman who was supposed to meet him there. She'd just wait in the car. She admitted to herself she was a little bit attracted to Selby, but then asked herself what healthy twenty-something isn't at times attracted to random twenty-somethings of the opposite sex.

There was none of the awkwardness she expected when he arrived. He parked near her and waved her over to the administration building. They didn't talk during the short walk to the office inside. Selby signed her in as a guest and retrieved Mallory's rifle from the locker he had stored it in. Lilly cast her eyes down when the man behind the counter glanced at her. But she was not normally a shy person. She dealt with people of all kinds every day at work. She wondered if the strange frisson she felt might be caused by being around firearms.

"So, have you seen more of your friend Mallory lately?" Selby's smirk was gentle. They were walking very slowly from the office to the range.

"No. Not lately. He's going to the therapy meetings by himself now. Now that he's used to it, I guess." Somehow that sounded impersonal, so she went on. "I started him on that idea, going to therapy." She realized this sounded like she was bragging, but she decided to give herself a pass on that.

"You started him on that?" Selby seemed impressed. "I don't know if therapy is what that man needs, but he sure needs something."

The way he flatly stated his opinion was calming to her. It seemed to be okay in their conversation to have different opinions. "I think therapy might help him. He's so alone. Having a friend like you probably helps, too."

"Friend?" Selby huffed. "Okay, I guess you could say he's a friend. He started off as a suspect, though." Selby told her the story of arresting Mallory carrying a ferret in a cage down the street at night while wearing a white plastic bag over his head and with a rifle in the open trunk of his car. She laughed out loud, picturing the confrontation in her mind.

"It must be tough, being a cop."

He stopped walking and looked over at her. "No. Not always. There are a lot of good days. I love being a cop."

Lilly tried to visualize Selby going through his day, meeting people good and bad, mostly good. She could tell he thought most people were good. She could tell he thought she was good. She just knew that. She had thought she'd be jittery, shooting a rifle for the first time in her life, and being taught by a policeman she had met only once. But no.

He didn't act surprised that she remembered all the instructions from the last time. He handed her the gun and the bullets and watched her every movement carefully, but he didn't interfere. He didn't need to. "Am I ready?" she asked, and he sent the targets out over the range. The gun was heavier than it looked, and the kickback was rough on her shoulder. She aimed as well as she could but missed the target completely three out of eight times.

"Oh," she breathed out the word. "Embarrassing. Hey! Stop smiling." She could see he was trying not to laugh. She punched his chest with her open hand. Selby turned and walked a few steps away. She could see his shoulders shaking.

"Quit laughing, please, and come back here." He obeyed. "Let me try again. I think I didn't have it sighted in right."

"All right. All right."

She hit at least somewhere on the target every shot this time.

"I think you were right about the sight," Selby admitted. "And really, this is not bad at all for someone who has never shot a gun before." They didn't stop until they had used up the whole pack of Mallory's Serbian bullets.

Lilly was amazed at how high she felt when they finished. Selby had been patient and kind but not obsequious. Still, she didn't want to show herself in the gun range office, so she waited out in the parking lot while Selby put the rifle in his locker. She could have just driven away, but she wanted to thank him properly.

"They say you grow up, and you do the same job every day, and you don't have many new experiences," she spoke to him through her open window when he finally arrived back at her car. "Well, they're wrong. Thank you for this experience, Officer Selby."

"It was fun to teach somebody who really tries."

"You know, I can't afford to get really good at this, either time-wise or money-wise."

"What does it matter? We had fun this one day. Didn't we?"

"Yeah," she said. "This one day." Her voice came out differently than she expected.

Chapter 10: Hard Truth and an Easy Lie

Mallory was beginning to understand that no woman had ever fully and properly surrendered herself to his virile powers. He had been so focused on his plans to seduce Nell with cognac and lies that he hadn't noticed she wasn't interested in guys at all. Bad mistake. Then he had simply assumed that Lilly would sleep with him to save her brother's job. Total misjudgment of her character. And he had thought his old girlfriend Rose would do anything for a home and a husband, but it turned out she wouldn't stand for being made an accomplice to his schemes. Three strikes, and he was out.

It had never occurred to Mallory that other people, ordinary people without his outstanding sensitivity and extraordinary urges and passions, could suffer as much as he did from a failed love affair. He had suffered for Nell, tried to change himself for her, only to be rejected in the most mortifying way anyone could imagine. But they had forgiven each other. Now it was Nell who was suffering wrenching doubts about her new lover. He thought it was his manly duty to help. He sat down across from her in the UniCast breakroom.

"How many times have you been out with Kathie on a Saturday night?"

"Why do you care?"

"The answer is zero, I know. And you've been to her apartment only once. You told me all this." He knew Nell would appreciate his factual insights. "I know she talks to a guy on the phone every afternoon on her breaks. She's not into you anymore."

"You fucking, jealous, sicko liar!" Nell hissed.

The last part, about Kathie talking to a man on the phone every afternoon, was a lie. But Mallory felt like he had to say that to convince Nell of the seriousness of her situation. He knew Kathie had never been seen in public with Nell. He knew Kathie had withdrawn from Nell's Employee Cheer Committee and didn't appear in the breakroom as often as she used to. He knew Kathie had never lost her crush on Brad Pitt. And he had seen with his own eyes, while spying on them through the window of Nell's house, how excited Kathie had been in her first passionate encounter with Nell – but he also had seen that Kathie was dead drunk at the time.

When Nell didn't just get up and leave the break room, he knew he had hit a nerve.

"I'm sorry this is happening to you."

Nell put her face in her hands. Then she rustled in her pocketbook, came out with a tissue and wiped her eyes. Her face was blotched red. He once would have given anything to be the object of a passion this strong from Nell. He would not have let her down. Seeing her so heartbroken over Kathie confirmed his idea that they lived in a twisted world. They were both victims, and they couldn't help each other.

"But, in a way, you might be luckier than me," he said. "You had a time when you believed it was true. Maybe she did, too. I didn't have that, not for one minute, with you."

"I never told you that I loved you. Kathie did, to me."

"You act like you have nothing. Did you forget about Koko? You at least have Koko. Koko loves me, but you won't even allow me to see him. I'm the one who has nothing at all."

*** ***

Harrison intercepted Mallory just outside the break room and ordered him to come to his office. He told him to sit down.

"I just got a call from Chub. He's leaving tonight on a flight to San Diego. He's not coming into work the next two weeks."

"What?"

"He said he located his missing wife and daughter in California. He has a custody order for his daughter, and he's going there to pick her up. This is the same guy who missed fourteen straight days of work two months ago. I told him he'd be fired if he did that."

"You're all heart."

"Don't give me that, Mr. Mallory. Corporate is big on attendance. He's lucky I didn't fire him the first time."

"You're lucky you didn't try."

"You should watch your mouth, Mr. Mallory." Harrison batted his half glasses back up his nose with an energetic gesture that did not seem to bode well for Mallory. Harrison was a lot younger than his predecessor, Teitelbaum. He wouldn't be as vulnerable as Teitelbaum had been to Mallory's threats of suing him for his retirement fund. The pained, aggravated look on Harrison's pasty face did not bode well for Chub, or even for Mallory's future at UniCast.

"And I've been looking into your file. You don't have any official status as an employee representative. According to your job description, you're supposed to be on the phones full time, assisting customers."

"Well, there's a reason for that." Mallory paused while he tried to think of a reason. He scanned Harrison's face and noticed the angry lines around his eyes had softened a bit. "Sometimes an employee's role has to change over time." He checked Harrison's expression again. "You might not realize what chaos UniCast Cable was in before I started representing employees. We've had three interim managers in the six months before you got here. And do I have to remind you again that the last permanent guy who had your job, Teitelbaum, was fired for his inability to handle a personnel issue."

The personnel issue that Teitelbaum had been fired for was his failure to fire Mallory. Still, that was a personnel issue. Mallory was surprised that everything he had said so far was technically true. But he didn't yet have enough faith in himself to rely completely on the truth, so he added a blatant lie. "And Teitelbaum's supervisor, Starganoff, was pushed out because of the poor morale of this division as a whole."

"Hm." Harrison broke eye contact with Mallory and glanced all around the room, seemingly circumnavigating the huge world of problems he had inherited when he took over the Customer Service section of UniCast Cable. "You're basically saying letting you do as you damn well please would make my job here a lot easier."

"It certainly will, Mr. Harrison." Mallory's voice became much more confident as he journeyed farther away from hard facts and into his world of pure imagination. "Take Chub's case, for instance. You could fire him and face years of appeals and lawsuits, and ultimately go down in history as the cruelest manager of all time. Or you can let me find another employee who can take over his position for the two weeks he'll be gone."

"Are you telling me you can find another employee who's qualified to handle Chub's job while he's gone?"

"I already know the perfect person."

"You do? And who is that?"

"Kathie …." A sudden panic seized Mallory when he realized he didn't know Kathie's last name. "Miller, I think. Or maybe that was her married name, when she was married." Mallory had no idea if Kathie had ever been married. He felt a surge of panic that his old habit of making up reality as he went along was taking control of him again.

"Kathie … Miller? What's she do for us now?"

Although Mallory had talked with Kathie in the break room and in the Cheer Committee and in Nell's house many times, he had visited her in her cubicle only once, during their ill-fated quest to find a suitable image of a ferret for the holiday party flags. All he knew was she did something with computers. He knew Chub was a programmer, and that programming had something to do with computers. "She's an associate programmer, and she's really good."

"Okay. I'll talk to her."

"Um, let me talk to her first. Smooth the way, you know. That's kind of my real job here, anyway. Right?"

*** ***

"I'm not a programmer! I'm a statistician." Kathie's look managed to combine both resignation and disgust.

"Isn't that kind of the same thing?" Mallory always enjoyed being in Kathie's presence. She was one of the most attractive of UniCast's 226 employees, with her long, thin frame, massive blonde hair, green eyes. She had also in the past defended his ideas about how the Cheer Committee should be run – thereby showing, he believed, an incredible amount of common sense, for a woman.

"Not even close."

Not having the slightest idea about either programming or statistics, Mallory thought a detour in the conversation was in order. This might allow him to indulge in some of his more turgid fantasies about Nell and this hot woman who, he now suspected, was a screamer. "Okay. Put that aside. Let's talk about Nell for a minute."

Mallory and Kathie had stayed on relatively good terms, even though she had ruined Mallory's only chance for true love. Mallory blamed only Nell. He had exacted revenge only on Nell. Now, curiously, he sensed that Kathie was pulling away from her.

Kathie's eyes flicked over to him, then down. "Why do you want to talk about Nell?"

"You are all she talks about. She's head over heels. You know that."

"You're still jealous?" Kathie's exasperated sigh filled the space between them. "You're still trying to blame me for her dumping you?"

"Ha!" Mallory's guffaw was so loud it could be heard three cubicles down.

"What's so funny?"

He knew their affair had not been Kathie's idea. And he didn't quite understand himself why he kept focusing on the night of his own ultimate humiliation, the night he watched as Nell introduced Kathie, step by step, to the world of women-on-women love. It was the worst indignity he had ever suffered. The actions he later took to revenge himself on Nell were not legal, or even sane.

"It's not funny. It's sad." Then he thought he'd impart some of his expert psychological advice. He lowered his voice. "Funny thing. After all that, it seems like you're not into her anymore."

"This is none of your fucking business!" she hissed. "What are you trying to do, break us up so you can get back with her?"

"No. No. No. It's just …." He couldn't explain why it bothered him so much that Kathie was playing games with Nell's heart. He had previously had enough common sense to ignore the entire world of women whining about their relationships. He was sorry he had stuck his nose into this business at all.

He still had to convince her to substitute for Chub. He told her that Chub would lose his job if he couldn't find somebody to take his place for two weeks.

"I've always thought Chub was a nice guy," she admitted. "But I don't know a thing about programming."

"How hard could it be, if Chub can do it?"

"You have no idea, do you? People go to school for years to learn these things."

"You can fake it. Chuck missed fourteen straight days of work earlier this year, and hardly anybody even noticed."

"Do you know exactly what he's been working on?"

"Some kind of …." – he wracked his brain for a scientific-sounding word – *matrix*, I think."

"I never heard of that. I don't think I could do it."

"Kathie, look. I know you can fake it." *You're good at faking it, like you've been faking it with Nell*, he longed to say, but he held his sarcasm in check for the benefit of Chub and little Stephanie.

"Kevin, I just don't have the skills."

"Think about Chub," Mallory implored. "His wife Janice is a heroin addict, and a crack whore. She followed her drug dealer to the West Coast. She took little Stephanie with her. If Chub can't go and get her back, little Stephanie will be dragged along into that life. At best, she'll be living in a crack house. At worst, she could be sold into child prostitution." Most of these new details he told her were made up. Mallory was trying to stop his habit of lying about everything, but he still thought it was okay to do it for a good cause.

"What am I supposed to do if they ask me to write a program?"

"Just stall them. Take a couple of days to get your passwords set up. Then say you are getting oriented to their programming language, which you will say you haven't dealt with since college. Use Google. Always show some programming crap on your screen. Then say you ran into a *glitch*. A good glitch should last you until Chub comes back."

*** ***

The main topic of discussion in Mallory's therapy group was whether it would be appropriate for Ramsteel (ne Mallory) to stay in the Healing Hearts therapy group, or whether he would have to move to the Sexual Addiction group.

"That man has no interest in this group except as a way to get laid," bald Peter immediately intoned, aiming his chin, and thus his pointed grey beard, in Mallory's direction.

Mallory was immediately inspired to fight for his right to stay in this group. "Some people say I have a sex problem. Others say I'm just a person with normal male hormones. Who knows? But I want this group to know I have other problems, too. I bet I have as many problems as any of you." Mallory's smile brightened. "Every time I drink cognac, I get so drunk I pass out. I've just maxed out my third credit card, but I'm still driving an Escalade I can't afford. I bought a gun, but I can't learn how to shoot it. The cops have a nickname for me. They call me 'Mr. Plastic-Bag-Head Man.'"

"That does it for me," said Michaela, the brunette with the blue eyes. "You sound like an interesting man. I think you should stay." Mallory reminded himself that she had to be pretty much starved for sex.

Peter twisted his mouth like he had just bitten into an onion. "I say, go away so we can focus on people who actually want to help themselves."

"I'd kind of like to know why the police gave Mr. Ramsteel that ridiculous nickname of Mr. Plastic-Bag-Head Man." Grace brushed her blonde bangs out of her eyes.

Mallory thought she smiled at him. He knew he'd like to engage with her. "Has your mother died yet?" he called across the room.

Grace jerked upright in her chair. "Um, no. But it's getting worse." She slumped down again, but not before catching the eyes of each member of the group. "To tell the truth, it's awful. It's really awful."

"Thank you, Grace," Sebastian murmured. "I know that's hard to talk about. Mr. Ramsteel, please try not to be so blunt in your comments."

"I don't mind," Grace went on. "It is awful. But that's why I come here, to be able to say that awful truth to somebody. Thank you, Mr. Ramsteel."

Chapter 11: It Took a Village

It was Lilly's turn to make dinner. They had moved together to a two-bedroom apartment and had to economize about food. They went out to eat only once a week. She thought she had developed into a decent cook. Tonight, she was making a chicken pot pie. Zach was always appreciative, but this feeling didn't seem to translate into an equivalent culinary effort on his part. Still, she would call his efforts pretty good. And she didn't think she had anything to complain about if the worst she could say about their relationship was that he made food for her three nights a week that was only pretty good.

Zach was usually chipper when he first arrived home from work. In that way he reminded her of her father, who always managed to lighten the mood in the house when he arrived home from his lab. Once she had become a teenager, she stopped jumping into her father's arms when he came through the door, but she had always made sure he noticed her.

Zach posted pictures of themselves on Instagram almost every day. For his job, he scoured his company's internet hits for possible new sales leads daily. His company had a sophisticated IT department that handled the technical side of things. His job was to transform these electronic connections into hard money deals. He was always talking to her about potential clients he had met. She sometimes felt a little tired of this endless list of prospects, some of whom, he often said, had enough money to set them up for life. But the cast of characters seemed to change a little too often for her to catch up. And some financial bonanza always seemed to be just around the corner.

She sometimes found herself complaining to him about her boss, McFadden, who was absent so often. Zach, however, did not seem interested in that problem.

"I do want to talk to you about this," she persisted one night. "It makes my job really hard when he's away so often."

"Honey, if the situation's that bad, why don't you just get another job?"

"What about all the other employees? What about our clients?"

"You're not responsible for Roof's other employees, or for Roof's clients. You should just leave."

But she knew she wouldn't be happy abandoning Roofs. He didn't seem to understand that. He seemed to think that work was just something you did for money. They were different in that way.

Zach and Chub seemed to get along well. Chub was already speculating that she might soon start a family. She begged him not to talk like that. Chub was a computer nerd, and he sometimes acted like he was intimidated by her much more flamboyant boyfriend. When she mentioned this to Zach, he just gave her his big smile. "It takes all kinds, doesn't it?" He did seem to like everybody. He was nothing if not an easy and affable man.

Through his business contacts, Zach had helped Chub find a reliable lawyer in California. Chub's wife, Janice, was not hard to find. She had taken Stephanie and run all the way across the country – but had still been unable to keep herself off the internet. Lilly kept in constant contact with Chub, who had arrived in Los Angeles and filed his custody order in the California courts. Lilly still worried a lot about Chub's chances. He had done the worst thing in the world, as far as custody was concerned, by going off the wagon the minute Janice deserted him. Fortunately, she had no idea about that yet.

Chub told her that it was Mallory who had gotten him his leave of absence. At the mention of Mallory's name, Lilly had an instant vision of Mallory swinging his loaded rifle around at the shooting range. He was even more than a crude, sexist jerk; he was a truly dangerous imbecile. But she needed to call him anyway.

"What?" Mallory sounded annoyed as soon as she identified herself. "You want me to go shooting again?"

"No, I don't want to go shooting with you again." She fought with herself to keep from hanging up. She worried that, in his one-track mind, he would think she was calling to have sex with him. She thought she'd better cut off that line of lascivious thought right away. "I'm calling about my brother. He told me you got UniCast to agree on a leave of absence to let him go to California. You don't know how much that meant to him. So, I'm just calling to thank you. You're a strange man, Mr. Mallory, but you're not all bad."

"Not *all* bad?"

"Oh. Sorry. I didn't mean it like that. And I'm glad that you're taking steps, like going to therapy, to gain some insight into … into at least into how other people perceive you sometimes."

"How do they perceive me?"

She really hadn't meant to get into this type of discussion with him. "I just wanted to say thank you."

"No. Tell me. How do they perceive me?"

The line went silent. She couldn't think of an adjective that wasn't hurtful. But she was experienced in talking to difficult people. "You're in group therapy, Mr. Mallory. In group, people are encouraged to say what they really think. So, you tell me, how do the other members of the group perceive you?"

"I never thought about that before." The silence on the line told him he was supposed to think about it now. "Okay, there's one guy, Peter, who hates me. There's this hot young blonde, but her mother's dying of cancer. Let me think. Oh, to be honest, some of the people in the group seem to think I'm a little crude."

Lilly had to suppress a laugh. "Well, I hope you keep going to therapy. You might find out some things about yourself, and other people, too." When he didn't respond, she told herself she needed to focus the conversation on something besides Mallory's deficits. "Have you seen your friend Officer Selby since we went to the shooting range?"

"Friend? Yeah, I guess he's my friend. He asked about you."

She couldn't deny the tiny thrill she felt at hearing this. But Selby was a kind man, so of course he had asked about her. And she couldn't let the conversation end just like that, without knowing what he had said. So, she asked about that, as casually as she could.

"He wanted to know if you had a good time shooting with him," Mallory answered.

"I did!" She hadn't meant to sound so enthusiastic.

But Mallory didn't seem to notice. "He asked me if he should get the rifle from the range and bring it back to me at my apartment."

"Maybe you shouldn't keep it at your place," she began. She remembered how clumsy he was with the gun. "There's no place you can legally shoot a gun near your apartment. Maybe it's better to keep it at the shooting range."

"I can't shoot. I'm thinking of letting Selby keep it."

"Just because you screwed up one time, that doesn't mean you can't learn to shoot as well as anybody." She could feel her counselor-self speaking. People who were down on themselves should be encouraged to think positively. Including even Mallory. At the same time, she sensed it might be to her personal advantage if he left the gun at the firing range.

She had been having thoughts of going shooting with Officer Selby again. When she had first admitted this to herself, a few days before, she had decided not to tell Zach. There was nothing to tell. She wasn't going to contact Selby. She didn't know his phone number, or even his first name. She liked the guy, but what was so unusual about that?

Over the next few days, Lilly found herself pursuing Zach more passionately than usual, but they seemed to be out of synch. "Can you give me a break?" he complained to her one night. She had never been turned down before. She had heard about this kind of problem, of course, but it shocked her to think this could happen to them.

She spent time every day helping Chub try to get Stephanie back. She did all the footwork for the local custody proceedings. She obtained the missing persons report that Chub had first filed with the police, certified copies of their marriage license and Stephanie's birth certificate, Stephanie's school and medical records, even their mortgage papers and utility bills – anything to prove the status quo that his wife, Janice, had broken when she disappeared with their only child. Chub could have gotten all of these things a lot earlier, but he had been drinking at the time. But he had shown up in court, sober, in time to get a signed custody order from the Howard County court. But it would mean nothing if Chub couldn't get the California police to find them and get the courts in that state to honor the order.

Chapter 12: Off Kilter

"Is she dead yet?" Mallory cornered Sebastian, the group therapy coordinator, just before his next therapy meeting.

"Are you talking about Grace's mother?" Sebastian's voice was hushed.

"Of course." Mallory realized his own voice was too loud. He glanced at the other group members as they bumbled their way toward the semicircle of chairs in the church basement.

"No, I don't believe she has died yet. Mr. Mallory …."

"Ramsteel."

"Mr. Ramsteel. Sorry. Mr. Ramsteel, last time you sort of yelled across the room to Grace, asking her in front of the group if her mother had died yet. An approach like that can be very distressing to someone who is losing a loved one."

"Oh. I thought we could say anything here."

"We can say anything about our own problems, Mr. Ramsteel. Grace is having a hard time. She has made herself vulnerable to us by sharing her private grief with us. We can help her by listening to her. Not by yelling insensitive questions across the room."

"Oh. You mean she's really hurting." Mallory studied Sebastian's eyes to see if he was sincere. "I'm sorry. I never had anybody die on me. I mean, my father died, but I hadn't seen or heard from him in three years by then. It didn't bother me."

Sebastian's soft blue eyes sought out Mallory's. "You know, that's quite an unusual response to a father's death. Do you think you might want to talk about that in the group?"

"God, no. I came here for a sex problem."

"… which you have denied having ever since the first meeting."

"A friend, Lilly, sent me here. I don't have a sex problem with her. I mean, I don't have a sex problem with her anymore."

"So, you're saying you don't have a problem with sex?"

"I don't know. Are you saying I belong in this regular therapy group with these regular sickos?"

"That's not a term we use here. But yes, I do believe you belong in this group."

This time, Mallory didn't ask Grace whether her mother had died. When it was Grace's turn to talk, she spoke again about her mother's illness, and a little about her boyfriend. Her boyfriend wasn't being as sympathetic as she thought he should be, but she wondered if she was expecting too much of him. Mallory focused on the fact that she had a boyfriend. She wondered if they did it or, for that matter, if anybody did it while their mother was dying. This thought distracted him for much of the rest of the meeting.

He did notice that Peter, his grey-fringed, pointy-bearded nemesis, was watching him closely. This gave Mallory a strong urge to do something to aggravate him. But he didn't want to do anything that would annoy Sebastian, who seemed to be a pretty good guy. So instead, he developed the technique of suddenly sitting forward in his chair, his hand half-raised and his mouth open like he was about to speak, drawing Peter's sharp attention like a vulture spotting a piece of dead meat. Then Mallory would slowly close his mouth, lower his hand and slump back in his chair, staring at whoever was speaking and nodding in sympathy. Time and again the vulture got his claws out, only to be unsatisfied. Mallory thought this was a pretty enjoyable way to pass the session.

"Mr. Ramsteel, do you have anything to share with us today?"

Sebastian's softly spoken sentence made Mallory jump. He hadn't been listening to what anybody was saying. He didn't know if listening was actually required. He guessed he was now supposed to contribute to this conversation he hadn't paid any attention to. But he didn't want to let Sebastian down.

"Um ... I guess we all have these feelings sometimes ... um ... that we're not appreciated, or ... um ... we don't deserve to be ... um ... loved, and ..." – he thought he should get a little more upbeat – "that we should try to see things clearly and get ourselves on the right path." Several of the group members nodded solemnly.

But they were looking at him as if he were supposed to go on. "I don't know if I can add anything else to the excellent discussion we have had today."

Sebastian was waiting for him outside in the parking lot after the others left. "I think you're starting to get the hang of therapy, Mr. Ramsteel."

"You mean I didn't insult anybody today."

"That's a start."

*** ***

Lilly had spent almost a decade living off "crumbs and charity," as Chub described it. She recognized that one of the ironies of her life was that people were now required to come to her to ask for money. She managed hundreds of thousands of dollars in grants and other funds. She was the only financial person in Roofs Over Our Heads who had worked closely with the clients themselves. As a result, she was probably the most influential voice in how the money would be spent. She remembered every crumb that had been doled out to her and Chub. She had seen the way in which compassion could in some ways be measured in dollars, and she took very seriously the privilege she had now of doling it out.

As with every other organization outside of the national security sphere (or, as she learned from Zach, outside of the area of finance) funds were always short, there were obvious unmet needs, and people were always leaving for better paying jobs. Two counselors had recently left, and she was in the process of trying to do her work plus their work and to hire their replacements at the same time. She didn't mind. She remembered how hard her father worked, literally up until the day he could not get out of bed. He was rarely home before nine at night. Still, she was thirteen before he stopped checking her homework before she went to bed. She had known she was his favorite, and she had spared no effort to keep that status.

Her girlfriends, always flattering her, joked that Zach was her reward for being a workaholic, goody two-shoes. Sometimes she felt like that was true. But she didn't want to start thinking of Zach as some sort of commodity.

Was it the stress of dealing with Chub's problems, or her flashbacks to Mallory swinging his rifle around at the shooting range, that was now adding an occasional little jump to her heartbeat? She told Zach one night she was feeling a little strange.

"Headache?"

"No, nothing like that."

"Oh. This is something new. Hmmm. You're not …. You couldn't be just a little bit … *pregnant*, could you?" His eyes lit up deviously.

"No, no," she laughed. "Definitely not that. Actually, I don't think it's anything physical at all."

"Problems at work?"

"No. I mean there are always problems at work, but I'm used to handling them."

"What, then?"

"I don't know. Really. Actually, it's been getting better the last couple of days. I guess it'll go away." She assumed he would ask her why she hadn't mentioned it before, but he didn't.

Chapter 13: Things Best Left Unsaid

"The Cheer Committee is looking for a place for the holiday party. Of course, we're not allowed in the Pirate Bar." It was a tribute to Nell's new, more mellow attitude toward Mallory that she would even mention last year's holiday party. That party had abruptly ended when a Cheer Committee member wrapped himself in a string of flags and pulled down from the wall a large artificial galleon which crashed and destroyed a neighboring table, sending all the customers from that side of the building running for their lives. Trying to impress Nell, Mallory had flipped out his credit card to pay for the damages. He still hadn't paid off that debt. Of course, that had not been even close to the most embarrassing part of Nell's day.

"I should tell you the truth about exactly what happened between us in my apartment after they kicked us out of the Pirate Bar."

Nell's entire face turned beet red. She had been standing in the corridor outside his cubicle, but now she stepped forward into the opening. "Please. Please. I don't want to ever think about that again."

"It's not as bad as you think."

"I've started a new life with Kathie. I need to forget all that stuff in the past."

"Come here. Sit down." Mallory cleared his bag of Dough and Go donuts from the tiny chair that was squeezed between his desk and the outer wall of his cubicle. She sat down, her face still flushed. She begged him to keep her in the dark about exactly what had happened after she blacked out in his apartment that afternoon. This put Mallory in a position he was not accustomed to. He had spent most of his adult life hiding his own misdeeds while accusing others of worse. Now, he was trying to ease Nell's anxiety by confessing to the creepy part he had played in the missing panties affair. He had taken her panties off after she passed out. He had been planning to use them in his nightly porn adventures, but he had reconsidered and put them in her pocketbook. Knowing that she woke up the next day and found her panties in her pocketbook, he had tortured her for weeks by advising her to take pregnancy and STD tests. It was cruel, but he had been too ashamed to tell her what really happened. Now he was trying to swallow his shame.

But Nell clearly didn't want to hear about it. She seemed more relaxed once he stopped talking. He decided that his urge to confess had been a mistake, an overreaction on the part of a neophyte just trying out various ideas of what it meant to be a decent human being.

"I've been talking to Kathie myself," he started again. Nell's color was returning to its normal blanched tint.

"You're not still trying for a threesome, I hope." She seemed more comfortable now, berating him.

"No," he scoffed. He had put aside the threesome idea some time ago, though he was still haunted by the idea of Kathie as a screamer. "But it seems like Kathie doesn't want to talk about you."

"Well, that's a good thing, as far as I'm concerned."

"But you talk about her all the time. I'm just wondering why she never talks about you."

*** ***

A few days later, Mallory was surprised to hear Selby's voice on his work line. "Do you want your rifle back, Mr. Mallory, or not?"

"Call me Kevin, please."

"Not Ramsteel?"

"Who told you that? I only use that name in therapy group."

"When you're a cop on the street, word gets around. Anyway, I can bring your rifle back, if you want it."

"Maybe I'm not the kind of guy who should have a gun?" Mallory stated this almost as a question. He was hoping Selby would contradict him. But he didn't.

"If you want, I could sell it for you. I'm friends with Gus, the owner of Guns-R-Us."

"No, keep it." He was now convinced he didn't have the right nervous system to become the expert marksman and hunter he had wanted to be. He had always assumed he had inherited at least that much from his father. He was beginning to wonder how his father had gotten so good at it. He had never once seen his father take any of his rifles off the rack.

"Your friend, Lilly, wasn't so bad at it. She hit at least some part of the target every shot, once we got the sight straightened out."

"Maybe give it to her."

"I wouldn't feel right, contacting her again. I hear she has a boyfriend."

Mallory wasn't focusing on what Selby was saying. He was still thinking of his father's rifles locked in that rack on the wall of their apartment his entire childhood. He was remembering that his father promised to take him hunting after the divorce but never did. It had always been in the back of his mind that he could be, and should be, the kind of man his father was. But maybe he just wasn't that sort of man.

Selby spoke into the silence. "But, you know, if she contacts you, and if she wants to shoot again, I'd be glad to take her as a guest to the range again."

Mallory snapped out of his reverie. "I bet you would."

The issue of what to do with the rifle was not resolved. Mallory sensed that his two new friends were attracted to each other, but he had no plan to help them get together. He could not see how that could be of any benefit to him.

Mallory's gross intrusions into the lives of Nell and Lilly had not turned out as badly as they might have. Both women at one time or another had told him that he was selfish, gross, immature, naïve, socially retarded, and pathetic. But the fact that he needed so much help was apparently inspiring some mysterious womanly instinct to rescue him. He wondered if he could make use of that.

*** ***

Lilly had planned to call Mallory monthly to see how he was doing with his therapy, but she found herself calling him sooner, and from work. "Chub took out a second mortgage on his house to pay his California lawyer's fees, and it seems to be paying off. His lawyer filed his court order in the California court. Janice didn't even file an answer. And he knows where she's keeping Stephanie."

"Oh. Good." Mallory knew that most people said they would do anything for their children. But he didn't have any children, didn't even know any children. He knew that Lilly cared about her little niece. That was the way good people felt. And Lilly was a good person. But he was surprised at the real reason for her call.

"And I want to ask you something about that Officer Selby. He taught me how to shoot, at least a little, and it went pretty well. I wonder if you could find out from him, very quietly, if he would be amenable to another practice session."

"*Quietly*?" Mallory's keen ear for human weakness picked up on the appropriate word.

"I just mean without making a fuss, and without saying I'm insisting on it or anything. I mean, maybe you could find out ahead of time if he would think it was an imposition to give me one more lesson. I mean, without saying that I asked about it."

Mallory could sense that he now had more power over Lilly than ever before. She was a better person than him in every way, but it seemed like she was stepping out on her boyfriend. He hadn't thought Lilly had any weaknesses. But he couldn't think of any way he could take advantage of this weakness. And he didn't want to hurt her. In fact, he felt a strange desire to help her.

The kindest thing he could do for her now was to cut to the chase. "Tell me the date and time that's good for you."

"Oh! Oh, thank you, Mr. Mallory. Now remember, don't tell

him I asked for this. Can I call you tomorrow to see what he says?"

"Sure. There's one condition, though."

"Oh" He could sense the dread in her voice. "What?"

"You have to call me Kevin from now on."

Chapter 14: Not Pistols

He's just a beat cop, Lilly told herself. He spends his life on the streets with the worst of the worst. What if some of that grossness has rubbed off on him? She'd run into that kind of grossness once years before, when she and her date were pulled over by the police on a deserted road late one night. She had learned to her shock what a search of the person entailed. Ever since then, she had made doubly sure not to give any cop any excuse to pull her over.

Bu she really couldn't imagine Selby doing anything like that. She tried to recall every word he said, every gesture he made, every facial expression, during their time at the gun range. She didn't remember anything objectionable. He wasn't as classically handsome as Zach, but she thought he was cute. He was close to her height, and that was kind of fun after months of being dwarfed by Zach.

About noon, she told her office manager she had a personal errand to run and wouldn't be back until three. At the parking lot of the firing range, Selby pulled up next to her car in a police cruiser. He explained that he was "sort of" off the clock, but he'd have to leave quickly if any emergency calls came in.

"What if we're way down there at the range and an emergency call comes in?"

"I can get back to the car pretty quick." His dramatic, dark eyebrows knitted. "But let me ask you one thing. The last time we were here shooting that rifle, you said you weren't going to keep it up. What gives?"

"You're a cop, so I guess you always remember what a witness says." She tried for a sarcastic tone, but she couldn't manage it because she was nervous about what she was going to say next. "Maybe we should do something different this time."

"Maybe pistols?"

"Maybe lunch."

It was just lunch, she told herself. She followed his cruiser to a little eatery. She had been there a few times before, when she was in college and on a stricter budget. They each got coffee and a sandwich. It felt strange to be back at this restaurant and to be eating with someone in uniform. She had a pleasant, hyper-alert feeling. She noticed everything about him. His ruddy face, thick, dark hair, the easy, sheepish smile he gave her when describing his job.

"You act like it's nothing," she corrected him. "You deal with the craziest, most dangerous situations."

"Crazy. Mostly crazy."

"I've seen you. When you took that gun from Mr. Mallory outside of the therapy group. That situation could have gone south really fast." She didn't mention she had also googled him and had read all about his intervention with the SWAT team that had resolved Mallory's standoff at the courthouse. But she didn't understand why she had felt compelled to investigate this friendly policeman.

"I guess we all have our talents," he said. She liked that he wasn't overly modest. "I've talked with Mallory about you some," he went on. "He told me about your job. To him – funny thing – he couldn't understand was why anyone would spend their career trying to help poor people."

"I think Mr. Mallory's needs to grow up."

"That's for sure."

"I should confess." She could feel herself blush. "I called him. I asked him to feel you out, to see if you wanted to go shooting again." And of course, she knew that Selby could do addition and subtraction: one request to meet him for shooting, minus one shooting, equals one request to meet him. "Look, I'm not trying to start something. I have a boyfriend. We're engaged, at least unofficially. I just thought you were one of the more interesting persons I've met recently."

"Yeah. I guess I feel the same about you. And your job is interesting, too. You deal with poor people. I bet we have a lot of clients in common."

"Oh, that's so *cop*. So prejudiced against poor people. We check the police records of every single client. You might be surprised to know that our percentage of people with criminal records is smaller than that of the general public."

He started to speak. Stopped. He had beautiful teeth, full lips. She knew there wasn't any harm in admiring him silently right then. The next twenty minutes was the total amount of time she would ever spend with him for the rest of her life.

"Have you ever been married?" She had noticed he never wore a ring.

"No." She felt like a detective as she checked his eyes. Very dark brown. Not evasive. Not troubled. "I had a lot of girlfriends when I was younger. One long-term one. Ended about a year ago. She's married now. We're still friends."

"So, you can be friends with a *woman*?" she teased. She guessed that was the very question between them right then. She wondered how many of the women he knew had experienced his gentle touch. She wondered if they had felt it to be as comforting as she had at the shooting range. She asked him about his most recent breakup, even about his girlfriends before that. He seemed very matter of fact, and a little regretful. He said he had been engaged to his last girlfriend, but she broke it off.

She heard every word he said, and she talked as much as he did. She told herself he was just one of those unusual, interesting people you run into every once in a while. She did like the way he looked into her eyes and actually listened to what she was saying. She couldn't really remember anyone who had ever done that before. She knew she had told him a lot about herself, and she hoped it wasn't too much. She reminded herself that she didn't need to feel guilty. She had told him she was engaged. But she didn't want to give him up. She wondered if there was any way she and Zach could somehow fold him into their group of friends.

*** ***

Mallory spoke first at the next therapy meeting. "Some of my problems are my own fault, I'm beginning to think." He hadn't really made up his mind whether the less than mediocre life he had been living was really his fault. But he knew that was what people in the group wanted to hear, and he wanted to get along.

"No shit, Sherlock," Peter of the Pointy Beard interrupted immediately.

Peter had somehow gotten under Mallory's skin. His quiet sarcasm sometimes echoed in his mind even when he wasn't in the therapy group. In the therapy group, in person, Peter had the ability to make him feel like he didn't belong.

Sebastian the facilitator cleared his throat and spoke from his position just outside the semicircle. "There's no need for antagonism here. We're all coming at life from different angles. We've all had different life experiences. It might benefit everybody to learn where each of us is coming from." Sebastian talked so much Mallory began to think he should be paying to come to the group just like everybody else.

"We don't know anything about your problems," Grace, the hot young blonde, surprised Mallory by speaking up next. "You haven't really talked at all, except it's obvious you want to talk about sex with the women in the group."

"What else would I talk about with women?"

"You don't think women are people, do you?" Grace tossed her short mop of unruly blonde hair defiantly. "You think we are just animals you can fuck?"

A silence fell over the room. Grace had never spoken before about anything except her devastation over the fact that her mother was dying. It seemed like they were getting a look at the spirited, pre-grief woman she had been, and might become again.

Mallory was as surprised as anyone. The tension in the room didn't let up. Many of the group members were now turning to him to see how he would respond to her accusations. He stood up to leave. But then he started gauging the embarrassment he would suffer by waddling his way across the center of their semicircle of chairs. Peter might well make fun of his weight. But mostly, he didn't want to miss this chance of talking openly with this hot young woman about his urges. He pretended he had just gotten up to straighten his suit jacket.

"Maybe you're right," he spoke directly to Grace. "Maybe I think like that a little bit. But you're wrong about part of it. I can't really get anybody in bed. Not without getting them drunk, or by lying. Mostly lying. Always lying." He sat down and looked at his feet for a long while in the silence. When he looked up, he was surprised to see that it was Grace who was blushing.

"I'm sorry." Her murmur could be heard across the silent room. "I shouldn't have attacked you like that. But you come across as so gross sometimes." Mallory noticed some of the other members of the group nodding.

"I've been thinking about that lately. Everybody says that." He couldn't believe that he was talking about this to this young girl, but she met his eyes steadily from across the room. "Some of my ideas came from a website I used to follow, Manly Man, but his advice never did me any good." For months, Mallory had been slowly weaning his way off his internet guru's dating advice. But this was the first time he admitted, even to himself, that if he had been looking for guidance, he had been following the wrong prophet. He was amazed that Grace had so easily gotten him to admit this.

Sebastian broke the spell. "Mr. Ramsteel, maybe we should explore why you did that, why you would blindly follow an internet guru you probably knew nothing about?"

"I don't remember," Mallory snapped, aggravated that the facilitator had interrupted his deep communion with Grace. Sebastian now looked askance at him. Grace and some of the others seemed interested, too. He decided to try harder to answer. "I just remember a feeling, the feeling that in Manly Man there was finally somebody who believed everything that happened to me wasn't my own fault."

Chapter 15: Faking It

Kathie could look great, with her mass of hyper-curly blonde hair framing her long face and intelligent green eyes. She was thin, and a good three inches taller than Mallory. But even before she turned gay, Mallory had never considered going after her. He'd never even thought about why. Maybe because she was too tall, or too outspoken, or too close a friend to Nell.

Now she was laughing. "You were right. I think I can do it, hang on, do Chub's job for two weeks. They want me to work on a program, something that is going to figure out the time of day each show is watched. They already know how many people are watching and how old they are, etc., but they're trying to break it down better for advertisers. I'm faking it so far."

"I wouldn't even know how to fake it."

"Oh, I did the password thing for a few days like you said. But then I realized they actually were dealing with statistics. So I gave them some statistical mumbo-jumbo and they've now decided to go back and look at their model." She laughed again. "But I'm glad there's only another week to go."

"Why don't you just call in sick next week?"

"I can't. I'm saving my time up for vacation." UniCast didn't have sick leave. Any time taken off sick was counted as vacation. "I really haven't minded this at all. It's kind of exciting. I feel almost like a spy."

"Like in a Brad Pitt movie?"

A strange, curious smile stretched across her face. "Why did you say that?"

"I know you follow Brad Pitt and all those other hunky, *male* movie stars."

Her voice dropped down an octave. "What are you saying?"

"I'm saying Nell is totally in love with you. And I don't think you love her. And I don't even think you're gay."

Kathie's expression was grim. A full minute passed in silence. Mallory was expecting her to slap him. But, as usual, Kathie surprised him.

"What do I do now?" Her voice was tiny. She knew he knew. And even though she asked for his advice, her tone of despair signaled that she had no faith that anyone could do anything to help her.

"You're asking *me* for lezzie advice?"

"I wasn't trying to trick anybody." Kathie kept her voice low so it couldn't be heard outside of her cubicle. "I thought it was just a girls' night out, like we told you." She went on, her voice breathier, less controlled. "I guess we were kind of flirting, but it didn't seem like a big deal. Then one night, I was pretty drunk. She just led me, step by step. I mean, I did like it, that one time. It seemed all so new and lovely. I guess I was out of control." Her lips tightened until they were almost invisible now. "I don't know what I was thinking." She sighed heavily. "I told her I loved her."

They sat there without saying much of anything for the next few minutes. Mallory recognized that he had no right to lecture anyone about honesty in relationships. And, as strong as Kathie had always seemed to Mallory, he was shocked to see her cry over the harm she was doing to another. "You should see her eyes when she sees me," Kathie broke the silence with a whisper. "I mean, they *light up*. I thought that was just an expression."

"You don't love her. You've been lying to her all this time."

"I do love her, as a friend. But not as a lover. It would *kill* her if I told her that. I just don't know what to do." Kathie held her head high and let the tears run down her cheeks. Mallory thought he might have been too blunt. He searched for a tissue to wipe her face. He couldn't find one, so he put his hand up to wipe away her tears, but she brushed off his offered hand and asked him to leave.

Mallory understood from his own experience the sharp pain of being rejected, but he had never considered the other side of the coin. Kathie was now in pain because she had to reject someone. He didn't want to learn about that kind of pain, or any more kinds of pain. The aura of sadness in Kathie's office followed him all the way back to his cubicle. He wondered if he should start an in-house therapy group.

*** ***

Lilly came back from lunch with Selby later than she had planned. She blamed herself. She remembered sitting in that restaurant, deciding not to check the time. Now, out of guilt, she stayed on at work a little later than usual. But she had always relished working alone anyway, without all the distractions and interruptions and phone calls that always consumed much of her day. She felt especially calm that evening. The tingling nerves that had bothered her off and on the last few days were gone. She finished her critique of a complicated contract that Roofs Over Our Heads was negotiating with an apartment management service, a chore that her boss, Rory McFadden, had said was too tedious and picayune for him to handle. The task had been hanging over her head for days. The management company obviously had a lot of management experience, but none of it was with non-profit housing. She sent an email to the lawyer who wrote it, pointing out provisions of the proposed contract they couldn't agree to, as well as some clauses she didn't really understand. She enjoyed making the effort to keep her responses on point and to set them out as concisely as she could. Finally, feeling entirely satisfied with her work, she left for home. She got a speeding ticket on the way home, the first of her life. She still thought it had been a good day.

"Surprise!" Zach greeted her at the door. "We're going out to dinner."

"Oh, you lazy bones," she laughed. "It's your night to cook. You're just trying to get out of it." She noticed he'd been drinking, and she wasn't sure she wanted to eat anything he cooked right then anyway. But she still felt that same strange fervor that had been flowing through her veins all afternoon. The day seemed to be getting better and better. "You're already dressed! I'm not going out wearing this rumpled work outfit."

"Well, change, then."

"But I'm so *tired*, Zach," she suddenly teased him. "I think you need to help me undress."

He followed her into the bedroom. She took off her dress and turned to face him, buried her face in his neck, made sure he could feel her heartbeat. "I think we need to do this now, Zach." She pulled him even tighter, kissed him sensuously, ran her hands up and down his back. She was giving in to a pulsing need that seemed to have been buried inside her for weeks. She needed him, right now.

"We're going to be late for our reservations."

"Fuck the reservations, Zach. It's been so long." She knew what he liked, what could make him weak in the knees. But she didn't feel him responding. Had he drunk too much Scotch? Or was it her fault for being so over-hyped? She leaned into him, sought his kiss again. But now he put his hands on her shoulders and gently pushed her away. Then, avoiding her eyes, he quickly turned his back on her and walked out.

This was the second time he'd rejected her. She walked into the shower and took her time, even washing her hair. He came to the door once, but she told him she would be ready when she was ready. Her fever for his touch felt more like anger now. He was drinking another Scotch when she finally came out dressed in a black, spaghetti-strap dress she had never quite had the nerve to wear before.

He drove too fast on the way to the restaurant, but that seemed to fit her mood. Even though they didn't talk, Zach seemed to have a trace of a smile on his face. She was guessing that he felt sheepish for turning her down. She was curious to see how that would work out, but it was a cold curiosity that wasn't connected at all to that strange heat she had felt earlier.

What was Rory McFadden, her boss, doing there? And why was Mary, her bookkeeper, together with most of their own personal friends, standing there in the dining room and staring at them the moment they arrived? It seemed like they had all been drinking, too. "We had to start without you," McFadden chuckled. "You're almost an hour late for your own engagement party!"

She found herself subjected to a flurry of congratulations, coy glances, and toasts. People told her she was blushing, but that wasn't why her face was red. She tried to just let go and ride the wave, dam the undercurrent of resentment she felt against Zach for breaking his promise to keep their engagement secret. She told herself that telling Selby she was engaged hadn't broken her own promise to keep their engagement secret, because she only did it to keep him from getting any ideas. Besides, she would never see that policeman again. She watched a smiling Zack, his arm around a new friend whose name she didn't remember, drunk with friendship and alcohol, pontificating about shorting utility stocks, all the while trying to draw her to his side. Zack seemed to want to show the whole crowd what a catch she was. She didn't know what his excuse would be for breaking his promise to keep their engagement secret, but she didn't care.

He was too drunk to drive home. They didn't talk in the car. Earlier in the day she had felt like an invisible gate had been opened inside her soul and her life was finally flowing along freely and naturally. But now she just felt exhausted, wasted.

Chapter 16: Stalking the Truth

Thomas, the college student, was Mallory's next-door neighbor. He lived right across the areaway from Mallory's efficiency on the second floor of the apartment complex. Sometimes, in the past, when he finished his daily practice runs in the neighborhood, he had waited for Mallory to trudge up the stairs returning from work. Even though he was twenty, thin, athletic, and Black, he had made friends with klutzy, thirty-three-year-old, white Mallory. And he had helped him escape the consequences of some of his most outrageous deeds. Mallory was now overjoyed to see Thomas waiting for him again.

"How's it hanging, Mr. Mallory?" Thomas was the only person who had stood by Mallory in the face of all his transgressions. Some of those transgressions had been against Thomas himself. And the worst of these offenses had occurred the night Nell had appeared at Mallory's doorstep with the police, demanding the return of Koko, her cat. Thomas had covered up Mallory's theft to keep him from being arrested. When Thomas's parents found out about that, they insisted that their son have nothing to do with their sketchy neighbor, but Thomas had stuck by him.

"I haven't seen you around much, Thomas. We used to be buddies."

"School. You know I'm at State now."

"Yeah, I knew that." Mallory had totally forgotten. He took a breath. It seemed he couldn't stop lying, even to his friend. He was still trying to get used to the idea that most people told the truth most of the time.

"I got that track scholarship. I'll be running the 800 indoors this winter, and outdoors in spring."

"Oh, that's great." He recognized that he was supposed to say something like that. But he hadn't got the hang of keeping up an interest in other people's lives. He did think of something he could say next. "I guess you don't have to run in the streets around here at night anymore."

"No. That was a crazy, crazy time. I don't know what I was more afraid of, the police coming after me or you escorting me in that Escalade." Thomas turned to him and ventured a laugh.

It had been the unanimous opinion of Thomas, Thomas's mother and father, and even Officer Selby, that Mallory had increased the danger to the runner by following him on the street in his Escalade, lights flashing, while carrying his unloaded rifle. Mallory still felt a tinge of resentment that Thomas hadn't appreciated his efforts to protect him. They'd had an argument about this once. Arguments with real people, as opposed to arguments with employers, had always frightened Mallory. But he hoped he could talk with Thomas now like he used to.

"I'm going to group therapy."

"Oh." Thomas hesitated. Mallory figured the young Black college student would naturally hesitate to interrogate a substantial citizen like him on such a personal matter. But Thomas went on. "You … um … did seem to cause a lot of trouble with some of your ideas. Maybe it's a good idea to have some of them checked out."

"Sex addict therapy."

"Oh. That." Thomas seemed at a loss for words.

Mallory changed the subject. "I did listen to you. I did give back the cat. Nell and I are friends now."

"Just friends?"

"Yeah. She's gay, like you always suspected. I made her announce it at the courthouse. That part of her statement really was true."

"My mother says people can get over almost anything, with time. That's good. I'll try to get my parents to speak to you again next time they come to visit."

"That's nice, Thomas. Stop and talk to me yourself sometime."

✳✳✳ ✳✳✳

Mallory had been puzzled by Grace's accusation in his therapy group that he thought all women were "just animals you can fuck." Didn't all men think that? What was the point of her remark? He decided to draw her out on the subject at the next therapy meeting. On the way to the meeting, however, he was distracted by a fantasy he had about one of his favorite porn stars, who was blonde and petite like Grace. This gorgeous and athletic actress could scream on the screen like he always fantasized a real woman would. He tried not to confuse her with Grace.

Fortunately, he had time to calm down, as Grace was not the first to talk. And when she did, she spoke about trying to deal with her mother's impending death. Mallory put his metaphysical questions about sex on hold as Grace talked about her mother's condition and her own guilt feelings over things she'd said to her mother over the years. Mallory could hardly remember anything he'd ever said to his own mother. Maybe in his case it would be his father he was supposed to have talked to. He didn't know.

Grace said her parents had divorced fifteen years ago. "My father's been remarried for years and hasn't been in touch much. I feel guilty for not contacting him about this until a few weeks ago. I guess I felt he wouldn't care, or shouldn't care, or didn't deserve to care or … I don't know." She stopped suddenly and cast her eyes shyly around the group. Nobody said anything. "Thank you all for not beating up on me about this. But I don't think he cares, and I guess I didn't want to waste my energy watching him pretend to care."

Sebastian reminded her that it was her mother who was dying and most needed her concern. "Your father made his choices long ago. You shouldn't feel like you have to babysit him now." A few people spoke up in agreement. More nodded. Mallory thought he agreed, though he didn't have much experience with death. He sat in a trance for the rest of the meeting, admiring this girl who had been to places he had never been.

But as the meeting closed, her realized he hadn't had the chance to question her about her "animals" remark. She was the only person who had ever described his mindset so crudely. He decided he had to talk to her, and he couldn't wait until the next week. But he came up the steps from the church basement well behind her. He didn't want to call out to her while all those other people were there, and there was no chance he could catch up to her. He rushed to his Escalade, started it up, and watched until he saw her get into a red Corolla and leave by the lower exit to the parking lot. He accelerated across the lot and followed behind her, but not so closely that she would become suspicious.

He hadn't realized she lived twenty minutes away. Twenty-five. Thirty. Finally, she turned into a huge parking lot. He stopped at a green light so she wouldn't spot him, but the honking horns behind him threatened to expose him even more. Still, he kept his foot on the brake and tried to keep his eye on her car. When he saw where she parked, he powered through on yellow and parked as far away from her as he could while still keeping her in sight. Crossing the lot on foot, he kept his head down and tried to watch her out of the corner of his eye. Her building was huge, and he followed her across the large lobby at a distance, head still down, shrugging off the calls of the receptionist and hoping that his suit would protect him from being immediately evicted. Grace got in the elevator alone. He didn't dare jump in behind her. He saw that it stopped on the sixth floor. "Sir? Sir?" he heard the receptionist call out, but he quickly jumped into the other elevator and pressed the button to close the door.

He was surprised when Grace turned to him outside the elevators the second he exited on the sixth floor. "What are you doing here in this hospital?" she insisted.

"Hospital?" Mallory looked around. Nurses' stations, machines, carts. He sniffed the air. Disinfectant. He had thought this was her condo. He had just wanted to talk to her because he admired her.

But now she would think he was a complete idiot if he told her the truth.

"Um ... I'm visiting .... I'm visiting my father."

Grace immediately relaxed. "Oh, what a coincidence." But then she dropped her chirpy tone. "I'm here to see my mother. She's ... she's probably going to be put in a hospice soon, today or tomorrow. I just want to have a last chance to see her before she goes into that place."

"I'm sorry." He really was. He completely surprised himself with his next sentence. "Can I go see her with you?"

"Don't you need to see your father?"

"He's supposed to be discharged today. If I haven't already missed him this afternoon, I'll catch him at his house tonight."

Mallory had never set foot in a hospital before. He didn't think he was the kind of person who would ever get so sick he would have to go to a hospital. He'd also never seen a dying person before. He hadn't even known his father was sick until he heard that he had died. He was ashamed he had told Grace his father was here. He admired her courage in coming to this horrible place, every day. He wanted to be with her just a few minutes longer. But she cocked an eyebrow now like she thought his request was really weird.

"No, I'm being ... silly." He tried to meet her eyes. "You want to be alone with her." He didn't understand why she would want to be alone with her sick and dying mother. But he expected that relatives did this all the time. Maybe he should have noticed before that some people had real feelings for others and weren't as narrowly focused as he was. Or maybe Grace was the only one like that. He wasn't sure.

"I kind of want my alone time with my mother." Grace seemed determined, but also apologetic.

"Of course." He turned back toward the elevator, but then he stopped. "I need to tell you something."

"Can it wait?"

"Oh. Sure. I'll wait in the lobby downstairs."

He spent an uncomfortable half hour standing downstairs while being subjected to suspicious stares from the reception people behind their plastic shields. Fortunately, nobody seemed willing to confront him. His back ached, and he finally found a chair around a corner in a hallway. As soon as he sat down, a security guard approached him. Fortunately, Grace appeared at just that moment, and the security issue seemed to disappear as soon as the cute little blonde started talking to the guy in the suit who had seemed suspicious two minutes before.

"You didn't have to wait for me." Grace's face looked drained. "We could have talked at therapy next week."

"I need to apologize for something." Mallory looked directly at the floor. "My father isn't in this hospital." He looked up. She didn't flinch. He searched her eyes. "I tend to lie about things."

Chapter 17: Nuclear Family/War

Mallory sat on the top step of the landing between his apartment and Thomas's. This was the opposite situation from last year, when Mallory would often come home to see Thomas waiting for him there. Their friendship had survived Mallory's initial prejudice against him, Thomas's arrest and beating at the hands of the police, and Mallory's impersonation of a lawyer – at first to get Thomas free, and later to entangle his neighbor more deeply in the legal system. With the help of a real lawyer, Thomas had eventually gotten a substantial settlement. Mallory still felt that his own contributions had been valuable and that he was owed something, at least gratitude. Thomas's parents had felt differently and had warned their son to stay away from their erratic neighbor.

Thomas now bounced up the steps and sat down next to his neighbor. "Hey, Mr. Mallory. What's up?"

"Thinking."

"Oh." Thomas was obviously trying to hide the surprise in his voice. Mallory was not known for his thinking. "What about?"

"Do you remember that beautiful woman you were talking to on the steps who was waiting to see me?"

"Yeah. Name's Lilly, right?"

"Right. I admit I was after her at first. But now she's like a sister to me. I can even think about her now without, you know, imagining her naked."

"That so?" Thomas didn't sound impressed.

"Anyway, she keeps bothering me about Officer Selby."

Thomas's eyebrows lifted. "She knows Selby?"

"Yes. I introduced them. Now she wants to call him. She's run out of excuses to call him at the police station, and she doesn't have his cell number."

"So, why don't you hook them up?"

"I don't know. What good does it do me to see that nice piece who blew me off get boinked by that nice cop?"

Thomas stood up, leaned back against the railing. "I don't know, man. Maybe so you can get her out of your mind, move on?" He shifted his weight. Thomas was six inches taller than Mallory, thin, well-built but not muscular, the perfect body type for a runner, Mallory had learned. "Something I gotta tell you. I'm having a party in my apartment. I had to invite my parents. They told me not to invite you. But I'm gonna."

"Didn't they move out? Didn't their house get built yet?"

"Yeah. It got built. Big new house. I don't know. I let slip about the party and my mother right away says 'What should I bring?' That's just how our family is. I can't say no." Thomas's eyes went dull. "Maybe they want to keep track of what I'm up to." He hesitated. "And they want me to meet some girl, some daughter of a guy who works with my father."

"Is she hot?"

"I don't know, man. Never seen her. They're treating me like I'm twelve years old."

Mallory sought out Manly Man's advice that night on his computer. He, of course, was familiar with Manly's general advice on how to deal with parental demands once you reach the age of eighteen: "Don't take any shit off them." It didn't really apply to his father, because his father had not made many demands on him and Mallory had always had something wrong inside that made him almost invisible to his father. His mother was a different story. She had controlled almost his every movement. And set him up once with a woman who made him feel like an obedient robot sex doll. Mallory had long since broken free from his subservience to both of these women.

But he was now looking for advice on how to help Thomas. He had found out that his parents were not just inviting themselves to his parties and pushing a girl on him and telling him he couldn't deal with Mallory anymore. They were also controlling his money. Thomas had been awarded a settlement of $100,000 for his police

129

brutality suit against the county. This was more than enough to pay his way through the two years of college he was doing at State. On top of that, Thomas had won a track scholarship to State, so Mallory figured he'd be rolling in money. But Thomas told him: no, his parents had taken control of the settlement money and were "saving" it for him, even though Thomas was nineteen and legally an adult when the incident happened. Mallory thought Manly Man needed to be consulted about this.

In his years of consulting Manly, Mallory had never clicked on any of the icons except the video of the tattooed muscleman holding in one giant hand a hot blonde with pouty lips and a long tongue and in the other two hot blondes whose two long tongues were tasting each other. He had always thought that Manly's six-word advice about parents had been enough for him. But he noticed for the first time there were other icons around the edges of the screen. The image that caught his eye now was that of a mushroom cloud with the caption: *Nuclear Family/War.*

*** ***

Grace crumpled down in the chair next to Mallory in the hospital reception room. "I'm too drained to be offended." She stared straight ahead, breathed deeply and stared straight ahead at the blank white wall across from their chairs.

Mallory continued his confession. "My father's been dead for seven years. I didn't go to the hospital when he was sick. I didn't go to the funeral." He turned toward her. "I guess I'm afraid of death. That's why I wanted to talk to you. You don't seem afraid of anything." When she didn't move or speak, he added, "Even me."

"I don't mind talking." She was almost whispering. "You don't know me or my mother, but it feels good to talk to somebody."

"You come and see her every day?"

"She's such a good, good soul. I miss her already."

"I followed you because you said I was treating women like animals or something. You're the only one in that therapy group who has the guts to speak her mind."

"*Animals you can fuck*, is what I said. What? Do you want to argue that point with me here?"

"No, I'll go." He stood up to go. But he turned back toward her. He had been honest with her. This was a new experience for him. It didn't feel as humiliating as it could have. But he didn't know how to put that feeling into words, so he turned back around again and walked away.

Chapter 18: Community Fun Day

Lilly went to lunch with Selby again. It was rushed this time because they actually did go shooting first. She wasn't happy that shooting would cut into their lunch time, but shooting was something you could explain to your boyfriend better. When Zach got home that evening, he said she smelled like gunpowder. He did seem especially interested in cavorting with "Annie Oakley," as he called her, that night. Lilly's feelings were all jumbled. This time, she hadn't felt that strange connection with Selby she'd felt before. But what was wrong with that?

Roofs Over Our Heads owned a sixteen-unit low rise apartment building in the county. It backed up to a field of brush that was bordered by a slim line of woods between it and the county dump. It was twenty years old and had outlived its commercial usefulness as a haven for young singles. Roofs had bought it from the bankruptcy court. With a grant, and with the help of a lot of paid and free work from local contractors, Roofs had rehabilitated it into decent living units. Lilly had driven herself half crazy handling the complicated project over the last two years. She was still looking for a contractor to mow down the weeds so they could do something with the back yard.

The complex was now full, and Director McFadden decided it was time for a "Community Fun Day" celebration. Lilly, having worked closely with housing clients for years, was all in favor of social occasions where the tenants would get to know one another. But her enthusiasm was curbed when McFadden decided to go to the national Non-Profit Housing Conference in Denver for that entire week and told her she had to handle Community Fun Day. She had already been having a hard time keeping up with her regular work.

She contacted a low-budget catering company that specialized in hiring ex-convicts. She had used them before with great success.

She interrogated all the mothers in her organization for ideas on how to entertain the kids. This resulted in the community donating several minivans full of kids' toys, games and athletic equipment. She arranged for them to be stored in the utility room of the building. She contacted two teenage girls who lived in the building and hired them for $75 each to help watch the children. She spent two afternoons going door to door in the building explaining the event and asking for recipes and, especially, for food. She then re-contacted the catering company and drastically reduced the amount of food she was asking for. She contacted the lawn service and made sure their schedule wouldn't interfere with the party. She arranged for audio equipment in case there was any hidden talent in the building. She asked at each apartment if there were any teenagers who would know how to run it. She prayed it wouldn't rain.

There still wasn't much for teenagers to do. She knew this was a critical age for kids and she didn't want them to be left out, but she knew nothing about teenagers. When she mentioned this to Zach one night, his face lit up. "Games, of course! Set up a basketball hoop in the parking lot, a volleyball net on the lawn."

"I didn't think of that. I'm so not into sports."

"Yeah. You torture yourself with workouts. But you have no idea why sports were invented. Sports were invented so people can have *fun*."

She didn't want to ban alcohol, but she was worried about things getting out of hand. Undoubtedly, some residents would invite their friends, and there was no telling what kind of characters would show up. But asking the police to show up would probably alienate a lot of the residents. Some of the cops treated her poor clients like they were dangerous criminals. She wished she could assure herself that every officer who showed up would be like Officer Selby.

"Look, I want to get something straight between us," she told Selby when they met again for lunch. "Although I've enjoyed our lunches, I'm really not into shooting." A puzzled look came over

Selby's face. She thought she should get to the point. "I know you're a community outreach officer. I'm wondering how I could contact the police and have them … sort of come to this Community Fun Day without, you know, coming on so strong the residents feel like they're being watched."

He smiled broadly. "This is right in my wheelhouse. This is what I do." He asked her how many people would be there, their demographics, especially the number of kids between seven and eighteen, the physical setup. "You need some sports activities," he said right away, echoing almost exactly what Zach had told her. He asked her the address and the physical arrangement. The next day, three off-duty policemen came with tractors and mowed down the brush behind the building, then put up a volleyball net. The following day a portable basketball net appeared in the parking lot complete with cones and crime scene tape keeping anyone from parking right underneath.

When Lilly watched Zach playing basketball against some of the cops and some of the residents at Community Fun Day, she wondered how he considered it fun. His expression was deadly serious when he drove for the basket or leaped to block an opponent's shot. Maybe it was fun just because he was pretty good at it. Selby was on the other team with one other officer and three residents. He was a lot shorter than Zach, but he seemed to be pretty good, too. He laughed when Zach blocked his hook shot. The next time he faked it and went under Zach for the basket. He kept up a running patter with the residents on both his team and Zach's. But nothing Lilly saw made her want to play basketball. She thought about going out back and trying volleyball, but the party was over before she had a chance to get back there.

Zach was so exhausted he let her drive home. She thanked him for coming.

"No problem, honey. It was fun."

Mallory Goes to Therapy

*** ***

With the help of a Howard County Court order, a California lawyer, a private detective, and with the cooperation of the Los Angeles Police Department, Chub not only located Stephanie but was able to bring her home by the end of his two-week leave of absence from UniCast. He beamed with pride when Lilly picked him up at the airport, laughing even at the credit card debt he had run up to get his daughter back. Lilly suspected this was the first time he had ever really stepped out of his humble programmer mode.

Chub later made the rounds at UniCast, thanking Mallory, Kathie, and even Harrison for giving him the chance to get his daughter back. The following day, Lilly made the same rounds. Mallory was astounded. "I can't believe she took time off from work just to come and thank us," he said to Kathie.

"Yeah, she's really something. But we did good. We all did," she said. Mallory smiled, but Kathie's look turned anxious. "So, Lilly's invited you and me, and a lot of other people to a party at Chub's house to celebrate them getting Stephanie back. Are you going?"

"Why not? Free booze, free food."

"Everyone at UniCast Cable will eventually find out about this party. Including Nell."

"You don't want to bring her?"

Kathie dropped her face in her hands. Mallory thought he saw her thick blonde curls trembling. "No," she mumbled finally. Then she looked up at him as if he would understand. "I've been trying to think of a way to gradually end it. But the more I pull back, the harder she clings to me. There's no way to gradually end it, is there?"

Mallory had never had a relationship that ended in a gradual way, or nicely at all. He was at a loss for what to tell her.

"I'm going to break up with her today." Kathie stared blindly past him, her voice struggling to register her determination.

"Good."

"I never thought I would ever have to do anything so cruel."

*** ***

Selby showed up early for Lilly's party. She and Zach were still setting out the food and drinks. He asked if he could help, but Lilly quickly brushed him off and made him sit down. "I'll get you a drink," she said.

"Honey, go talk to the guy." Zach's voice was loud enough that Selby could hear.

She sat down next to Selby. "Can you believe it?" she started. "Mallory actually helped Chub. He somehow got their boss to give Chub a leave of absence to go get Stephanie back. I mean, I used to think that guy was nothing but some demented sexual pervert."

"He's got women problems, for sure," Selby agreed. "But I don't think he's dangerous."

"You don't know how he tries to seduce women." She was almost whispering. "He shows them gross porn movies. He thinks that's a good way to get them in the mood."

Before Selby could respond, Zach called Lilly over to ask her what he was supposed to do with the salad. When she came back, Selby was no longer interested in talking about Mallory. But he kept talking, almost in a whisper. "You know, I had no idea you already lived with your boyfriend."

"Oh. Should I have mentioned it to you earlier?"

Selby's mouth dropped open. He clearly didn't know what to say now. If he said yes, it would be an admission that he was taking too much of an interest in her personal life. She smiled at his discomfort.

"I guess," he finally said. "I guess …. Never mind. It's none of my business."

Lilly did not really want to torture the man. "You know," she said, reverting to a more conversational tone, "It's kind of funny that you and I both know Mr. Mallory pretty well, but we've each seen a completely different side of him."

"But neither side's too great, in my opinion."

"You're right," she laughed. "So far. But he did put me in touch with you. He had nothing to gain by that. Maybe there is the tiniest bit of kindness in his heart."

"Kindness? Huh. Hard to believe. But I guess I've seen stranger things." Then he suddenly changed his expression and motioned her closer, now speaking almost in a whisper. "I have to tell you something. This is not the time or place, but I figure I might not ever see you again."

She inclined her head toward him. She told herself she was an idiot for feeling both excited and frightened to hear what he had to say. She shook off these weird feelings. "What is it?"

"I need to tell you something about, you know, real life. This comes from my experience on the street. Chub probably hasn't seen the last of his wife. The mothers come back. Doesn't make any difference if they're junkies, crack whores, whatever. The mothers almost always come back, sometimes even years later."

Lilly swallowed hard. "I guess we don't need to be talking about that at this party tonight."

"No. Of course not. I just thought you might want to be on the lookout, for your brother's sake. I don't mean to put a damper on things tonight."

"Oh, come on. You're never a damper! I saw you playing basketball, and it looked like you were having fun. In fact, you inspired me. I'm going to try volleyball, if I ever get the time." Her legs were crossed, and she was embarrassed to realize she was wobbling her foot like a nervous child. She quickly stood up and went back to helping Zach in the kitchen.

Mallory was the next to arrive, and he sat down next to Selby. "Getting any of that yet," he sniggered.

Selby stared him down. "You didn't tell me. This is the apartment where *she lives with her fiancé*."

"Oh. I didn't know she was taken." Mallory was becoming re-

137

signed to the fact that he knew almost nothing about women other than their body parts.

    Kathie came to the party alone.

Chapter 19: Lessons from a Funeral

Grace spoke up first at the next therapy meeting. "Okay. I should tell you all something that happened after I left this group session last week."

Mallory had deliberately sat down next to her in the hope that she wouldn't talk about him. He had always admired how she would speak her mind about even the most embarrassing things, but he was afraid this didn't bode well for him now. "After I left this group last week, I drove to Arundel Hospital to see my mother. By the time I came out after seeing my mother, I realized that Mr. Mallory, er, *Ramsteel*, had been stalking me."

"Jesus! Did you call the police?" Pointy-bearded Peter leaned forward in his chair, his face red, twisting his head back to focus his stare on Mallory.

"I just wanted to finish up a conversation we started in here," Mallory explained.

"Justification. Rationalization. Every stalker has a reason." Pointy Beard pulled out his cell phone. "This man shouldn't be allowed to remain in decent society. I'm calling 911 right now."

"No, please …." Grace pleaded. "It wasn't so bad."

"Yes. Put your phone down," Sebastian the facilitator raised his voice for the first time in all of Mallory's therapy sessions. "I think this can be our chance to explore a whole range of Grace's feelings as she faces her mother's imminent death."

"It wasn't so bad," Grace repeated.

"And what was it that Mr. Ramsteel wanted to talk to you about?" Sebastian barked quickly, probably to keep people's minds off calling the police.

"You know, we never actually got to that. He told me a lot of other things."

"Can you tell us some of those things, Grace?" Sebastian was obviously intent on keeping Pointy Beard out of the conversation.

And Peter did sink back into his chair and seem to lose interest in calling the police. But Mallory was terrified. He had slipped up by telling Grace the story of how he had failed his father. That confession had just spontaneously poured out when he sat next to this brave young girl in the hospital facing the death of her mother. He hadn't imagined that his weakness would later become fodder for discussion by this whole group of losers.

Sebastian kept talking fast. "I'm assuming Mr. Ramsteel wouldn't mind you telling us what he said."

"Yeah. There's no secrets here." Pointy Beard's glare at Mallory was vicious.

Mallory started to get up and flee. The only thing that stopped him was Grace's hand on his leg. He quickly turned to look at her, then sat back down. But Grace kept her focus on the facilitator even as she withdrew her hand. "I guess I want to say what's really on my mind." There was a catch in her voice that caught everybody's attention. "I didn't think I could talk about it today, but my mother died last night."

"Oh, I'm sorry." The words came to Mallory spontaneously. Then, slowly, most of the others said pretty much the same thing. Even Pointy Beard mumbled something. Mallory had never been in a room where the feeling he had was the same feeling everybody else had. He felt disoriented. And he was still in shock that Grace had kept his secrets, even touched him. Maybe she even had feelings for him.

Sebastian asked her about the funeral. Grace admitted that her mother had made all of the arrangements herself before she became too debilitated. "I guess she spoiled me my whole life, even to the end. Nobody could have had a better mother." They let her cry. But she pulled herself together quickly. Grace's bond with her mother seemed stronger than any connection Mallory had ever had with anyone. He wondered why he had always been alone. He wondered why nobody had ever really loved him. And he wondered what it meant that Grace had touched him that day.

*** ***

"Have you ever been to a funeral?" Mallory felt he had reversed the natural order of things. It was Thomas who was supposed to wait for him on the landing at the top of the steps. At least, Thomas had done that often when they had first met the year before. Thomas was now busy with his college courses and his track practice most afternoons. Now, Mallory practically had to stalk him to talk to him. They sat on the top step of the landing, staring out across the parking lot.

It had been Sebastian the Facilitator's suggestion that the therapy group members be allowed to go the funeral. Mallory had never been to a funeral. He had never seen any use in crying over spilt milk. But he was going to go because he thought Grace liked him, and because he couldn't imagine how horrible it would be for her if Pointy Beard was there without him there to protect her. "What is a funeral like?" he asked his young friend now.

"Been to a lot. They're all different."

"I mean, what do I do?"

"I dunno. Listen to the choir. Sing if you can. Say you're sorry to the family when you get the chance."

"Do I have to know any prayers?"

"No. Don't think so. People pretty loose at funerals." Thomas looked at him. "Why're you going?"

"A woman's mother died. A friend of mine. She's been pretty good to me." He left out the part about her being cute and young and blonde.

"The worst that can happen at a funeral is you sit there, and you don't even know the guy who died, and you don't get to talk to your friends – but even then you hear some good singing, and then you go home. That happened to me once."

That didn't seem so bad to Mallory, though it sounded lonely. He suddenly turned to Thomas. "You have experience with this. Will you go with me? Go with me to the funeral?"

*** ***

Thomas looked around warily. "Is this a church? Where's the choir?"

It was a round building, clearly not a house, but not a church either. Thomas read the pamphlet they had been handed at the door. "Wynnewood Community Center. Guess it's not a church."

There was an aisle between the two groups of chairs, and the coffin was in the aisle, toward the front. Mallory was terrified to see that one half of it was open, allowing a close-up view of what looked like a wax figure of a very old, pruned-out white lady. Mallory picked a chair as far away as he could. He didn't see Pointy Beard or any other members of his therapy group. There were some depressing speeches about what a wonderful woman Grace's mother had been. Then they closed the coffin and wheeled it out. There was an announcement that there would be a reception in the next room.

Grace stood up in the front row. To his surprise, she caught his eye and nodded toward the reception room. Mallory stood up and bolted towards it, gesturing for Thomas to follow. They were two of the first to get there. Mallory immediately went over to the punchbowl and ladled out some kind of fruity red punch for himself. Thomas declined the punch and moved a little off to the side. He definitely stood out in this crowd, Mallory noticed. There were only two or three other Black people in this crowd of about thirty, and both were women who were at least fifty years old. And they each had about forty pounds on this young, thin, muscular kid with that engaging smile and that clean, close-cut do.

"How long do we have to stay here?" Mallory's whisper was loud enough to be overheard by an elderly couple standing near. They gave him an ugly stare, and he stared right back. To his surprise, he now saw Thomas on the other side of the room engaged in conversation with an old, white-haired man he couldn't possibly know. The man's crooked yellow teeth showed themselves in reaction to Thomas's wide smile. Mallory could not see Grace anywhere, and he gestured to Thomas that they should get going. But just as they neared the door, Grace came in, turning away from an elderly woman who seemed to be clinging to her.

"I'm sorry," they heard her say. "I need to talk to the other people here, too." Her eyes seemed to light up when she saw Mallory and Thomas standing there. She tore herself away from the woman and rushed over to greet them. She put her hand on Mallory's arm. "Thank you for coming, Mr. Mallory! No one else from the group came. And who is this?"

"I'm Thomas. I'm a friend of Mr. Mallory. He told me about your mother. I'm sorry for your loss."

She put her hand on Thomas's arm, too. "Thank you for coming with him."

"Your mother was a fine woman. A great mother. It's gotta hurt to see her finally lose her battle with cancer. Real sorry. Just real sorry." Mallory was astounded at Thomas's speech. How did he know anything about Grace's mother? He was even more astounded at what happened next. Grace muttered something he couldn't hear, then walked into Thomas, clung to him, and sobbed into his chest.

Chapter 20: Pots and Pans

The party to celebrate little Stephanie's return had gone on longer than either Zach or Lilly expected. Neither of them was the type to leave a party mess until the next morning, but Zach seemed especially intent on cleaning up. Lilly was content with this state of affairs at first, as she could focus on gathering the glasses, plates, silverware and food in their living room while Zach loaded the dishwasher and dealt with the leftovers. Lilly was happy that little Stephanie seemed happy to be home, though she wondered when it was going to sink in that her mother was gone. She had vowed to help Chub stay sober and keep her little niece busy. She dreaded Selby's prediction that Janice would one day return to cause trouble about the little girl, but she was glad he'd told her. She was thinking about this and vacuuming the wall-to-wall carpet when she heard the sound of pots and pans crashing in the kitchen.

"What's wrong? Are you all right?" She couldn't understand the situation. There had been more than one crash. Zach crashed the lid of one pan on top of another as she watched.

"You don't know what's wrong?" His voice was acid, his face red. "You don't know?"

"No. I don't."

"We just had a party. Some of my friends, some of your friends. Our personal friends. Every one of my friends asked me quietly why you weren't wearing your engagement ring. That was embarrassing enough. But your policeman friend didn't know we were living together, and your friend Mallory didn't even know we were engaged. You're hiding our engagement as much as you can. And I don't know what that means."

She was not going to cower in the face of his rage. "No. I told you from the beginning I didn't want to make our engagement public." But she couldn't stop the quiver in her voice.

"I don't know." He crashed the last pan onto the pile. "Maybe

I'm just insecure. Maybe I'm not the kind of guy you want." He turned toward the bedroom. "I can't talk about this anymore. I'm going to bed." She moved toward him, but he was gone. She stood there in the kitchen doorway, shaking, thinking. She wasn't sure who was at fault.

She knew keeping an engagement a secret was not a normal thing for a woman in love to do. She had acted like she wasn't in love – but when Zach was hurt, as he obviously was now, she felt the hurt herself. She was confused. In bed that night, she promised to wear his ring. She told him she really wanted his touch, right then. He acted reluctant at first, but she knew what he liked. She felt exhausted, spent, as she drifted off to sleep later. But she dreamt of something else entirely.

*** ***

Mallory had felt uncomfortable at the party for Chub. He had long since given up hope that he could ever make time with Lilly, but he was still depressed to find out that she had a live-in boyfriend. Up until that moment, he had been rooting for Selby, but now he knew Selby would be wasting his time even talking to her.

He sat next to Chub on the sofa during most of the party. Chub was tired, but he'd taken the trouble to bathe and put on a button-up shirt and douse himself with some manly perfume that didn't smell too bad. People pulled up chairs or sat on cushions on the floor to hear him talk.

Chub, who never spoke a word that wasn't necessary at work, was on a high from retrieving Stephanie and was eager to tell his story. He couldn't recite all the sordid details with Stephanie sitting close by on the arm of his chair; but he somehow managed to tell the story on two levels, one sanitized version for when his daughter was near and the more sordid and interesting version when she was across the room.

"I knew Janice was getting worse. The drugs, I mean. I just …

they became her whole life. She was getting worse, lost her job, never home. I knew her dealer was from California. I knew when she took off she wouldn't go far from him. Her mother still lives in a house in Simi Valley. I figured they'd inevitably end up in a place where they could live for free.

"I asked Lilly to have this party so I could thank all the people who have helped me. So many people have helped. Lilly, mainly. But even my attorneys, here and in California, and even the LAPD. And I guess I should thank Visa, too, for extending me all that credit. It seems like the whole world came together for Stephanie. I can't thank you all enough. I owe you. And I'll try to find a way to make it up to you someday."

Lilly was beaming. "This is great. This is so great." Every time she nodded her head, her fabulous French twist distracted all the men in the crowd. "And little Stephanie is great, she hasn't changed. But, Chub, you don't even know yet all the people who helped you. Kathie here held down your job while you were gone."

"*Pretended* to hold down your job," Kathie corrected her.

"Ha! And Mr. Mallory here arranged that whole deal somehow with Harrison."

People filtered away from Chub, who appeared to be crying, or sweating, or both. Lilly encouraged people to get drinks or food. Kathie sat down next to Mallory.

"I see you didn't bring Nell," he started.

"I know. I did the deed. I just couldn't fake it any longer."

He envisioned Nell sitting alone in her rented house with her two dogs and three cats. He wondered if she would spend her whole life sitting alone with that menagerie. He thought he might understand the pain she felt.

*** ***

The following Monday morning, Mallory stood in the opening to Nell's cubicle and asked her to talk with him in the break room.

"What about?" Her expression was tense, suspicious.

"Something you need to know."

She followed him to the break room. "I've been talking to Chub," he said. "We're all in trouble."

Nell breathed a sigh of relief. "I thought it was something else. I thought you were going to torture me about Kathie."

"No. Listen. It's about Algonquin J. Tycoon." He saw Nell roll her eyes at his pet name for the billionaires who manipulated the economy – mostly, Mallory believed, by furiously trading assets and dumping employees like pawns sacrificed on a chessboard. "This time it's real. There's this hedge fund, Everdine, that's thinking about buying UniCast."

"Aren't we already owned by some hedge fund?"

"Just a part. But UniCast is now dying to sell itself completely, and it thinks it can get a better deal if it cuts costs and shows more profit."

"Who told you all this crap?"

"Chub. He knows a little about business. And after he told me, I've been looking up this stuff on the internet all weekend." He didn't mention that this was practically the first time he had ever used the internet for anything but his porn site or Manly Man. "Look, we're all in trouble. I saw a guy talking on the internet. He said UniCast's new philosophy is 'Every dollar spent on customer service is a dollar profit lost.'"

"Maybe that has something to do with them taking the tape off the surveillance camera."

Mallory jerked around in his chair to look at the camera looming over their conversation. The camera had been there for years. No one knew why UniCast would want to spy on its employees during their lunch breaks. Mallory had mooted out the mystery the year before by standing on a chair with a white plastic bag over his head and taping over the camera lens. The employees had laughed about it for a few days and speculated – even took bets on – what would happen. Nothing happened. The tape had stayed on the lens for months.

"They're looking to cut jobs," Mallory insisted. "I saw it on the internet. So far, I've convinced Harrison that his best bet is not to make waves. But now? Now he thinks his best bet to keep his job is to cut as many people as he can. This will change everything."

"Kevin, I'm sure you'll survive, even if no one else does." Her look was sour.

"Thanks. And, Nell, I hope you do, too."

"I wonder if the statistical department will be cut." It seemed like Nell was talking to herself, looking away from him.

Mallory knew what she really wanted to know. Talking about the statistical department was her way of giving him an opening to tell her what he knew about Kathie. He knew Nell was hoping against hope that Kathie would change her mind. He knew the answer. He didn't know whether to tell her or not. He had nothing to gain for himself either way. But he still hesitated. He didn't want to hurt her.

"Oh, come on," she turned back to him. "I know she talks to you. Just tell me."

But he didn't have to say a word. She could tell just by the look on his face.

Chapter 21: Tell, No Tell

"I'm calling to thank you, and your police officer friends, for all your help on Community Fun Day. And if you'll give me their names, we want to send each of them a letter of appreciation. It's the least Roofs can do."

"You don't need to do that, Lilly."

Just thinking about making this call had made her jittery. But strangely, the jitters went away as soon as Selby used her first name. It was good to have a friend. A friend who agreed to go to lunch with her to discuss having a similar Community Fun Day at one of their other apartment buildings.

As often as she found herself worried, aggravated, and frustrated in her work life at Roofs, and even in her home life with Zach, she seemed to be getting a break from those feelings that day when she met Selby for lunch. They met in the same little pizza and sandwiches joint they ate in before, both of them grateful for the cool air conditioning after braving the sultry weather outside. She found herself hoping they would sit at the same table they sat at before. That didn't work out, but the new table felt as serenely comfortable as the last one had. Selby carried a large black notebook with a calendar fastened to the front cover. She was disappointed to see that. She was afraid he was in a hurry and would want to get down to business too soon. But he said he had plenty of time, as long as his cell phone didn't go off.

She thanked him again. He thanked her for inviting him to her party.

"Zach and I got into an argument when we were cleaning up, because I hadn't told you we were living together." She was suddenly grateful she hadn't mentioned Zach slamming the pans around. The last thing she needed was to get Selby's cop antenna up.

"Oh." If he was surprised, he did a good job of hiding it. His dark eyes seemed noncommittal. "Yeah. I was kind of surprised you hadn't told me that."

"Zach says being engaged is a public thing, by definition. So is living together. I guess I agree, at least in theory. So, I'm kind of wondering why I wanted to keep it all a secret. Normally I'm a person who does everything by the book."

"I can tell."

"What? With your street cop radar?"

He smiled. "Yeah, maybe something like that." He leaned back and put his notebook aside so the waiter could supply them with glasses of water. "I have this feeling," he went on when the waiter left. "It's not just cop radar. It's personal. I feel like I'm really getting to know you."

"So, you know me, do you?" She felt like she should probably deflect this kind of talk. But she didn't. "So, if you know so much about me, what's your diagnosis for my weird behavior about my engagement." She knew that this conversation was somehow inappropriate, but she told herself they were just bantering. There was no reason she couldn't have a silly talk with this guy, this guy who she knew wouldn't judge her.

"Well, speaking as a guy who was once engaged …. No. Never mind. My situation's got nothing to do with yours."

"What? Your fiancée shouted it to the rooftops, right?"

"At first. At first, she told everybody and their brother. And then, when she changed her mind and dumped me, she told everybody even faster."

"Oh. I'm sorry. That must have hurt."

"I glad she didn't leave it to *me* to tell everybody." He shook his head slowly. "I don't blame her. She said she decided she couldn't be married to a cop."

It seemed to her that their food was taking forever to arrive. She wondered if this meeting was a mistake. There was no urgency at all about the additional Community Fun Day, which wouldn't be scheduled for months. They hadn't even talked about it yet. Neither of them seemed interested in it.

"If I'm engaged, why would I want to keep it a secret?" She realized this was going beyond friendly bantering. This was the serious question she had been asking herself.

"I can't answer that question. Maybe you're too shy for all that kind of hoopla."

The food came. He began to eat his pizza delicately and slowly, with a fork. Lilly picked at her salad equally slowly. The conversation changed to her work at Roofs. He seemed really interested in her tales of the clients and their troubles, of the office work that had become such a burden ever since her boss had begun attending more and more conventions. He listened without volunteering any easy solutions. He seemed to understand that most real-life problems could not be unraveled by simple suggestions over pizza.

"Oh. I've been talking about myself too much," she grinned. "I'm sure you have a much more interesting job. What's it like, being out on the streets all day?"

He raised his thick eyebrows. "I do run into some interesting characters. One of the most interesting recently is your friend Mallory."

"Oh. Do tell! I have some stories of my own about that guy."

She described Mallory's attempt to seduce her by playing the sound of that woman screaming in ecstasy on his porn site. Selby laughed so hard she thought she saw tears come to his eyes. She was pleased that she could tell a story good enough for even this street cop to appreciate. She decided not to tell him the even more incredible story of Mallory's attempt to trade sex with her for Chub's job. She was content with the reaction Selby had already given her. She didn't need to strain to get his attention. But she hadn't expected Selby to one-up her. Her jaw dropped when Selby described how Mallory's obsession with Koko the cat led to a standoff at the courthouse with the SWAT team.

"My God. Is he actually dangerous?"

"He's never hurt anybody. I think he's just a ... blundering idiot, if you don't mind me using that phrase. And he's going to therapy now." He shrugged.

Lilly thought about reminding him that she was the one who had convinced Mallory to go to therapy. But she knew that wasn't necessary. Selby already liked her, she could tell. It wasn't necessary to try to get him to admire her more. There was no kind of work or effort at all involved in their conversation.

Selby didn't talk about himself. He seemed so interested in her that she probably revealed more about herself than she should have. They stayed a half hour longer than they had planned. But as they left the restaurant, the blazing sun, the stifling air, and the smell of melting asphalt in the parking lot reminded her of the sticky, complicated world she actually lived in. She worried that she had told this man too much. But then she told him more.

"I still don't know why I wanted to hide my engagement," she called to him from the safe distance across the roof of a couple of parked cars. "But I did. I realize it's my problem. I'll figure it out."

*** ***

"Listen," Nell leaned so far into the opening to his cubicle the ends of her stylish bob were brushing his face. She was whispering. "Harrison's now requiring us to keep records of the Cheer Committee Meetings. Including attendance. And to turn them in once a month."

"Let's talk in the break room."

"They have that camera there now."

"I'll take care of that." Nell followed him to the break room. They stopped in the doorway so they were in the camera's blind spot and glanced upwards.

"What are you doing?" Nell was still whispering.

"Same thing I did last year." This time Mallory dispensed with the white plastic bag he had worn over his head last year. He knew the camera angle better now. Besides, he didn't want Nell to think he was a coward. He grabbed a chair from outside in the hallway, reached up, pulled a roll of tape out of his back pocket, and taped over the lens.

"You? It was you who did that last year?" Nell looked impressed. "But what if they try to monitor the camera now and see the tape?"

"I don't know. What's this about the committee attendance records?"

Mallory had consistently used his duties as a member of the Cheer Committee as his excuse for being off the phone or away from his desk. He had brilliantly outmaneuvered Harrison's predecessor, Tietelbaum, by simply throwing away all the records of the Cheer Committee, thus assuring himself of an all-purpose excuse for not being where he was supposed to be. Later, he had given the reins of the Cheer Committee completely over to Nell as part of their rapprochement. He had assumed she had enough sense not to keep records after that. But he had been wrong.

"Harrison's after me," Mallory griped. "Didn't you say you'd put me down as present for every meeting of the committee?"

"They have some sort of program to keep better track of things now. Harrison said you were away from your phone seventeen times in the last two weeks, for over an hour each time."

"I'll figure out something." Mallory feared he was losing his fight with management. He hadn't represented any inadequate employees since Chub, and he suspected Harrison was making sure he wasn't informed of any personnel moves he was making. Mallory had also been distracted by his therapy. He felt it was now his duty to lead the therapy group members, especially the female group members, into a more common-sense approach to sexual relations. He thought he had worked wonders with Grace, and he felt he was making progress with Michaela. He hadn't gotten either one into his bed, but in his new wisdom he felt he had an expanded timeline in which to accomplish this.

He hadn't said one word to Nell about Kathie lately. Nell had betrayed him with Kathie, and he liked nothing better than seeing the tables turned now against Nell. He had the impression Nell was shrinking. She didn't seem to walk or talk with the same self-satisfied female swagger that had always annoyed him so much. He suspected her failed lesbian affair had dried her out.

"You should come to the next Cheer Committee meeting," Nell said now. "We need a quorum. At least, when I tell Harrison you come to the meetings, it won't be a total lie."

"Does Kathie still come to the meetings?"

Nell bristled. "No, she hasn't come in a while. Why are you torturing me?"

Chapter 22: Attraction

Thomas was insistent. "It's my crib. It's my party. My parents can come if they want, but there's no way they're telling me who I can invite."

Mallory had been afraid it would come to this. Thomas's parents, Ava and Edison, had long ago instructed their twenty-year-old son not to have anything to do with Mallory. This might have been because Mallory, pretending to be a lawyer, had tried to get their son to plead guilty to a felony he didn't commit, then had bungled his civil case against the police officer who brutalized him during the arrest. Mallory didn't see why they should still be angry. After all, the charges against Thomas had eventually been completely dismissed, the officer had been fired, and the young man was awarded $100,000 in damages.

"It ain't all that," Thomas explained. "It's that I had to lie for you about Koko. When the cops came to get that cat."

"What's the big deal? I gave Koko back to Nell."

"Uh ... yeah. A couple weeks later. So, you're coming to my party, right?"

Thomas was his only friend. Even with his limited understanding of family dynamics, Mallory understood that Ava and Edison were wonderful parents. But he didn't like the way they seemed to be trying to control Thomas's life now. A year before, he might have pretended to be a lawyer or a therapist and advised Thomas directly on how to get his hands on his own money and keep his parents in the dark about his social life. Mallory knew he could be a therapist now because he had been to four therapy sessions and because he had experienced himself a whole lifetime of controlling parenting from his mother. But there was no chance that Thomas would listen to his advice now. The only thing he could do to help him was to come to his party.

Mallory expected Edison to slug him when he arrived, or Ava

to deny him access to any of her delicious food. At the very least, he expected Thomas's parents to shun him. But the party didn't go like that at all. The crowd was mostly Thomas's college friends. Ava did not put on a big spread; she brought only one large plate of tacos. And Edison greeted him cordially, even shook his hand – but without offering him the huge glass of cognac that Mallory had been hoping for. Thomas's parents mingled with their son's friends for a while, but then they sat by themselves on the balcony, waving any of the younger generation who stepped out there to come over and talk.

Mallory felt out of place at this party. Most of the kids were Black, half of them looking at their phones the whole time, and he didn't understand what they were talking about most of the time. He did sight a neighbor couple from the apartment complex. They had been at the earlier meeting that Ava and Edison had held in this same apartment to talk about starting a Neighborhood Watch program. Mallory remembered he had had a conversation with them, but he didn't remember what they talked about, or even who they were. At least Grace was with him now.

*** ***

Grace had called him two days after her mother's funeral. "I want to thank you. You are the only one from the therapy group who came to the funeral. I didn't know most of the people there. They were mostly my mother's old friends from way back."

Mallory was not used to a woman initiating a conversation with him. When he had first taken to wearing a suit and tie everywhere, he had attracted some attention from the women at work. They had stopped acting as if he were a dangerous animal that needed to be avoided. But the women's interest seemed to have faded over time. Manly Man had said this was to be expected. Sustained female interest, Manly advised, often required a constant parade of shiny new objects, and he had only two suits.

"Um … okay." He racked his brain for something to say. He had to push out of his mind the erotic images her unexpected call had stirred up. "I guess you're having a hard time." He just guessed this from the way she had looked at the funeral. He knew he didn't qualify to speak about what she was going through.

"Yeah. You know, the people at therapy, they're so nice to let me go on about it, but I think I'm taking up too much of their time."

Mallory agreed. But he thought this was the perfect time to allow full rein to his reflex to flatter her. "No, you're not. Not at all. People are moved by your story."

"Oh, that's so kind. Now that the funeral is all over, I feel like I'm kind of at loose ends."

"Don't you have a boyfriend?"

"He didn't come to the funeral. Does that answer your question?"

"I'm sorry." She didn't respond. He couldn't think of anything else to say. At work, he just cut off customers if the conversation got tedious, but he didn't want to do that to her.

Then Grace brought up something they had talked about at the hospital. "You know, you told me your father left you and hadn't contacted you in years. I don't think it was so bad of you not to go to his funeral."

"Not that anybody even told me about it." He had never mentioned this to anyone before.

"Oh. That's so awful. Sorry."

Now he remembered why he had never mentioned this to anyone before. The last thing you needed was to seem pathetic. He was feeling pathetic now. He had to change the subject. "You know, I have a friend. You met him, Thomas. He lives right next door. He's a good kid. I'm going to a party at his house tomorrow night. Why don't you come with me?"

*** ***

She said she would just meet him there, so it wasn't exactly a date. She knocked on his door first, as he had arranged. He was still in fear of Thomas's parents at that point, but he figured they wouldn't dare attack him if he had a little white girl on his arm. Mallory's suit and Grace's blonde hair did stop the conversation for a second when they first stepped in. Mallory assumed all the young Black men were lusting after her. He didn't include Thomas in this. But Thomas was the first person to talk to her.

"Good to see you." Thomas was polite, but he seemed a little shy. If he remembered her sobbing into his chest at the funeral home, he didn't show it.

"Thanks for having me, Thomas." He seemed to brighten when she remembered his name. She went on in a lower, private voice. "Nice to see you outside of the funeral home. But don't let me put a damper on the whole party."

Thomas's face looked strained. "You can talk about whatever's on your mind."

Grace sighed. "She *is* on my mind. But I'm not going to talk about her – except maybe to you and Mr. Mallory."

Thomas walked away and brought them each back a beer, then stood and talked with them. Mallory had never noticed what a good conversationalist Thomas was. Hearing her respond, Mallory found out more about Grace than he could have found out in a month of dating. Grace had been a receptionist, then an office manager for a medical office, but her mother had insisted she quit and promised to support her if she went to community college full time.

"What college?"

"Community Tech."

"Hey! That's where I just graduated from. And Mr. Mallory, too."

They discovered more common ground. Each of them was an only child. But Grace and Thomas each had a lot of cousins, while Mallory had none. He didn't have much to say in the cousin-talk part of the conversation, and from that point on it seemed like he was being edged out of it. He had never seen Grace so talkative before. Her eyes lit up and she tossed her head as she spoke, mostly with Thomas. Mallory thought Thomas was too young for her – but then, he himself was too old. Thomas circulated around among the guests but always came back to Grace, his smile tentative but gently expectant. Grace obviously liked him. She smiled at his sudden shyness and countered his every lighthearted remark. It seemed like he was succeeding in making her forget about her grief for a moment. Mallory felt that his own fantasies about Grace had been foolish. He was a foolish old man. He was lucky enough that Grace hadn't reported the full story of his failure as a son to the therapy group. He couldn't be angry at her. The best he could hope for was that Thomas would appreciate the manly powers he had used to bring this sweet young thing into his life.

*** ***

Lilly couldn't get her conversations with Officer Selby out of her mind. She called and asked him out to lunch. She didn't pretend to have a work-related excuse. "I had a good time when we went out to lunch last time, and I want to do it again."

"Lunch? Or the shooting range? Or what?"

"What."

No matter what silly thing they did, she was sure she would have a good time. It was that simple. Lately, she had been trying to recreate within herself the calm sensations she always felt in his presence. That was perhaps because her relationship with Zach seemed to be going in the opposite direction. She really couldn't blame Zach for being disappointed that she was showing so little outward enthusiasm about their engagement. She was beginning to wonder if their problems weren't more deeply rooted. He had apologized for his temper tantrum after the party. And he had obviously been trying to be more romantic. If there was an almost imperceptible rough edge to each of their encounters, she told herself it was just because they were two real people, in the real world, trying to make a real life together.

She had been focusing on all the work she had to do at Roofs in the absence of the director. She was starting to believe that she could handle McFadden's job if the opportunity ever came up. This extra work detracted from her time together with Zach, but he didn't seem to mind. "You'll go far. You'll be director soon. Between you and me, we'll be rich before we know it," he joked.

"I don't care if we're rich. I wouldn't take a promotion unless I was sure I could make the organization better," she responded. When Zach looked askance at her, she had to laugh at herself. "Oh God, I sound like such a do-gooder. Of course, I'd take the job if they offered it to me."

Selby's house was pretty small, an old wooden cottage with brown shingles. It stood on a tree-shaded street along with other small houses of all different styles. She was standing several steps back on the porch, looking it over, when he opened the door and stepped out, wearing just a pair of khaki shorts and bright red Ban-Lon shirt. She noticed he was a little bowlegged. She decided to focus on the house. "Wow. This is not exactly the bachelor pad I expected."

"It wasn't what I expected either. It was supposed to be ours, Paisley's and my starter home. I hated living here alone at first. But I'm really getting used to it."

"Oh. I'm sorry. I hadn't realized how serious …?"

"Yeah," he interrupted, catching her attention with a sharp look. "Engagements are serious."

She felt like he was warning her. He stood next to her and pointed out all the faults at the front of the house. "I have a ways to go, but I started on the inside. Come on in and see." He kept talking about home repairs as he ushered her in. "I've lived here almost three years now. With a house this old, you have to keep working on it all the time. But I got some friends on the force who are real good at this kind of stuff." He stood facing her in the living room with his hands on his hips like he was about to direct traffic. He was exactly her height when she wore kitten heels.

"When I was growing up, my father always insisted we live in a new house," she said, smiling at this memory. "My father was a researcher, really smart, and a real hard worker, but at home he refused to even pick up a hammer."

"I heard your parents died when …."

"I was fourteen. I'm not really an orphan, if that's what you're thinking." She didn't want him feeling sorry for her. She had been lucky to have had them for as long as she did. "I was practically an adult by time they died."

"You're talking to somebody who knows the streets. Fourteen is *not* practically an adult."

He had a beautiful circular oak table in the modern kitchen, a sofa and an intricately designed Oriental rug in the living room. The chairs across from the sofa were plush, the patterns bright. They looked nice, but she thought the whole ensemble didn't exactly fit together. She wondered who he entertained here. There were framed photos on the walls. He gestured generally in their direction. "Nieces, nephews. I got tons of them." There were pictures of his parents also. The place seemed to be very neat and clean. When she commented on how beautiful it was, he shrugged. "I'm too old for the beer bottle décor."

He asked her to sit down in the kitchen. His empty holster was hanging on the back of a kitchen chair, his gun locked away. The wonderful smell from the stove was the lasagna he was baking. He had put it in frozen before he went to work. He made her a simple salad while it cooled, talking all the while about the food. He sat down next to her. He smelled like he had just shaved and showered. She knew she should be nervous in this situation, but she wasn't.

"I'm sorry about your fiancée. Her name was Paisley, right? You told me she didn't want to be married to a cop. But, you know, I've been thinking about that. A lot of women couldn't stand that lifestyle, being married to a cop."

"She did marry a cop. A different cop."

Lilly took a slow breath. "I'm sorry," she said evenly as she watched his eyes seem to harden. "It's none of my business anyway."

She felt like she already knew him well enough. She didn't have to know all the details about his past life. She knew she felt comfortable in his house, eating his food. She loved that he had family pictures on the walls. It seemed more like a real home than any place she'd been in a long time. She hadn't realized how much she missed a real home. She couldn't help wondering if she'd been here before, or if she'd just dreamed it. He served her the lasagna he had baked, and even his cooking was good. He talked about the department, even the things he didn't like about it. She told him she was going to apply for a director's job somewhere. She was acutely aware of the nuances in everything he said; but when she spoke, she didn't need to censor anything. He was not as handsome as Zach, but she was starting to wonder if he was the man she had always been waiting for.

Chapter 23: Footies

"Oh, Mr. Mallory?" He looked up. It was Ms. Marcie, Harrison's assistant. She had been the assistant to every supervisor since Teitelbaum. Mallory thought she was decent enough looking, with nice, thin, black hair not quite down to her shoulders. His theory on her was she was too skinny to attract real male interest. He had always avoided her anyway, because she worked too close to the boss.

"Harrison wants to see me?" He couldn't keep the little quiver out of his voice.

"No. No," she whispered. "Can I sit down?" She sat down on the tiny metal chair squeezed between his desk and the cubicle wall. "It's about Harrison, though. He's being so unfair. I think he's looking for an excuse to fire me."

Mallory breathed a sigh of relief that he wasn't the target this time. *Problem solved* was his first reaction. But then her realized that Ms. Marcie was still sitting there. She had always been nice to him. Now she was gritting her teeth in anger.

"I have a scheduled vacation in Mexico all next week. My husband and I have reservations in the Riviera Maya. Hotels, plane tickets, transportation, everything. Now Harrison is saying I can't go. My car had a flat tire last week and AAA was very slow and I was four hours late. Harrison is charging that against my vacation time. I told him I don't have any other vacation time other than that one week. He says he doesn't care. If I'm not back from Mexico by noon on Friday, I'll be fired. He knows I can't be back by noon."

A shiver of terror ran from Mallory's head and down to his toes. Harrison was obviously determined to make the 15% cut to the workforce needed to keep the Algonquin J. Tycoons of the Everdine hedge fund happy. He wondered why the supervisor was starting with Ms. Marcie. Harrison and Ms. Marcie had always seemed to get along well. "I know you have some influence in personnel matters around here," she continued. "I'm asking if you could possibly help me. You know, I'm just the first one, but I hear that he's going to fire a lot more."

The hedge fund acquisition plan seemed to be going through, and Harrison was being cruel to Ms. Marcie just to prove he could downsize with the best of them. Mallory knew there was no defense against a hedge fund acquisition. But there was always the option of offense.

"Get me the personnel complaint forms. Get me two copies. Meet me in the break room. If the tape is still on the surveillance camera, I'll meet you there in ten minutes."

Mallory sat across from her while she filled out the form, setting out her complaint in what seemed like excruciating detail. "Don't you think I should type it up?" she asked after she had finished writing it up in beautiful longhand. "Is that why you told me to bring two blank forms?" Mallory assured her he would get it typed on the other form if she would sign that one also. But as soon as he got back to his cubicle, he threw Marcie's version of the complaint in the trash and typed out on the other signed form a version of the complaint that he thought would have more of an impact.

> *I Marcie Hofstater, do declare and affirm under the penalties of perjury that the following is true and correct.*
>
> *I am employed as a Management Assistant at UniCast Cable. My supervisor is Mr. Gregory Harrison. From the first day of my employment, Mr. Harrison has harassed me.*
>
> *He began by making me remove my shoes and walk around without them. He would hide my shoes in his desk and watch me as I went through his drawers to find them. Then he began making me look for them on my knees. He insisted on me taking off my underwear and putting it on him. At first over his clothes, then later under.*
>
> *When I asked him if this was a normal part of the job, he said yes, it was UniCast Cable's policy. He threatened that if I complained, he would transfer me to Customer Assistance.*

Mallory Goes to Therapy

As a result of this harassment, I ruined several pairs of footies, and I had to buy new panties because mine were all stretched out. I would like to be reimbursed for the cost of these items.

Mallory warned Ms. Marcie not to contact anyone at UniCast Cable while she was on vacation. He took her phone and, with Chub's help, blocked Harrison's home number, every number he could find for the UniCast corporation worldwide, and every number at UniCast's lawyers' offices. As soon as he was sure her plane had taken off, Mallory mailed his version of the complaint to the main personnel office of UniCast Cable in Texas.

*** ***

Mallory didn't know whether to sit next to Grace or not at their next therapy meeting; but when she met his eyes with a smile, that decided it. He knew she was more attracted to Thomas, and Thomas had said he was going to ask her out. But he had heard this younger generation was much looser about sex, and he still nursed a faint hope that she'd keep him in reserve, if only on her second string. He sat down next to her. But Peter of the Pointy Beard immediately took offense.

"Grace, don't be intimidated! You don't have to sit next to that cretin."

Mallory wasn't surprised at Peter's animosity. What shocked and depressed him was that he had immediately recognized that the *cretin* being referred to was himself. Was he starting to suspect that description was true? Was Peter getting into his head?

Mallory did not want to look like a coward in front of Grace. "All the other chairs are taken," he lied.

Pointy Beard rose from his chair, stood in the middle of the semicircle and pointed to three vacant chairs. "One. Two. Three." He didn't say another word. He didn't have to. Mallory was mortified.

"Okay. Let's all take a breath," Sebastian, the facilitator, interjected from his own chair at the center of the room.

"I enjoy sitting next to Mr. Mallory ... er, *Ramsteel*," Grace spoke into the tense silence. "He came to my mother's funeral. We had a nice talk. I consider him a friend."

Mallory didn't remember anything that was said during the rest of the meeting. He had a visual memory of Pointy Beard fading back down into his chair. He was utterly confounded that Grace had taken his side. He couldn't wait to talk to her after the meeting. But she stood up quickly when it was time to go.

"Can I talk to you outside?" He put his hand on her shoulder. She looked back at him coolly. He chalked that up to the therapy setting and followed her out of the room and up the stairs. "I consider you a friend, too." He spoke to the back of her head as she walked across the parking lot. She didn't turn around until she got to her car.

"Yes, you came to the funeral. I appreciate that." She gave him a little smile and looked up at him with those pale blue eyes. He felt a warm pulsation of excitement.

"You're the kindest girl I ever met."

She had her fingers curled around the door handle of her car, but she didn't open it. "That's a very nice thing to say, Mr. Mallory."

"In the hospital, remember? We talked. I told you some of my deepest secrets. My most shameful secrets. You're the only person who knows that stuff about me. I feel like we're connected now."

"Yes, maybe. But not in *that* way."

"You think I'm too pathetic to date?"

She let go of the door handle and turned to face him, audibly sighing. "I'm dating Thomas. I was hoping he would tell you first."

He stared at her. "Of course. I should have seen that coming. You're a good kid, and so is he. Of course. Of course."

"You're a good man. You'll find somebody. I'm sure of it." She put her hand on his chest briefly before turning around and opening the car door. "I don't understand everything myself. Maybe just keep going to therapy."

Chapter 24: Slipping

Lilly tried to spend some time every weekend with her niece, Stephanie. The little eight-year-old girl had been through a lot. Lilly and Chub were trying to keep up a pretense that her journey to the West Coast had been just a crazy adventure that her mother had taken her on, but Stephanie always asked why her mother hadn't come back yet.

"We don't know, honey," Lilly tried to keep to the party line. "She's kind of sick right now."

"You mean she's on drugs."

"What do you know about drugs, honey?"

"I'm not stupid, Aunt Lilly."

Aunt Lilly decided she didn't know enough about children. Some of her girlfriends were pregnant or had just had babies. She had noticed the change in their eyes, but whether it was a glow or a glaze she hadn't decided yet. Zach wanted a family. She wanted to finish her master's degree first, which would take at least another year. Secretly, she wanted another two or three years after that so she could get her career on a faster track. She told herself that being without a family since she was fourteen had been good for her career and had given her time to learn about people who were not as fortunate as she was. And now she had Stephanie to love. Maybe that was enough for now. Besides, watching Chub and Janice struggle in their early years with baby and toddler care had diminished any desire she had to rush into it.

Stephanie's disappearance had reminded her how easily everything she cared for could be taken away. Her solution to her parents' deaths had been to shuffle off her grief and to soldier on, just as her parents would have wanted her to. She and Chub had soldiered on when Stephanie disappeared. They had fought with all their hearts, used up all their money, done everything possible they could do themselves, then asked for help from friends and lovers, and even co-workers, to get her back. They had gotten Stephanie back from that horrible situation in California, and just in time. Lilly was the kind of person who soldiered on, and she was more certain than ever that that was what life required.

She wanted to talk to Zach about his losing his temper the night of the party.

"You scared me that night, Zach." They were sitting on the sofa having a drink after dinner. This seemed to be their new custom whenever they were home together at night. Until now, they'd never had nerves that needed to be calmed. "I never saw anything like that in my house, growing up. Not once."

But Lilly blamed herself for expecting everything between them to be perfect. To show him that he was forgiven, she began wearing her engagement ring everywhere. She could tell that made him happy. And he wasn't the only one. When she went for a girls' night out with her best work friends, they drilled her about why she'd kept her engagement so secret.

"I can't explain it. I guess I'm more of a private person than most people."

"Private from us, even?"

"I'm sorry. Zach and I both promised we would keep it secret." But she could tell from the looks she got that it had never been a secret from them.

She started meeting Selby for lunch once a week, something she no longer mentioned to Zach. She wanted to tell her work friends about this, too, but she hesitated. She found herself counting the days until she could see him next. She loved that his life was an open book to her. Having a conversation with him was like speaking with an attractive stranger from a different country, one who was trying to learn her language and so was watching her intently as she spoke, hanging onto her every word. And there was nothing wrong with two people sharing feelings, experiences, stories. Selby seemed more rooted in his neighborhood, in his house, in his family, in his job, than she would ever be. She told him this.

"Ha. I guess that means I never got more than a hundred miles from my hometown. And my job? I kind of fell into that because I had a friend on the force. Guilty on both counts." But his face creased into a smile as he said this. "Your family sounds like it was really sophisticated by comparison."

"Hmm. My parents took us to London once. They were both going to the same medical research conference. Except for those kinds of things, they stayed home and worked hard."

"I guess they were into that corny old idea of working hard to make the world a better place."

How did he know what she was thinking? She met his eyes. "I miss them still."

"You're close to your niece, right? And … and you'll have your own family soon. Congratulations." He looked down. "I'm happy for you. I guess I never said that before."

"Thank you. And Selby, I wish the best for you, too."

He took her for a ride on the bay on a small boat. She noticed he wore the same red Ban-Lon shirt and khaki shorts. She couldn't help but check to see if he'd washed them since last time. He owned the boat with one other officer. This wasn't the officer friend who persuaded him to come on the force in the first place. "That guy's now running a home improvement business." He didn't pretend to be much of a sailor, but she loved the confidence with which he tackled all the little arcane chores that seemed to go along with even the shortest boat ride. He unhooked, rolled and stowed the tarp covering the cockpit of the boat, jumped in and bailed a little rainwater out, wrestled with the large gas cans he brought to fill the tank of the outboard engine, untied the ropes from the cleats on the pilings, started the engine and kept it burbling slowly, then stood up and, working the gaff like a lance against the pilings, slowly guided the boat safely to the open water. They powered slowly down what he called a river. The water was green, calm, flat, and a mile wide, without any noticeable current, fringed everywhere with tall, green pines, and slowly heaving and sparkling in the bright noonday sun. He opened a cooler he had brought and handed her a can of seltzer water. She had told him she drank it all the time.

"You come here often?" she joked as she took the drink from his hand.

"Used to go out every weekend. Learned to fish. And crab. Not so much anymore." He killed the engine and they just slowly rocked on the glittering surface of the river.

"What do you do now?"

"Work some overtime. Work on my house. Go see my family in Frostburg. Sometimes there's community events like the one you had. I'm in a basketball league."

"You know, what you said about my family, people working hard, trying to make the world a better place ...." She sat there in that gently rocking boat, wondering for a second why she was going on like this. "I think you're doing the same thing."

He shrugged her off. He anchored in a quiet cove near a stand of tall pines and introduced her to the idea of doing nothing on the river. They lay across the front of the boat and watched the surface of the water as the reflections of the white clouds were gently distorted by the ripples. The warm breeze and the slight heaving of the boat had a hypnotizing effect. Soon, she heard a soft, rhythmic sound and turned to see Selby asleep, gently snoring. She tried but failed to suppress her laughter. Even this didn't wake him up. She had to fight off a strong urge to creep her fingers over and touch that red polo shirt. Then a cloud passed over, its deep shadow allowing her to see under the surface of the water. She was dreamily surprised to see the river teeming with life, with seaweed and minnows and jellyfish, and one crab, slowly playing out their own lives in front of her, in their own time. She had the delicious feeling that she, too, was a natural creature, living her real life, right now, on this river, with a sleeping Selby gently snoring next to her. She forgot about rushing back to work.

*** ***

She had to stay behind her desk to hide the brackish smell on her jeans when she did get back to the office. They met again the next week for lunch at his house. They never touched. She thought he was beautiful, and she sometimes fantasized about being in his arms; but he was already opening up about his life and letting her in. She told herself that was all she needed. But even their platonic relationship had its limits. He once invited her to do an all-night, police officer ride-along, but she didn't want to have to hide this big a thing from Zach.

She didn't want to compare Zach and Selby or even think about both at the same time. To keep them apart, she created two separate spaces in her mind. She loved her current life with Zach, but she couldn't shake the feeling that Selby knew her better than anyone she had ever met. That feeling was with her twenty-four hours a day. She wondered what her parents would have advised her to do. The right thing, of course. It broke her heart to realize she had bickered with her mother most of the last year of her life. Mothers and daughters were supposed to come together after those teenage years. She told herself that would have happened. She sometimes dreamed she was a teenager again; sometimes she dreamed she was just a young child. She'd never had these dreams before; they must have been stacked away somewhere in her brain. She started to dream about Selby; but in those dreams, he was always far off, unreachable, working a crime scene, or on a ladder at his house, or fishing from his boat. She lay awake at night long after Zach was asleep, half afraid of what she'd dream next.

*** ***

"I won my complaint." Ms. Marcie, back from vacation, gave him a shy smile. "Mr. Harrison told me he hadn't really meant that I would be fired for going on vacation."

"Of course. He can't do that. You were right to complain."

"But before that, he had 100% promised he'd fire me. It was the complaint that changed his mind. Thank you for helping me with it, Mr. Mallory."

"My advice is, don't take any shit off Harrison from now on."

Ms. Marcie blinked hard at Mallory's crude words; then she went on, but in a quieter voice, as if she had done something wrong. "He doesn't treat me the same way anymore. He won't close the door when he's talking to me, even if it's about a sensitive personnel matter. He calls Peggy to come in with me even if it's some simple thing each of us could handle by ourselves. It's like he's afraid to be alone with me. The whole situation seems weird. My complaint was so simple, but it seems like he's taking it personally."

"He *should* take it personally. He tried to fire you."

"You know, he's under a lot of pressure. I don't think he really meant it."

Mallory shook his head at the naivete of this simple but honest woman. Of course, it was obvious that the corporate personnel department had not contacted Ms. Marcie yet about the revised complaint he had filed over her signature. He had enjoyed writing that scurrilous complaint so much he had neglected to think through how he would handle the situation when the truth came out. It was not like him not to have a backup lie ready, but he had none. A vague feeling of unease gathered in his stomach and spread slowly through his whole body. He wondered if he was slipping.

Chapter 25: The Importance of Backup

"They took all that money I got from that lawsuit, and they say they'll put it in my college fund or something." Thomas's look was sheepish, as if he knew what Mallory was going to say.

"You're already in your third year of college. And – wait a minute – you got a track scholarship anyway!"

"They say I might need it if I go to graduate school."

Except for Lilly, Mallory had never even personally known anybody who went to graduate school. He wasn't even exactly sure what graduate school was. But he didn't want to appear ignorant in front of Thomas. He thought he'd bring up the one thing he knew about Thomas's school career. "Are you going to run track in graduate school?"

Thomas's brow furrowed. "No, man. I'm a business major. There's no money in track. Track is for fun – and maybe going to the Olympics someday. What I want to do is take that money and start up my own business. And now they're saying if I don't go to graduate school, they'll take the money and put it in a retirement account I can't touch until I'm 59 ½."

"You ought to sue them."

Thomas laughed. "Yeah, maybe I can get my famous attorney Mallory to go to court for me again." Mallory had to laugh himself. He had lucked out once pretending to be an attorney, but his impersonation of a lawyer from that point on had been an almost complete disaster for Thomas's entire family. *Almost*, however, had been the operative word. Although a little knowledge of the law was supposed to be a dangerous thing, it had turned out that sometimes you could luck out with no knowledge at all.

"My parents have their own house, but they're still coming to my parties at my place." Thomas complained now. "They're trying to control everything I do. You know Grace, that hot little blonde girl whose mother died, that you brought to their party? They saw me talking to her. They gave me crap after the party about messing with her."

Mallory had no clue about how to get Ava and Edison off their son's back. Facing them directly was out of the question. He was terrified of both of them. That night, he consulted Manly Man, specifically his *Nuclear Family/War* section. Manly Man had just posted that an overly controlling mother is often the cause of family dysfunction. An overly controlling mother can drive a father to drink, Manly taught, and such women are lucky the men usually take out their rage on someone else. But Mallory really liked Ava, and he couldn't relate these teachings to Thomas's family at all.

But then Mallory started to wonder if maybe his own mother was partly to blame for his father's departure. Maybe it wasn't entirely his fault that his father had abandoned the family. Mallory himself had not been able to live with her once he reached adulthood. Just thinking about sharing the blame with his mother made him feel better. But as he delved more deeply into *Nuclear Family/War*, he came upon a pronouncement that made him wonder if he had been thinking wrong about the whole family mess from day one. "The only manly way to deal with a controlling wife is to face the bitch head on. Running away to drink or divorce is the coward's way out."

*** ***

Mallory was awakened a few hours later by a loud clanking noise in the parking lot of his apartment complex. It seemed to come from right under one of his windows. He crawled out of his sofa bed and worked his way across the room, untangling his feet from the computer wires as he stepped cautiously in the darkness toward the far side of the room. There was a tow truck parked right near his Escalade, but it wasn't flashing its lights as tow trucks usually did. He studied for a minute the shadowy man who was making all the noise. The man was hooking up chains to his Escalade.

He called Officer Selby's cell phone. "Get me my gun! I need my gun right away!"

"Who is this? Oh, of course. What's the problem, Mr. Mallory?"

"Somebody's stealing my car. Right now. I need my gun."

"The gun range isn't even open. I'll come over right away. But, Mr. Mallory, promise me you won't do *anything* until I get there."

Mallory was too enraged to wait. He threw on his suit without bothering to put on underwear. He didn't have time to button his shirt. He put on his shoes without socks. On his way out, he stopped and banged on Thomas's door and yelled "Help! Police!" He could now see clearly in the parking lot floodlights that the man had hooked some chains on the Escalade and was dragging another chain around. He noticed Thomas coming out of his apartment and an old woman coming out onto the third floor landing.

"Get off my car! The police are on their way."

The man looked like what he thought a tow truck driver should look like: heavyset, sleeveless, ripped and greasy khaki shirt, big shoulders, tattoos, shaved head. He completely ignored Mallory's shouts. Mallory edged closer. He knew the man could probably beat him up with one hand tied behind his back, but he had faith that his suit would show he was the superior being.

"You're stealing my Escalade! The police are on the way!" He felt a surge of anger so strong he forgot to be afraid. He approached closer. "Get your fucking chains off my car!"

As the man continued to ignore him and started pulling levers to tighten the chains, Mallory had the sudden realization that it wasn't just the car. It was his life. It was his crummy job that he was about to lose. It was Nell. It was Lilly. It was Grace. It was all the women in the world who didn't want him. It was all the bosses who tried to get rid of him. It was all the Algonquin J. Tycoons behind it all. Everything had always been stacked against him. He had tried all his life to measure up, to be a man. And his father, the one man he had been trying to measure up to his whole life, had been a fraud.

The only good thing left in his life was that car. He rushed the repo man and crashed into him. His face hit the man's elbow, and he fell back to the asphalt, tearing his suit. His whole body hurt, and the frightening man was standing over him, but he felt alive. And at least he stopped the steal for a few seconds. And, a few seconds later, to his utter amazement, Selby arrived with his police lights flashing.

"Whoa! What's going on here? Sir, are you hurt?"

"This little fat something ran into me and fell down."

"Can you get up?"

Mallory slowly got up. "Officer Selby, this man is stealing my Escalade."

The big man with the shaved head shook his head. "Car's being repossessed. Dealer says lease payments haven't been made in three months."

Mallory could feel his rage flaming back up. "No! No! It can't be! This is the only thing I have! The only thing I have in this fucking world besides this fucking suit!" He ripped off his suit coat and threw it on the ground. "Here. You might as well take that, too!" Then he took off his shirt and threw it toward the Escalade. Before Selby could stop him, he unbuttoned and unzipped his pants.

"Take everything! I got nothing! Nothing." He dropped his pants to throw them at the Escalade too, but they got caught around his ankles. He tried to step out of them but tripped over himself and fell down flat on the asphalt. The woman on the third-floor landing shrieked. The repo man backed up a step and glanced toward Selby.

"Mr. Mallory, you're under arrest for disorderly conduct." Selby started to put handcuffs on him, but then he stopped. "Pull your fucking pants up or I'll charge you with indecent exposure, too."

Selby looked away while Mallory slowly rose off the parking lot, rear end first, in an attempt to pull up his pants before anything worse showed. The repo man snickered. Mallory knew he had degraded himself more than he could have ever imagined. The whole world was against him, had always been against him. It had worn him down. Nothing he had tried had ever worked. He was a defective human being. When he finally managed to stand with his pants up, he held his wrists up close together toward Selby.

"Go ahead. Cuff me. Take me away. I give up. I just give up."

"You gonna arrest that fat little fucker, or what?" the repo man called out.

Selby's glare shut him up. "Sometimes citizens have a hard time distinguishing repo men from car thieves. Sometimes I can't blame them." He then turned and called to Thomas, asking him to bring the lady down from the third-floor landing.

"I heard you scream a minute ago, ma'am. I'm deciding if this man should be charged with indecent exposure. I want to get to the point, so we can all go back to sleep, or whatever we were doing. Did you see his ding-dong?"

"I saw something. I'm not really sure what that thing was."

Selby decided to let him go. The repo man finished hooking up the chains and towed the Escalade away. Thomas escorted the old woman back up to her apartment. Selby shined his headlights on the scene and made Mallory pick up the rest of his clothes. Then he followed him inside. "You owe me one."

"Yeah, I guess so. Thanks." Mallory threw his suit jacket on the sofa. "It doesn't matter. My life is over. I don't have a car. I don't have a girlfriend. I'm gonna be fired for a scam I pulled at work. I'll be evicted. Nobody has ever liked me."

"You have friends," Selby contradicted him.

"You?" Mallory murmured. "Are you my friend? You could have arrested me."

"I'm not talking about myself. What about Lilly? She's been really nice to you."

"Yeah. If you don't count the part where she turned me down."

"What are you saying? She's worthless to you because she won't sleep with you?"

"No, no. She's good. Good as a friend. I didn't get to hit that."

A little smirk crossed Mallory's face. "But I don't think you did, either."

"You're right, she's just a friend." Selby paused, and his sharp glance melted into something unfocused, hazy. "But don't you think having a friend like that can make your day go a little nicer?" When Mallory didn't answer, Selby sat forward and seemed to shake off his trance. "Anyway, Lilly is my friend now. And it's thanks to you I met her. You can thank Lilly you aren't locked up in jail or in the psycho ward right now."

*** ***

Ms. Marcie's normally pale skin flushed beet red as she looked over the single sheet of paper that had just been handed to her. "No, this is not the complaint I filed. This isn't it at all."

"But that's your signature at the bottom, isn't it?" The woman from the main UniCast headquarters in Houston was being politely cautious. Mallory recognized the reasons why. There could be any number of reasons for the discrepancy between the written complaint they had received and Ms. Marcie's story now. Could she have filed that bizarre sexual harassment claim just to get corporate attention to her case? Could Ms. Marcie have been hired by a corporate insider to create a potential legal roadblock to the Everdine takeover? Was there actual sexual harassment, and was she now being intimidated by Harrison into changing her complaint into just a little tiff about four hours of leave time?

"Yes, that's my signature. But Mr. Harrison didn't do any of these things."

"Then how did your signature get on this paper?"

"Oh, I remember now. I was getting ready to go on vacation and I was in a real hurry to get it done because I didn't have enough leave time, according to Mr. Harrison. Mr. Harrison has now fixed that leave problem, by the way. I wrote my complaint in pen on the form – but then I signed another form, too, because Mr. Mallory said it needed to be typed up and to get to headquarters so I wouldn't lose my job by the time I got back from vacation."

"So, you didn't even see this printed form?"

"No, I signed a blank form."

"Who filled in the information on this printed form?"

"Mr. Mallory kindly did it for me."

They were meeting in Harrison's office: Harrison, Ms. Marcie, the corporate investigator, and Mallory. Mallory's suit had been torn in his confrontation with the repo man. He had reverted to his old uniform of jeans and T-shirt and hoodie that he wore both indoors and out. He knew he wasn't making a good impression on the corporate investigator, but he hardly cared. He'd had to ask Thomas to drive him to work the last few days. There was no chance anyone would lease or sell him a car now. The only thing of value that he owned was his rifle. The first place Thomas had driven him was to the shooting range, where he had met Selby and insisted on getting it back. He'd put it up for sale online but was frightened by the responses he got.

He was frightened more by the prospect of losing his job. There was a simple way for him to get out of the Marcie dilemma, but he didn't know if he could take it. All he had to do was flat-out lie and say that he had printed out exactly what Ms. Marcie had told him. Harrison's career would be forever tarred by this allegation. Mallory thought the supervisor richly deserved it. The problem was that Ms. Marcie would then be forever marked as a liar, or at least a flake, and would probably never be able to get a job anywhere else. And he would have to look her in the eye as long as he worked at UniCast Cable. Mallory had absolutely no scruples about lying to or about his supervisors and managers, all of whom he considered to be the paid lackeys of the Algonquin J. Tycoons of the world, but he had never thrown a fellow employee under the bus. And he liked Ms. Marcie, who had always been nice to him. And his life was going down the tubes anyway.

"Um ... I think this misunderstanding might be my fault," he started. Harrison jerked back in his chair in obvious surprise to hear Mallory take the blame for anything. Ms. Marcie opened her mouth like she was about to form a question, and her eyes went wide. The corporate investigator looked like her day might have just become a lot easier. "We were both in a hurry," Mallory went on. "I couldn't really read what she wrote, but she had already left for vacation. I just typed it up the best I could from what I could interpret from her chicken scratch."

"So, you are the one who actually typed up and mailed this phony complaint." Harrison's smile was triumphant.

"I typed up what I thought she had written."

"Did you know Ms. Marcie is famous in this office suite, and in fact on this whole floor, for having the most beautiful, easiest to read handwriting? And you couldn't read it? And you didn't even call her, did you?"

"She said it was an emergency because otherwise you'd fire her before she even got back. And I tried to contact her on her cell phone, but I couldn't get through."

Harrison lost his smile, sat back. He didn't want to draw corporate personnel's attention to his threat to fire a longtime employee for basically having a flat tire. Mallory was satisfied with this temporary stalemate with Harrison. But would corporate ever believe his story, ever forgive him for filing this false complaint?

Ms. Marcie spoke up into the silence. "What Mr. Mallory said is true, I turned off my cell phone the whole time I was on vacation. I was just too upset about Mr. Harrison firing me. And my handwriting. I don't remember exactly, but I do remember my whole body was shaking when I was trying to write it out."

The investigator seemed skeptical. "Ms. Marcie, the complaint says Mr. Harrison was wearing your panties. Did you write anything at all about panties in your handwritten complaint?"

"No. But …. Um, you have to remember how upset I was. I mean, I was being fired, and I was rushing to pack, and I had a list. I'm sure I had panties on that list. Maybe somehow, you know, I

181

don't know, I got confused and … I don't know, maybe … maybe the list got mixed up in my mind with the complaint, or maybe the papers got mixed up, or … I don't know."

"I guess your answer would be the same about the word 'footies?'"

"I guess so."

Mallory wanted to crawl across the room and kiss Ms. Marcie's footies. She was making up excuses even he couldn't have dreamed up. The investigator audibly sighed. Everyone in the room knew exactly what had happened, but nobody could prove anything. Harrison had been exposed as a cowardly tyrant. His attempt to fire Ms. Marcie in order to pander to the Algonquin J. Tycoons of the Everdine Fund had failed. Ms. Marcie had not had to lie. Mallory's impulsive act had done a little bit of good, and he still had his job. For now.

Chapter 26: Candy Bar

Lilly felt she had to merge the two halves of her soul obsessed with the two men in her life or else go insane. She knew she had found something in Selby that she needed – but what was that worth? She'd missed out on a lot over the years in her personal life, but in the meantime, she'd built a career, made lot of friends, loved a niece, found Zach. She'd been happy, or she thought she'd been happy, all those years before she met Selby. Why did she think about him now every time a police officer appeared on the news, every time she saw a police car, or a pickup basketball game, or when someone mentioned a boat, or even ordered lasagna?

A serious problem at Roofs took her mind off her troubles. Roofs was a member of an alliance of non-profits. One of the requirements of membership was an annual audit of their finances. McFadden, the director, was again away on a business trip, and she was responsible for overseeing Roofs' response. Mary Salinger, the bookkeeper, had been preparing the records for days – for too long, it seemed. And she had been ducking away whenever Lilly came near. Lilly finally confronted her, made her come into her office and sit down and talk.

"Why is this taking so long? We keep good records here."

Mary, an older woman and former client of Roofs, squirmed as if she had done something wrong. "Um, there's $20,000 I can't find."

"What? Where is it missing from?"

"It's the grant for the roofing from the Community Development Fund. They gave us $100,000. It's mostly spent on roofing contractors. It all adds up, except there's $20,000 missing."

"Something must have happened. I'll find out." It took her three days (and three long evenings working late at her desk) to figure out what happened. The $20,000 had been originally designated as overhead. This overhead amount was a much higher percentage than Roofs had ever charged for such a job. This high overhead percentage was a problem they could probably explain away. But the real problem was there was no record of the $20,000 being deposited in Roofs' main bank account at all.

She discovered that the $20,000 had been deposited in a special new company account termed "professional development" and kept off the books. The funds had been spent on trips to Chicago and Houston and Denver. She remembered that the director had attended conferences in these cities. But there were also trips to Miami and Pocatello, Idaho. There had been no conference in Miami. She then looked in the personnel records and discovered that the director had been born in Pocatello and still had parents living there.

If he had just outright stolen the money, she would call the police. But, of course, the situation was a little murkier than that. She downloaded the information into a separate file without telling Mary what she had found. To be fair to McFadden, she'd have to talk to him. She considered asking Zach about the situation because his company dealt with auditors all the time, but she didn't want to do anything that might complicate their relationship right then.

She went out on the boat again with Selby. Same shirt, same shorts. He told her he rarely went fishing anymore. "I just like to cruise on a gorgeous day like this." She felt a little guilty because she could barely afford the time for another two-hour lunch. But they went out into a wider area where the river merged into the bay, which now spread out its sparkles in heaving swells for miles. The boat rocked a little more out here. When a giant freighter loomed far out in front of them like a huge grey wall, they turned back. The calmness that suffused all her meetings with Selby came to her again. She didn't see any reason why she shouldn't ask his opinion of the audit problems she was having at work.

"You're a cop," she said. "Is what he did a crime?"

"I'm just a street cop. You know that." She loved his easy smile, his full lips, his not-so-chiseled face, his thick, dark hair. She loved the way he didn't pretend to be something that he was not. "The state police do have a financial crimes unit. But they won't even open a case unless the amount is over $250,000. Funny, I had to arrest a kid once for stealing a candy bar."

"You didn't!"

"I did. The owner insisted. He'd caught the kid red-handed. On video, too."

"I mean, what happens in a case like that?"

"You know, there's cops who administer instant justice, slap the kids around, leave them off in the middle of nowhere."

"Is that what you do?"

"Of course not. I just ride them around, talk to them, wait for them to cool down. Turn up the volume on the dispatch calls so they can hear what's going on. Sort of a police ride-along – like the one you didn't go on."

"Does that really work?"

"Sometimes. I say I'll tell your father. They say they don't have a father. Or they say their father doesn't give a shit. Or they say the cops are picking on them. I don't have any magic answers. I just talk to them for a while and let them go."

"What if they keep doing it?"

"I don't know. I don't have all the answers. Just, you know … day by day … trying to keep the neighborhood on an even keel."

"So, you're the candy bar cop. I didn't realize how important you were."

"We had a murder a couple of weeks ago. I was the first on the scene. You never want to see that."

She felt appropriately chastised. "Oh. Little me. I've never even seen a dead body. My father wouldn't even let me see my mother when she was dying in a hospital bed."

"He was right. You don't want to see even that."

"Why do men always want to protect me?"

He didn't answer, just motored the boat slowly back into the wide river mouth, the afternoon sun now blindingly bright on the water, the banks fringed with green trees, docks, houses near the shore, houses on high bluffs. He docked the boat, and they opened their sandwiches at a picnic bench at the marina. She knew she was spending too much time in this alternate life. She also knew how dangerous it would be to try to merge her two lives, but she couldn't help it.

"I'm afraid," she began, "I'm losing my reputation in the office as the only person who's there all day, every day, to answer questions and make decisions. It's not fair to them that I'm taking so much time off for lunch during the week."

He was looking away toward the trees on the other side of the river, the sun's wavering glare off the water flickering across his face as he sighed. "Sorry. This has been really fun for me, but I shouldn't have done this to you."

"No," she added quickly. "It's not you. At least, it's not *just* you. It's with Zach, too." She hadn't started this conversation to end their secret meetings. What she wanted was to share with Selby some of the mysterious undercurrents she felt tugging at her, day and night. She told herself it would be okay to share a little something about her life with Zach. This little tidbit, she told herself, was a true thing that would put some proper distance between her and Selby. "I've skipped work with Zach, too. We both took off work yesterday afternoon. Totally unscheduled. We met back at the apartment for ... you could call it, let's say, an *afternoon delight*."

*** ***

Lilly came to work early the next few days. She felt full of energy and sure she could make up for her recent lunch hour escapades. She decided to be proactive and request an informal, virtual meeting with the auditors to explain what she found. She was told, as she expected, that the director's trips to Miami and Pocatello did not appear to be legitimate overhead expenses. McFadden, the director, was away on another trip, but she kept calling until he returned her call. She explained what she had found and what the auditors had said.

"Lilly, tell the auditors I'll close the separate account. I'll pay back the money for Miami and Pocatello. I always meant to use my own money. It was just quicker to use the Roofs account for that at the time."

"Great. I'll think they'll be happy with that."

"And Lilly. One more thing. Do not, under any circumstances, tell the Board of Directors about this."

"Oh. Well …."

"Lilly, I've supported you all along in your career. I got Roofs to help pay for your graduate school. I've promoted you to the top job in finance at Roofs. If you report this to the Board, I might be fired, my career ruined."

Even this small moral dilemma could not ruin Lilly's mood. It was a mellow feeling that came over her after every meeting with Selby, but it lasted only a day or two. After that, her mind would settle down, though it would still sometimes rock, like Selby's boat, between thoughts of the two men. Through it all, she still felt like she was getting a better feel for the right path. And the most important path of all led to little Stephanie.

"Aunt Lilly, do you think my mother is ever coming back?"

"Oh, Steph. We all hope she will, someday," she lied.

"Mom left me with Grandma out in California. I didn't have anything to do all day."

"Oh darling, you must have been very lonely. I'm so sorry. Your Dad will never leave you alone. And I'll always be here for you."

She was always there, at least in the sense that she worried about Stephanie all the time. When Chub seemed flummoxed about after school care, Lilly found someone by using her contacts at Roofs. When Stephanie didn't like it there, she found her a better place. She had faith that her niece would eventually make friends there. But she hadn't anticipated the relationship between her and her niece.

"Your mother's sick," she told her again the next time Stephanie asked.

"If she's sick, why can't I go see her?" It was more of a challenge than a question. "I know where she lives. In Grandma Fitz's house." This was not the same naïve little child Lilly had known even six months ago.

It must have been easy for Lilly's own parents to tell her the truth always. They had never had anything to hide. Lilly had found herself relying on her own gut feelings in personal relations lately, and she now told Stephanie truthfully that her mother was a serious drug addict. "That means, right now, she doesn't care about anything at all but getting more drugs. It's hard to get better once you're on drugs that bad. It might take a really long time."

"I kind of knew all that. She's not coming home."

When he found out about this conversation, Chub was furious. "What the hell were you thinking? She's my kid, and it's my job to tell her …."

"Tell her what? Anything different than what I just told her? She's not stupid, Chub, and she's growing up."

"Yeah, but I'm her father. You don't live with her. You have a sixty-hour-a-week job. You're engaged. Are you willing to quit all that and be a mother to her instead?"

Chapter 27: Discretion Be Damned

Manly Man's *Nuclear Family/War* website was proving more valuable than Mallory had ever expected. He had learned that his failures at love, at work, with finances, with friendships, and in his standing in the community, were all the fault of his father. Algonquin J. Tycoon was at fault, too, but Tycoon's misdeeds were just the icing on the cake.

It was three miles from his efficiency apartment in Glenwood Flats to the desolate industrial park where he toiled at UniCast Cable. Thomas drove him to work and picked him up for a few days, but he couldn't keep it up because of school and track. Mallory practiced walking at night, one block a day at first. He was slowed down on these practice walks by having to carry his rifle which, he was proud to say, was now loaded with bullets, but Thomas persuaded him not to carry it to work. Mallory's first day of commuting by foot started badly. After three blocks his feet hurt so much he had to stop and sit down on the curb. It was still almost three miles to UniCast. His body, encased in his hoodie, was slimy with sweat, and he was so out of breath he hardly noticed when a car pulled up beside him.

"Get in." It was Kathie. She said she lived right behind Glenwood Flats. He confessed that his Escalade had been repossessed for non-payment. "I always wondered how you could pay for that on a UniCast salary," she commented.

"My suits, too. I couldn't keep going with them, not with the cleaning bills."

"That's too bad," she said. "You looked good in them."

Mallory was stunned when Kathie next offered to pick him up every day at his apartment complex parking lot and drive him to work. "It's not a big deal," she told him. "I drive right by there every morning."

He immediately started imagining Kathie in his bed, her wild blonde curls splayed out against the pillow, those green eyes begging for more. He had to look away from her for a minute so he could calm down. He realized he had made this mental mistake before. He was always craving something that was never going to happen. It didn't seem fair that his deepest needs didn't incite even the slightest interest in the women who could satisfy them.

** ***

"Zach is very supportive about my work at Roofs." Lilly and Selby had broken their promises to each other and were meeting again, this time just for a quick 10:00 a.m. coffee. "But I can tell he still resents all the time I'm spending there."

"I can understand that. He just wants you to save a piece of you for himself."

"He doesn't want me just for himself. He wants me for his friends and his customers, too."

Selby sat back. "What do you expect me to say to that?"

"Nothing. Nothing." She sipped her coffee very slowly. She wasn't feeling the soothing tranquility she usually felt talking with Selby. All her relationships seemed jagged at that moment. "You know how I told you about our 'afternoon delight?' Well, I can tell that's going to be our last one."

"Maybe we shouldn't talk about …." His ruddy face was growing redder.

She persisted. "I mean, it all just seems sort of anonymous now."

"Um. I guess, you know … routine …. I'm no expert." He wasn't meeting her eyes. "But you should go on one of my domestic disturbance calls if you want to see passion really gone wrong."

"I'm not talking about crimes. Just, you know, about … less than thrilling. God, I know I sound like a teenager. What's wrong with me? Forgive me for talking like this. But sometimes I wonder what happens to a couple, you know, if one of them starts to feel this way."

"I'll tell you what happened to me." The sudden growl in Selby's voice caught her attention. "Paisley dumped me. It happens all the time. Apparently, it's not a crime."

"I can't imagine anybody dumping you."

"That's what people do."

"I don't want to be just *people*."

*** ***

Mallory stood in the break room, staring at the vending machine in shock. He looked back and saw Nell leaning against the edge of the arched doorway.

"They've taken out the cinnamon buns!" He looked back. He saw the smirk on her face. "What happened to the cinnamon buns?"

Nell walked very slowly up to the machine where they both stood and stared at the apple crisps that had replaced a staple of Mallory's diet. "The Cheer Committee has decided to replace the cinnamon buns with a more healthful product."

"The Cheer Committee? That means you, Nell. And you did it just to get even with me." She didn't deny it. "What am I supposed to eat on break now?"

"Is that my problem? And if you had actually attended any of the Cheer Committee meetings, you could have objected."

"Why are you so angry at me?"

"Why are you bad-mouthing me to Kathie?"

"I'm not. She gives me a ride to work every day. I don't have a car, remember? We talk. Never about you. If she doesn't love you anymore, it's not my fault. It must be something you did."

"I've never done anything but love her." Normally stoic Nell seemed on the verge of tears. "Ever since you started talking to her, she started pulling away."

"I guess that hurts." There was no sympathy in his voice. "I know about hurting. Welcome to the club."

"I wish I could scratch that smirk off your face. I don't think I can be happy until I get you totally out of UniCast."

"Who's going to get me out of here? You? You and Harrison? You and Harrison and Algonquin J. Tycoon? Trying to get rid of me? Good luck with that. It has never worked yet." He made a face, turned and started to walk away.

"And you can forget about Koko," she shouted after him.

He stopped, turned around. "Don't you have the decency to leave the cat out of this?"

"There's nothing decent about being in love with a cat."

He was surprised how quickly she acted. Before he even left work that afternoon, a technician installed two cameras in his cubicle, giving management a real-time view of anything that happened there. Mallory answered his customer assistance phone that afternoon, but he deliberately slurred his words so badly that all the customers hung up. The next morning, he brought in cinnamon buns from the Dough and Go and smeared the sticky goop a quarter inch thick on both camera lenses.

*** ***

Good morning, this is the automated messaging service for UniCast Cable. Your call is important to us. All of our assistants are currently assisting other customers or haven't made it into work yet. But I am pleased to be able to give you the personal cell phone number of our supervisor, Mr. Harrison.

*** ***

Michaela was the first one to talk at the next therapy meeting. "I took Mr. Ramsteel's advice. I knew the rest of you thought it was crazy." Michaela stuck out her chin like a recalcitrant child. "I put a GPS tracker on Fred's car. Then I followed him next time to the address of his girlfriend. Boy, was I surprised. She lives in an ordinary house, not near as good as ours. She must be ten years older than me. Streaks of grey hair. Way too skinny, and I'm not just saying that because … you know."

"So, you have proof now. You're getting a divorce?" Mallory was thinking: if she loves to eat, she must also love to cook. He hadn't had a really good meal since Thomas's mother had moved out of the apartment complex. He found he was still charmed by Michaela's pretty blue eyes. And as much as he was put off by her less than glamorous figure, he admitted to himself that his was worse. But then he had the terrifying thought that she would reject him like all the other women had.

"No. I didn't confront him right then. I waited until the next day. I came up behind him in the mirror as he was dressing for work. 'What do you see in her?' was all I said. He collapsed back down onto the bed. He said he didn't know. He said he just felt sorry for her now." Michaela looked up. "I think we're going to be okay."

"I told you GPS was the answer," Mallory grumbled.

"He said he knew I knew. He'd been trying to break it off." Michaela seemed suddenly at a loss for words, as if waiting for Sebastian the Facilitator to interpret this event in her life for her.

Mallory was deeply disappointed. He had counted on Michaela as his backup plan after he realized he couldn't get Grace into his bed. He had lowered his standards for her, but now even she had rejected him. What good was therapy?

"What a wonderful story." Sebastian the facilitator nodded his grandfatherly approval.

"How do you know that?" Mallory challenged. "For all you know, he's a psycho killer just stringing her along until he gets a chance to kill her for her money."

"I don't have any money," Michaela interrupted.

"Kill the wife. Inherit the money. Marry the much thinner girlfriend." Mallory had seen this plot on numerous crime shows. "You admitted she's thinner."

193

Peter Pointy Beard stood up so fast he knocked his chair down behind him. "You blithering idiot. You don't understand anything. Why don't you just get out of here and leave the rest of us alone?"

"You want to get me out of the way. You don't even want to look at me. That's what you always wanted, isn't it?"

"*Always*? I've only known you for two months."

"You act like I don't count. Like I'm not even worth your time. You can't fool me, disguising yourself with that pointy devil's beard."

"*Disguising myself*? Are you having some kind of hallucination? Who do you think I am?"

"You're following after me everywhere, inside my head. You just want to tear me down from inside because it makes you feel better about yourself." Mallory turned his attention to the stunned, silent group. "And you all just sit there and let it happen. I never want to see any of you ever again. Except for Grace."

He waited outside in the parking lot, fantasizing that Grace would come out to calm him down. But she didn't.

Chapter 28: Just Ask a Cop

Lilly hadn't gotten any definitive guidance from Selby about what to do about Roofs' auditing problem. The director, Rory McFadden, paid back the money for the personal trips he took to Miami and Pocatello. The special account he had set up for his travels was closed, and the books were now in pristine shape for the outside auditors. McFadden was pressing her not to mention the incident to the Board of Directors. "No harm has been done," he insisted. He didn't mention that he had been paid for the two weeks he was away on these trips.

She had always prided herself on being meticulously honest. That was the way she had been raised. But she didn't know if it was right to apply those tough standards to everybody. McFadden had run Roofs for the last three years, and the organization had done a lot of good. He had been absent a lot while attending conventions and meetings, but there was some advantage in Roofs having connections around the country. And he had trusted her to run the organization herself when he was gone, and she had learned a lot from that.

She knew she was chickening out when she asked Mary, the bookkeeper, if she could put a note in her report to the board simply saying that a special account had been set up but had later been deleted as unnecessary. But Mary, who was about the age her mother would have been had she lived, looked at her over the top of her glasses like her mother would have looked at her. "Honey, I'm just the bookkeeper. I don't put in special notes to the board. That would be you, the chief finance officer."

She steeled herself and walked into McFadden's office and told him she had to report the bogus account to the board.

"Lilly, you know I've worked day and night for Roofs for three years now. We now serve 20% more people than we did three years ago. Our revenues are up 25%. I've traveled the country to make connections and dig up those grants."

"I know. But I just think I need to tell the board what happened." Her voice was tremulous.

"Do you realize I could be fired for this. Some of those board members are so strait-laced. Do you think I deserve that?"

"I don't know if you deserve it or not." It took all her courage to let that hang in the air.

"Come on. This stuff is done all the time. It's so small, compared to our budget. And I've already paid it all back. This morning. And don't you think you owe me something for all the responsibility I've given you over the last three years? For all the trust I've placed in you?"

"I owe you a lot, Rory. But I've thought a lot about this. I think I have to report it."

His tone changed immediately. "Don't you want to keep your own job?"

She had prepared for the worst. "I'm going to report it whether you fire me or not."

"You'll be just a disgruntled employee to them. They won't pay any attention. And meanwhile, I can promise you, you won't get any job of any responsibility in any non-profit in the entire country."

When she returned to her office, Mary was sitting just outside. "I heard everything. I'm so sorry dear." Lilly stormed to her desk and gathered her things. Mary turned to her as she was on her way out. "If I would have known, I would have just put in that note."

*** ***

"Am I just an idiot?" Lilly had called for an "emergency meeting" with Selby right after her conversation with McFadden. It was early afternoon. They met in a bar, and she ordered a beer. He listened. He seemed dispassionate and almost skeptical at first, but he listened, so she went on. "I mean, I have to do the right thing myself. I know that. But do I also have to tell on other people?"

"You're the accountant. Isn't that what accountants do when they see a discrepancy?"

"But he paid it back. And it wasn't that much money, considering."

"It wasn't a candy bar."

She was going to have to face the fact that he was right. It wasn't just a candy bar. She took several fast sips of her beer as if waiting for the alcohol to help her face the future. It didn't help much. "Roofs was my whole life."

He came back to the table and put a fresh bottle next to her empty one. "You won't lose your job. He wouldn't dare fire you. Even if he did, there's a thousand places, a million places, that would rush to hire someone with your smarts and your integrity."

"It's kind of you to say that. What about you, Mr. Beat Cop? What's your career trajectory look like?"

"I'm getting there. I'll have my B.A. in criminal justice by December." He shrugged. "Took a long time, I know."

"You have a tough job."

"Sometimes. But I like it. And I also spent a lot of time goofing around, playing basketball, going to bars." He raised his eyebrows comically. "Chasing women."

"I bet you caught a lot of them."

"Some. Some I had good times with." She kept quiet, hoping he'd keep talking about his history with women, but he changed the subject. "I want to make it a career, rise up in the ranks. All that stuff. I'm hoping I don't have to get my master's degree to do that."

"Could you really be happy in a desk job?"

"It always helps to know the streets, even if you're the chief."

"But would you like it, sitting behind a desk?"

"I honestly don't know. You're getting your master's degree, right?"

"I'm working on it. I took the summer off, though." She wondered what her summer would have been like if she had kept her nose to the grindstone and driven to State three nights every week for her master's program. There would have been no boat rides, no shooting range, no Mallory. Maybe no engagement.

"I can tell you're really committed. You're going to the top, Lilly."

"You're talking to a woman who doesn't even have a job."

She'd eventually have to tell Zach what happened at Roofs. She felt her usual sense of calm right after talking to Selby, but its half-life was shorter now, just a few hours instead of a couple of days. She wasn't sure these talks were helping her anymore. They now seemed to be splitting the two halves of her soul further apart. Zach deserved to know she might be fired. She imagined him showing up at Roofs and telling off McFadden, maybe even hitting him, but she didn't think that would help.

Chapter 29: Normal Business Practice

That night, Lilly did not tell Zach what happened at Roofs. She just wasn't up to dealing with his reaction. They spent what seemed like a normal evening in their apartment, but she felt like she was acting. She stayed up long after he had gone to bed.

She thought she was facing a real moral dilemma at Roofs. Was she just being super conscientious about reporting McFadden? Would McFadden really fire her if she reported what he'd done? She wondered what her father would have done. That was probably why she had a dream about him that night. In the dream, he was laid out in a coffin – though he looked fine, as if he were just sleeping. It was somehow a good dream. She felt better in the morning, even though she still had no idea what to do. At work the next day, she avoided McFadden, and even Mary. She would feel for one second like her life was falling apart, the next second she would feel her old confidence that she could overcome anything. But even though she had a good partner in Zach, and a good friend in Selby, she had never felt so alone.

Mary came into her office uninvited and sat down very primly on the chair across from her desk. "I need to warn you. After what happened the other day, I asked around at the last place McFadden used to work. Bookkeeper to bookkeeper, you know. He's real nice to everybody until he gets called on something. Then he'll cut your throat." She sought out Lilly's eyes. "I'd just forget about it, honey. Don't report him. He paid back the money. He can make it really hard for you."

Lilly knew she should be discussing this with her fiancé, not her bookkeeper. But she put it off for another day, even though she knew a 24-hour delay could not possibly make the situation any better. She knew keeping her problem from Zach was not helping their relationship. He went to bed alone again. The next morning, as they were standing at the kitchen counter, silently consuming their breakfast of coffee and toast, he briefly turned away from her and stared out the tiny window over the sink overlooking the parking lot below, absently thumbing the rim of his cup. His powerful form looked authoritative, relaxed, gorgeous in his white dress shirt. She admired even this man's back. But she found herself hoping he would keep looking away. When he turned back, she'd have to tell him.

"I'm probably going to be fired," she began. She explained that she had to report her boss's manipulation of the books to the board, and that he had threatened to fire her if she did.

"Oh, honey." He put his arm protectively around her shoulders. It felt really good – but only for about one second. "I wouldn't worry about this at all. He gave the money back. It's not a big deal."

"It's a big deal to me. My job is to give an accurate picture of the finances to the board. And to point out any discrepancies. And to warn them of any irregularities. This is a big irregularity, engineered by the executive director himself. They need to know this."

"Sometimes in life you have to go along to get along."

"You're not taking me seriously." She could feel her heat rise. "If you think I'm the kind of person who can let her boss fudge financial accounts …." She was afraid to finish her thought. But then she did. "If you think my ideas are so stupid, I guess you must not think much of me."

"Honey, you know I love you."

"I don't know what that means. If you don't respect me …." She slammed down her coffee cup, grabbed her purse and keys and hurried out the door.

Yes, she was angry at Zach, angry at his breezy, go-along-get-along advice on a matter that was important to her. Was this just a one-time disagreement like all couples occasionally suffered through, or was it a sign of deep character differences? She was so lost in thought she suddenly found herself pulling into in the parking lot at Roofs without any memory of driving there. She hesitated to go in. Was her problem at Roofs a tiny thing or a big thing? If it was a tiny thing, why was she making such a big deal of it?

She had to go in. She assured herself again she had to do what she thought was right. She opened the door and took the stairs to her second-floor office. She closed her office door after saying just a brief hello to Mary, who was sitting at her own desk outside. Nothing Zach had said had changed her mind. She couldn't hide the director's dishonest scheme from the board. It would be dishonorable to hide it. That was her opinion. Zach's was apparently different.

*** ***

Mallory sat on the steps outside his apartment. He was not feeling very happy or successful at the moment. He had struck out with Lilly and Grace. He had struck out in therapy. Nell hated him. Harrison was trying to get rid of him. He was waiting for Thomas. He couldn't be angry at Thomas for sweeping Grace off her feet. Thomas was younger, thinner and more handsome and, unlike Mallory, he hadn't stalked the young blonde or told her a fake story about his father being in the hospital. Mallory wasn't sure if it was manly to remain friends with a man who had stolen your woman, but Thomas was the only man friend he had, and he wasn't going to give that up. He smiled to see the young track runner bounce up the steps.

"What's up, Mr. Mallory?"

"Not much. You know they repossessed my Escalade. Kathie, a woman at work, is driving me to work every day now." He thought a manly man should mix in at least one optimistic scenario for each admission of failure.

"You got the hots for her?" Thomas was half smiling and looking away. He didn't even seem to take his own question seriously.

Mallory considered this an important issue. Of course, in one sense, he had the hots for every decent looking female between the ages of 16 and 45. In recent times, however, he had come to realize that, surprisingly, he didn't care for a number of them, and that it was even possible he could like a woman whose looks weren't all that great.

"Kathie's being nice to me. She's pretty, too. But she's not interested in me. And she used to be a lezzie."

"Yeah. You don't want to get caught up in that mess again."

Mallory stared out over the parking lot for a minute before he asked the question he had been torturing himself with. "Are you going out with Grace?"

"Yeah." Thomas made eye contact. "Sorry, man. She said she never went out with you. Said you two were not a thing."

"Yeah. That's right. But, you know, sometimes my imagination jumps ahead of reality."

"Don't I know that!" Thomas laughed. "But really, man, I'm sorry. I should've maybe given you more time on that."

"Forget it, Thomas. She probably thinks I'm crazy now, anyway. I told all those people in the therapy group what I really think of them."

"Uh, isn't that what you're supposed to do in therapy?"

"Not like I did," Mallory admitted. "So, you got in that hot young blonde's pants yet?"

"A gentleman never tells. But no. We talk about her mother a lot. She's still hurtin'. And we talk about community college. But that was different for her. Much harder. She was working full time for three years before she even went there."

"She's a good kid."

"*Good kid*? Huh, tell my parents that. They keep saying she's too old for me."

Mallory kept silent because he agreed with the parents on that. She was five years older than Thomas. When he was still a randy 30, she'd be fat and over the hill at 35. Still, it made Mallory sad that there was friction between Thomas and his parents. He had never had an idea of what good parents could be like until he met Edison and Ava. He didn't like anything that challenged this one model of a functional family. Their recent disagreements were a disappointment to him, and they seemed to be getting worse.

"What about your money? Your $100,000. Are they giving it back to you?"

"Oh, man, it's awful. All they ever say is I'm gonna buy a big-ass BMW and drink the rest of the money away. I don't even drink at all except in the offseason. Who do they think I am?"

"Like I said. You should sue them."

"Ha ha, *Attorney* Mallory. *Mr. Plastic-Bag-Head Man.* You're gonna represent me?"

"Shut up." Mallory didn't like to be reminded of the nickname Selby had given him. "But really, it's your money. I know you won't waste it." Secretly, Mallory hoped Thomas would waste at least a little of it on him.

"No way I'm wasting it. See, I got a plan."

Mallory was sorry to hear that. Now he'd have to listen to it. He didn't believe a twenty-year-old college student could have a plan. Still, he asked what the plan was.

"NIL. The new thing in college sports. The Supreme Court says colleges cannot stop players from selling their names, images and likenesses for money. To advertisers. It's going like crazy in Division 1 college football and basketball."

Although Thomas was a good-looking kid, Mallory couldn't imagine anyone paying to put his picture on a package of hot dogs. He didn't want to say that to his best friend. But he had to say something. "Um … how much do you think you can sell your picture for?"

"No. Not that." Thomas's smile was so magnetic Mallory almost felt his picture actually would be worth money. "I'm starting a company to represent college athletes. Sell their NIL to advertisers."

"Aren't there a lot of big PR companies already doing that?"

"Yeah. In football and basketball. Not track. Usain Bolt has less commercial media presence than a mediocre Big Ten lineman."

"Yeah, but isn't that because track's boring?"

"That's what the big PR firms think. But it's not boring. It just doesn't get enough PR exposure. Exposure breeds exposure. I think I can get in at the start, get people to see track stars for who they are. Sign them up before the big PR firms know what hit 'em."

Mallory had no idea if Thomas's plan made any sense. All he knew was he had gotten through life without being one of those suckers who paid extra money for sweatshirts with the names and numbers of pro football players. He was not the target audience for this sort of thing. A lot of people seemed to have some team or group or tribe they were faithful to. Maybe most people had faith in something. He had always relied only on his immediate gut reactions, which were pretty much limited to lust or fear. He wasn't in the same category as Thomas, or anybody who had faith in anything. He was disqualified from having an opinion. He had no idea whether there were people ready to buy stuff endorsed by track stars.

But he knew the chance they would follow track stars would be much higher if Thomas asked them to. "That sounds like a great plan, Thomas. Get in on the ground floor. You got to get your hands on that $100,000 to get the ball rolling." Mallory had no idea what these cliches meant. All he really understood was he was on Thomas's side.

Chapter 30: Fixed

The Board of Directors of Roofs was scheduled to meet in two weeks. Lilly could put off her report until the day before, but she dreaded working the next two weeks with McFadden. He set the tone the very next day by acting as if she didn't exist. He didn't directly order her again to suppress her findings, but he didn't have to. He had made things very clear. If she reported him, he would know this before the board meeting, she would be fired, and he would explain to the board that she was just a disgruntled ex-employee who had been angling for his job. He would claim the creation of the special bank account to fund his travels had been her idea and that she had done it for the sole purpose of setting him up. Mary had told her that's how he treated employees who crossed him in his former job. Lilly would not be at the board meeting to tell the true story, nor would Mary.

"Thank God, McFadden's going to another convention tomorrow and will be out all week," she explained to Zach that night. This was her way of continuing their conversation about her job. They had been avoiding the subject all through dinner. They were now sitting on their tiny balcony overlooking the parking lot of their apartment complex. Zach was having an after-dinner Scotch. Lilly felt she needed something like that, but she didn't want to put this off any longer. She didn't know exactly what *this* was.

"I wish you could support me on this," she started.

"I love you, Lilly. But if you go through with this," he laughed, "I probably *will* end up supporting you."

"You know that's not what I mean." She traced with her fingertips the curlicues in the little cast iron table between them. When she looked up, he was searching her eyes. She avoided his. They didn't seem to take such constant joy in each other's company anymore. She knew that was supposed to be normal. Why had she started noticing it now? Was she just on some kind of an ego trip, feeling she deserved more than almost everybody else? Or was there some real flaw in her relationship with Zach?

She reached for his glass and took a sip. He jumped up, went back to the kitchen and came back with another glass of Scotch and placed it in front of her. They sat staring at each other, slowly sipping – and waiting for courage? She remembered the exact words Zach had used: *go along to get along*. She didn't agree with that philosophy, though she admitted to herself it wasn't totally crazy. Was she just exaggerating the problem, unconsciously creating a rift between them so she could go somewhere else, maybe go with the man she hardly knew but with whom she felt more comfortable? Why would she do this when Selby himself had refused to give her his opinion. She thought about Selby's tales of street life as a cop. Was she endangering her job, and her whole relationship, over a stolen candy bar?

"Give me two weeks," she said suddenly.

"So, you're still thinking about it." Zach's tone was hopeful.

"Yeah," she said. But she had just told her fiancé a lie. She wasn't thinking about whether she should do the right thing at work. She was thinking about whether she should leave him.

*** ***

One morning, as Kathie walked to the UniCast building with Mallory, as usual, Nell stood expectantly just outside the doorway.

"He-ey!" she called out. But Nell wasn't very good at acting surprised. She had obviously been waiting there for Kathie to arrive. Mallory thought it was pathetic that she'd cling so desperately to a faded love. Women were so much weaker than men like him, who could brush aside past loves and be all the stronger for it.

Kathie gave her an awkward hi but slowed down for only a second before brushing past. "We have to get to our desks in time. Harrison's watching Mr. Mallory like a hawk. I don't want to be responsible for getting him in trouble."

Nell froze for a short minute before she turned and followed Mallory to his cubicle. She waited until he sat down and could no longer ignore her. "It's your fault. You're poisoning her mind against me," she accused him.

"You got her drunk once and practiced a little lezzie hootchie-coo on her. That's all there was to it. Get over it."

"That's so cruel. You used to say we were still friends."

Mallory pointed to the surveillance cameras in his cubicle. "I know you're responsible for these cameras. You're trying to get me fired." He noticed that the goop he'd put on the lenses had been cleaned off. He made a mental note to muddy them up again. "You want to get rid of me even more than Harrison does."

"You're deliberately trying to hurt me by flaunting your friendship with Kathie right in front of my face."

"I'm not trying to do anything but get to work. She gives me a ride every day."

"I hate that you're enjoying it so much, seeing her pull away from me."

He paused. "You're right. I am enjoying this." It felt good to speak the truth. It seemed to be a sign that his character was improving. He guessed he had learned something from his therapy group. "I feel sorry for Koko, living with you."

"You *should* feel sorry for Koko. I'm having him fixed next week."

*** ***

Later that morning, Mallory was startled to see Ms. Marcie standing in the entrance to his cubicle. Shy as always, Ms. Marcie didn't say a word until Mallory looked up in surprise. Her thin, timid figure standing there filled him with anxiety. Harrison, of course, knew that Mallory had written and filed the fake harassment complaint from Ms. Marcie. But corporate personnel was apparently happy to see the whole thing explained away. Corporate had exonerated Harrison. But even a fake complaint could someday raise its ugly head again and pose a danger to his future in the company, not to mention put a possible obstacle in the way of the pending and extremely profitable takeover of UniCast by the Everdine hedge fund. For that reason, corporate had also ordered Harrison to take no further action against Mallory for filing the false complaint. But Mallory was sure Harrison was looking for other ways to get rid of him.

"Um, Mr. Harrison wants to see you in his office right away." Ms. Marcie's tremulous voice revealed she was still shaken by the imbroglio over her sexual harassment complaint. She and Mallory had not spoken a word about it since the day of the meeting with corporate personnel. Mallory was touched by the way she had backed him up in that meeting – and without actually lying. It had never occurred to him to thank her. He guessed he should do that, but he was too worried about Harrison to thank her now.

"I know about the problem with the video cameras in my cubicle," Mallory began before he even sat down in Harrison's office. "It's probably my fault that the lenses got gummed up. You see, they weren't really aimed right, and I tried to fix that, and I might have gotten some stuff on the lenses."

"*Stuff on the lenses?*" Harrison parroted, a mystified look on his face. "I don't know what you're talking about."

"Those cameras in my cubicle. Isn't that what you called me in for?"

"Oh. Yeah. Those cameras. Your co-worker Nell suggested that. I don't think they got them hooked up yet."

Mallory sat silently. He didn't see any advantage in saying another word.

"I called you in," Harrison began, "to congratulate you. As you know, UniCast is a company that is very data driven. Your customer satisfaction rate has risen to 61%. For the last month, you peg out as the fourth highest customer assistant in this office. That's quite a turnaround."

Mallory was stunned. He knew it must be a mistake, but it was such a big mistake he couldn't figure out right away how to take advantage of it. He squinted at Harrison's face in disbelief. He began to think this was a trick, and he should keep quiet.

"Anyway, that's all." Harrison waved his hand like it was time for Mallory to leave. Mallory nodded, stood up, and exited his office. As he passed through the outer office, he caught Ms. Marcie's anxious look and gave her a thumbs-up.

Chapter 31: The Shirt

"Mr. Mallory, I'd like you to come to a dinner my parents are giving for me and Grace." Thomas hadn't settled for their usual quick greeting on the steps but had walked into Mallory's apartment behind him. Mallory was pleased with Thomas's familiarity. The world was becoming more complicated and confusing to him every day. Thomas's friendship seemed to be the one thing he could count on. But the suggestion of dinner with his parents was outrageous.

"They hate me. Why do you want me to go and spoil a nice dinner?" As soon as he said that, he had second thoughts, remembering Ava's cooking. But he kept quiet.

"They want to meet Grace again. Talk to her more, they say. They don't like her, I think. They're always polite, but … it's not looking good."

"So, bringing me is going to make things better?"

Thomas laughed. "I don't know, man. Might take the focus off Grace."

"You want me to be the punching bag?"

"Naw, man. Just take some of the pressure off. She's jumpy about it, says she won't go if it's just me and her."

"Have you talked to your father about the $100,000?"

"Yeah. Good idea. Distract them with talk about the money. Get my father talking about me using my money for my NIL business plan."

Mallory had forgotten what NIL stood for, but he was energized at the mere mention of Thomas's business plan. Mallory's sole source of information about the business world was Spike at the Dough and Go. Spike's tableside banter was full of scenarios of financial glory attained by young entrepreneurs who scorned the plodding advice of the older generation and struck it rich on their quick wits alone. Mallory couldn't remember any of the details of these stories, but he was sure Thomas was one of those budding geniuses.

"But Grace – is she afraid of me? At therapy, they say I stalked her. Is that what she thinks?"

"Don't think so." Thomas's eyes were suddenly downcast. "She told me some of the shit that went down in therapy."

"I followed her for about ten minutes one day after therapy was over. They acted like I was a rapist or something."

"She don't think so. Don't worry about her."

Mallory agreed to go on condition that they all go in Thomas's car. He rode in the back seat of the sporty little compact Honda, even though he would have fit much better in the front. Grace said hello to him nicely and peered around the headrest to talk to him first.

"You should come back to therapy. I think you're the most interesting person in the group."

"But I insulted everybody the last time."

"Oh, Mr. Mallory, you're not the first person who ever stomped out of therapy. In some ways it's like a family. Little kids throw tantrums every once in a while."

Thomas turned and looked at her sharply, but Mallory didn't take offense at the "tantrum" comment. He was more interested in the word *family*. People always seemed to be very interested in that. But he wasn't quite sure he got the concept of family.

"I'll think about going back," he said now.

"Grace, do you ever talk about me in therapy?" Thomas took his eyes off the road again as he spoke.

She met his eyes, then pointed ahead at the road. After he had focused on driving again, she answered. "Yes. A little. Discreetly, of course." Thomas smiled. Mallory too was charmed by her diplomatic response.

Mallory was pleased that the table was set for five, as this meant Thomas had warned his parents in advance that he was coming. He was even more happy that Ava was serving her special barbequed pork loin that he had been dreaming about ever since he first tasted it. The food was so good he had a hard time paying attention to the conversation. Ava seemed to be murmuring to Grace on the side, and Grace was responding like she was being quietly cross-examined.

"I know you lost your mother." Ava's voice was normal again, but still quiet. She extended her hand and slid it cautiously over Grace's. "I know that hurts."

"Oh." Grace held Ava's look as if she were the only other person in the room. She removed her hand only to wipe tears from her eyes. "I try to move on, you know, but I keep thinking about her. I still love her, and I'm afraid if I stop thinking about her, she'll be really gone. Do you think that's crazy?"

"You'll never stop thinking about her. She's in you, honey."

Mallory thought of his own mother. They hadn't spoken to each other since that humiliating public scene six months ago in the courthouse parking lot. His mother had once set him up with a work friend. Unlike Nell, she was a real woman. They had even lived together, but he had lied and lied and even got her to lie for him until he was forced to choose – and he had chosen Koko the cat over her. The only communication he'd had from his mother since then was an email from her saying she could get his torn suit pants fixed at the cleaners. He didn't bother to answer. He wasn't wearing his suits anymore.

Edison, Thomas's father, was too smart to have forgotten that he told his son not to associate with Mallory. He was probably still holding a grudge about all of Mallory's lies. His bulk was intimidating enough, but when encased in his white, short-sleeved shirt, and with his dark blue tie and his wire-rimmed, aviator glasses, he terrified Mallory. But, just as in the party at Thomas's place, he was unfailingly polite, as if he recognized that Mallory had been brought along only to save Grace from an unrelenting parental cross-examination.

He heard Thomas and his father talking about the $100,000

court settlement. Thomas's point seemed very simple. It was his money, and he wasn't going to wait until he was 59 ½ to get it. Edison seemed to believe this simple point had to be weighed against his own 55 years of worldly experience and that Thomas should put the money in a retirement account to assure himself of a comfortable living in his old age.

Mallory had always managed his finances on the theory that he would never get old. After all, his father had died in his late thirties. Ever since his Escalade had been repossessed, he realized that his method of getting a new credit card as soon as he maxed out the last one was not a good long-term plan. He had never taken any courses in school relating to finance, had never watched Suzy Orman or any other financial advice show, never looked up this tedious subject on the internet and had never in his life read a newspaper.

Lately he had depended entirely for financial advice on Spike. Spike often showed Mallory clips of his feats on the soccer field recorded by his friends. He was close to finishing his studies in business at community college. Mallory had bonded with him over their mutual hatred of the hedge fund billionaires who were dictating the lives of every poor drone working in the bowels of the American economy.

Spike was certain he was not going to follow in his father's footsteps as the owner of a small business. The key to escape this drudgery could be found in the world of finance, he often told Mallory. His plan was to get a finance degree from State and then take his MBA at Wharton or Stanford. His father, a first generation Greek immigrant, did not seem impressed with his son's plans to escape the family business. That afternoon, Mallory had taken the trouble to walk the mile and a half to the Dough and Go to seek Spike's advice about Thomas's problem, but Spike had seemed distracted by the televised MLS game playing on the single television screen hanging behind the counter. If Spike had told him anything worthwhile, Mallory couldn't remember it.

Edison was finished his meal and was leaning back in his chair, listening to his son's business plan, but it didn't seem as if he was really hearing it. Thomas explained that he would be the contact person with the track stars and his partner would handle the publicity. If they got into the game first, they would be the go-to NIL for track stars. They didn't even need to make money the first year. Once word got out, investors would be vying to get in on the action. "The whole thing's a new field. Nobody's tried it with track stars yet. But if I don't move fast enough, someone else will."

"What about your studies, son?"

"That's the beauty of business school nowadays. Next semester, an internship at a PR company. The following semester, an internship at my own company. If it goes well, I'll be *in* business instead of in business *school* within two years."

"But this all depends on you getting investors."

"Right, and for that you need three things: the right idea at the right time, knowledge of the business." Thomas smiled. "And charisma."

Thomas explained to his father how he was going to attract investors into his NIL scheme. Mallory didn't understand the plan at all.

"Fake it 'till you make it!" Mallory interjected, too loudly. He was proud he had suddenly remembered the main point of Spike's business wisdom. Ava couldn't have looked more alarmed if he had criticized her food. She excused herself to go back to the kitchen. Grace caught Thomas's eye before quietly following her out to help her in the kitchen. Thomas rushed after her. Mallory was terrified to find himself alone with Edison.

"What do you mean by that, Mr. Mallory?" Mallory was once again shaken by Edison's deep bass voice.

"I … uh. I don't really know. But your son understands all this shit. And I have faith in him."

Thomas came out of the kitchen pulling Grace gently by the hand. Grace rolled her eyes at Mallory. He stood up, hoping the party was over. Before they left, Ava came out and, looking only at Grace, said what a pleasure it had been to get a chance to talk with her. Edison put on a vague smile.

"Shit! Shit! Shit!" Thomas cursed his car into starting.

"What's wrong with it?"

"Not it. Them."

"I thought they were pretty nice," Grace offered.

"You don't know my parents. That's the coldest I've ever seen them."

*** ***

Zach spoke to her again about her problem with McFadden at her job. It wasn't so much a lecture as a series of observations, meant to be subtle, about career paths and getting along with those in power. But she had given up on arguing with him, and his roundabout approach just annoyed her.

She called Selby from her office, but he was on duty and couldn't meet her. She left the office anyway and found herself driving round aimlessly. Then she found herself cruising past one of their lunch places, then his house, then his boat dock twenty miles away. She had a strange conversation with herself as to whether she liked him better in his uniform or his red polo shirt.

She babysat Stephanie that evening so Chub could go to his AA meeting. She knew Chub had his share of problems, but she wanted to warn him that she might be losing her job. Chub was furious when he heard her story. He swore he'd take it up with McFadden.

"Don't do anything stupid, Chub. McFadden's not even in town until next week."

Zach was lying on the sofa, his long arms and legs overflowing the edges, when she got home. "I can't let you throw away your career."

She threw her pocketbook down on a side table and sat down facing him. "Zach, I've been through a lot worse things than losing a job. And I've learned some things. Just now, Chub and I got Stephanie back because we didn't give up. That's how the world works, at least for me. I might lose this job, but I won't give up."

"You are one tough lady, I know. That's why I love you so much."

She waited for him to say she was doing the right thing. He didn't. Was he waiting for her to say she loved him back? She didn't. There were now two reasons why she didn't want to sleep with him that night.

She woke in the middle of the night, strangely calm. She had that dream again about her father in his coffin. Everything in the dream was the same, except her father was wearing Selby's red shirt.

*** ***

"I have a subpoena here for the immediate production of all travel documents, hotel bills, phone records, email records, inter-office memoranda, correspondence and the cell phone of a certain Rory M. McFadden, who we have reason to believe works here."

"Oh." Mary looked frightened. "Oh. There is a Rory McFadden who works here. But he's not here now. He's away at a conference. What did you say your name was?"

"Ramsteel. Attorney Gregory Ramsteel. Mr. McFadden does not have to be here for us to get the material."

"I don't know if I have the authority to give this information out. We have a person in charge while McFadden's out. Lilly Pierce. But she's not in the office right now."

"This is a time-sensitive subpoena. I need the information right now. Anyone in this organization who fails to comply is subject to contempt of court."

Mary's hands were shaking. "Mr. McFadden's cell phone is not here. He always takes it with him when he's away at a conference."

"Well, what have you got, right now?"

"What have I ….? You mean here, in the office."

"Yes. And I'm advising you to stop stalling, Miss. This subpoena requires instant, good faith cooperation."

"I'm the bookkeeper. I have a lot of those records you are talking about. But I think I should phone Mr. McFadden first. Or at least Ms. Lilly."

"No can do. Haven't you ever heard of obstruction of justice? Do you know what it's like to be locked up in the penitentiary?"

Chapter 32: Frost in August

Lilly called in to say she was taking the day off.

"Lilly, please come in," Mary begged her. "I'm so upset."

"Why? You can tell me, Mary. Anything. Did McFadden already fire me? If that's it, just tell me now."

"No. No. But there was this lawyer here."

"Whose lawyer?"

"He didn't say. He had a subpoena for some of our records. McFadden's records, actually."

"Did you give them to him?"

"I had to."

"Maybe it's somebody from the state inspector general's office." She had a quick flash of hope that some government agency would take care of her problem with McFadden. But it quickly faded. "No, they wouldn't even open a case unless he stole more than a quarter million. You know, Mary, I don't care anymore. I have something important to do today. I'll be in tomorrow to start cleaning out my office."

"Don't say that."

Of course, she'd read a lot of books and seen a lot of rom-coms about women whose boyfriends or husbands gradually revealed themselves to be deeply flawed characters just as a nicer man stepped into their lives. But that wasn't her case at all. She suspected most people would agree with Zach: the best thing to do was go along to get along. Of course, most people weren't accountants who had a duty to report the results of an audit to the board. She wished she could quietly get a definitive professional opinion, but she didn't have any close ties to her night school professors, and she hadn't been taking classes this summer anyway. She was reduced to talking to Chub.

Ever since he was a drunken teenager, Chub always acted as if she were on a higher moral plane than he was. When they first lived together, he had tried to help her through every hurdle a kid who had lost both parents would face, all the while drinking his own life away. He always said she was the better person. She used to tell him that was just his excuse for his continued drinking, but he kept up that attitude long after he quit. It was just the way they related.

She and Chub could hardly have a conversation in the daytime now without little Stephanie overhearing, so she called him from the balcony of her apartment late at night. "I don't want to hear this *sister-you-know-better-than-me* talk. Tell me what you think, Chub."

"You asked me about this before. I'm not an accountant."

"Got it, Chub. This is not an accounting question. What should I do?"

"Okay, Sis. If you really want to hear my opinion …. Like I said, I don't know anything about your work, but I know how I've been making all my hard decisions lately. If questions come up, you know, about Janice's drug problem, or protecting Stephanie from her – or anything, really – I try to think about Dad, what he would do."

"Dad never had to face decisions this tough."

The line went silent. It seemed like Chub agreed.

"I know what I'm going to do, Chub. I'm going to think about you, and I'm going to do whatever *you* would do in my situation."

"But I don't even know …."

"I know what you would do, Chub."

This conversation answered only one-half of the questions that were torturing Lilly. As for the other question, she didn't want her life to be a rom-com. What would her father have said about Zach and Selby?

The next morning, she called Selby. He called back right away and said he wasn't going on duty until 4:00. He seemed reluctant to meet her again. He said he had something to do at his house. "What's her name?" she teased.

"It's not like that," he responded. "The damn dishwasher won't drain. You forget, when you buy an old house, that every single thing in it is old."

"I'll buy some carryout and bring it over. I have off today."

She could hear the smile in his voice when he agreed. But she could sense the ambivalence behind that happy note, as if he felt he was giving in to some weakness. She knew he felt something for her, but she didn't know exactly what, and she didn't think another lunch date would be any help in straightening things out.

Incredibly, he was wearing that same old polo shirt when she arrived. He apologized. "I was working on the floor under the dishwasher. I thought I could get it fixed before you got here. Let me change this shirt at least before we eat."

"No. Leave it on, please. I love that shirt."

He cleared his tools off the table, and they wiped it off. She set out his tuna salad sub and transferred her broccoli salad meal from its foam plastic container onto a real plate. He offered her water or soda.

"Don't you have anything stronger? I'm not working today."

"Hey, I'm no high roller like Mallory. No cognac in this house." They shared a quick laugh at the thought of their bumbling friend. He opened his refrigerator. "Hey! I have two beers. Want one?"

He handed her one and opened one for himself. "I've decided what to do at Roofs," she announced quietly. "I've decided to report McFadden. Roofs has been my whole life. My whole life will be different now."

"I knew you would do that."

"I've decided. For sure. It's not a candy bar, is it?"

"No. It's not a candy bar." He pushed his beer aside. "Lilly, if there's anything I can do to help, I'll do it. I swear I'll find you a job. I have a lot of friends, and family, too. It might not be as good as your job at Roofs, but I promise I'll find you something that can at least tide you over until you get one you really deserve."

"You're such a good friend. And I knew you would think like me."

*** ***

Nell reported to Harrison that Mallory had not attended a single Cheer Committee meeting since Teitelbaum left almost six months before.

"Why are you doing this to me?" He blocked the entrance to her cubicle.

She looked up with a stone-cold glare in her eyes. She had lately even started wearing those squarish, black-framed glasses he hated so much. He knew you didn't have to look good if you were an out-and-out lesbian.

"You're being immature, Nell. I had nothing to do with Kathie breaking up with you. I think she just doesn't swing that way. Besides, Harrison loves me now that I have a 61% customer approval rating. He won't give a shit about my Cheer Committee attendance record."

"I'll make sure he cares."

"Nell, what's the point in you hurting me now? I gave you back Koko, the one creature in the world that loved me. You won't even show me pictures of him anymore. You won't tell me anything about him now, except you're having his balls cut off."

"I'll give you an update on that," she sneered. "Koko died on the operating table."

*** ***

Good morning from the UniCast Cable Customer Assistance Department. You have reached the special assistance line of Nell Pickens. You are now speaking to her associate. I can arrange whatever special services you want from Nell at a very reasonable fee. Be sure to leave your credit card number and the address where these services can be performed at the beep. Oh, and if you are calling about cable service, you may as well forget it.

Most people hung up right away, but Mallory wasn't satisfied with that response. Not a single customer complained about Nell soliciting them over the phone. This was not surprising, as UniCast had made it almost impossible to file a complaint. He decided he could say anything he wanted.

Greetings from the UniCast Cable Customer Assistance Department. My name is Nell Pickens. I know this may sound like a man's voice, but that's none of your business. I can't help you with your cable problem, but if you need a cat exterminated, text KOKO KILLER to the following number.

Chapter 33: Resignation All Around

She didn't want to sleep with Zach once she decided to leave him. She wanted to put off telling him for a day or two, so she stayed up late and toyed with a glass of wine out on the balcony until long after the late August light disappeared from the sky. She felt that she shouldn't make alternative plans until after she told him she was leaving, but she couldn't help worrying about where she would live and what she would do for money once she was fired. Zach knew she was unhappy, but he also seemed to know he couldn't do anything about it. He seemed to be waiting for things to blow over.

Zach never condemned McFadden for what he had done with Roofs' finances, but he seemed obsessed over the details of McFadden's personal trips. Lilly didn't know that much about them other than that they were expensive weeklong trips, one to Pocatello and one to Miami, both taken at Roofs' expense and while he was being paid to work.

She had three more working days before McFadden was scheduled to return. She brought boxes to the office and started clearing out her personal stuff. She put the boxes in her trunk, but she left them there, as there seemed to be no point in bringing them back up to her and Zach's apartment. *Zach's* apartment, she decided. She was the one who was breaking up with him. She was the one who should leave. She was hoping she could get severance pay so she could put a deposit on a new place.

"I'm okay with losing my job," she told Chub that evening as they walked Stephanie to the corner ice cream stand near his apartment complex. "You and I have been through a lot worse things than that. But I want to tell you something else. I'm leaving Zach."

"Oh, Lilly! I had no idea." Chub face dropped. He instinctively ran his hand through his combover and stared at her with his mouth agape. But he had to shift his attention away to Stephanie, who was lining up for her ice cream. Lilly knew she couldn't explain, anyway.

"You didn't seem too happy at that surprise engagement party," he offered.

"I think you're the only one who noticed."

Chub ran over to the stand to negotiate Stephanie's purchase. As he walked back to her, holding Stephanie's hand and trying to fend off her offer of a lick of her peach ice cream cone, Lilly realized Chub had no time for a heart-to-heart talk. They never did that anyway. She thought she'd just cut to the chase.

"Chub, you told me I wasn't crazy for reporting McFadden. Can you please tell me I'm not crazy for leaving Zach?"

"You're not crazy, Sis. You can stay with me and Stephanie if you have to."

He called her again that night as she sat on her balcony staring at the parking lot. His tone was anxious. "Sis, whatever you do, do *not* quit your job before McFadden comes back."

"Why are you saying this?"

"We're working on your case."

"Who's *we*?"

"Me and Mallory."

"Oh, God! No!"

"You wouldn't believe this, Sis. He somehow got a copy of all McFadden's travel records and expense reports. We're going to write to the board and expose him ourselves, so you won't have to."

"That sounds creepy to me. Especially with Mallory involved."

"You don't have to do anything. You don't have to know anything. I'm just saying: don't quit, whatever you do."

As she approached her office the next morning, she saw Mary waving a piece of paper and gesticulating for her to come near.

"You won't believe this. I am so happy. McFadden's resigned! Look. Look at this paper. Read the whole thing."

McFadden had resigned to take a new position as Executive Director of the National Alliance of Non-Profit Housing Agencies, or NANPHA, effective immediately. Lilly couldn't repress a loud sigh of relief. She met Mary's eyes, but Mary gestured for her to keep reading.

> *I am also recommending that Lilly Pierce, who has served under me as head of our Division of Finance, and who has held down the fort at Roofs Over Our Heads numerous times as I fulfilled my national obligations, be elevated to become Executive Director as my replacement.*

*** ***

Lilly called Selby and told him she wanted to do lunch again and that she had a surprise for him. He wasn't wearing his red shirt this time. He was in his uniform, and there weren't any tools on his kitchen table.

"You won't believe this." She started talking before they even finished unwrapping the food. "McFadden quit to take another job. He even recommended that I be promoted to his job. This situation has come out, like, better than I ever imagined."

Selby didn't say anything until they were seated. "Wow. That's great. You stuck to your guns and the bad guy chickened out." But he seemed a littler suspicious of the sudden turnaround.

"But here's the part you really won't be able to believe. *Mallory* is claiming he did this. Yes, Mallory. Somehow, he got a hold of McFadden's expense reports. I think he was pretending to be a lawyer again. Anyway, somebody at Roofs – I won't say who – was foolish enough to give the expense reports to Mallory. That's all I know. I'm thinking maybe he blackmailed McFadden. But it's hard to believe Mallory is smart enough to do that."

Selby huffed out a laugh. "Did he tell you how he did it?"

"He didn't tell me at all. Chub told me. And now I'm afraid Chub had something to do with it, too."

"Lilly, I'm glad you don't know anything about how this happened. My advice is: you don't want to find out anything more about it."

"It's possible McFadden just took the chance to take a better job. He'll be making twice the salary he made at Roofs."

"It's very possible. Maybe you should just accept your own good fortune, Lilly. I know you deserve it."

"You *know* I deserve it?" She gave him a somber smile. "You do know a lot about me, don't you?" He didn't answer. She feared he had discovered that hard kernel of pride that she usually tried to hide. She hadn't thought anyone would ever know her that well. But the rush of being truly understood was tinged with fear. The table went quiet. They found themselves eating their sandwiches and talking only about the food. She didn't know how to start the next conversation because she wasn't sure how she wanted it to end.

"My parents lived a simple life," she began. "My life's not going to be like that at all, is it?"

He didn't answer. Why was she thinking so much about her parents lately? What did they really have to tell her? Maybe she had been half right when she ridiculed her mother, at age thirteen, for having such a pat answer for everything. Maybe her father's easy heart came from making so many easy choices.

He put his lunch down, folded his hands on the table like he was talking to a suspect. "I like you a lot. I look forward to these meetings. Afterwards, I remember and think about everything you said."

"I think about you, too."

"So, we're in a bad situation now, aren't we?"

*** ***

Mallory couldn't believe his luck. He was a hero now to both Chub and Lilly. And he was totally enjoying harassing Nell, though none of it seemed to have any effect yet on her frustratingly bland demeanor. Thanks to his customer rating, he was in good stead with Harrison, too. And Kathie didn't seem to mind driving him to work every day. He was still walking everywhere else in the sweltering August heat. He estimated he had lost twenty-five pounds, though he didn't have a scale.

He decided to go back to therapy. He asked Chub to drop him off. The therapy group went silent when he entered the room. He didn't see an empty chair in the semicircle. Grace was the only one who looked him in the eyes. She jostled her chair around to make room for a new one. She smiled at him, so he kept his focus on her and tried to ignore everybody else.

"How's it going with Thomas?" he whispered, but Grace made a sweeping gesture with her hand to indicate he should be interacting with the whole group. "I asked her how her hot new boyfriend was," he practically yelled to the group.

Her little smile showed she wanted to talk about it. "He is hot. He's awfully young, but he's a track star and he's got all these business plans. I like him so far."

"He came to her mother's funeral," Mallory added. "Like none of you did."

"The only thing is, his parents. They're so polite to me, I'm pretty sure they hate me." People smiled. Some laughed.

"That's not such a crazy statement," Sebastian the Facilitator ended the laughter. "Sometimes over-politeness signals caution, which signals fear, which arises from …."

"But let's talk about me," Mallory interrupted. "I've had a pretty good week. I saved my friend Lilly's job …."

"No. Wait." Grace insisted. "Sebastian, you're saying Thomas's parents might be afraid of *me*? That's impossible. You can't imagine how confident, how *solid* they are."

"I don't know his parents, of course. I'm just saying it's possible," Sebastian responded. Grace nodded and put on a sweet little smile that made it apparent to everybody that she didn't really believe it. Mallory was frustrated that the Facilitator was paying attention to Grace's ridiculous worries instead of paying attention to his own recent triumphs.

"I saved Lilly's job," he repeated. "I seem to have an instinct for knowing how to apply the right amount of force in the right place at the same time."

"Exactly how did you do that?" Peter of the Pointy Beard seemed intent on humiliating him again. But Mallory had learned something from therapy. He'd learned that some people built themselves up by tearing you down. He'd learned these people could sometimes get inside your head, and then you end up tearing yourself down. He wondered if that was what had been happening to him all his life, and who it was in his head.

"I did a complicated legal maneuver to save Lilly's job. You couldn't possibly understand it." He looked away. He realized he didn't have to stare Pointy Beard down. He didn't have to fight him, or run away. He didn't have to live in his world at all.

"Still no love life, huh?" Pointy Beard snickered.

"I am currently dating a beautiful French girl named Simone. Dark hair. Spectacular figure. She's learning how to let down her guard and follow her instincts and surrender to me." He was describing the latest porn site actress he followed on his computer every night. He had sworn off that site many times, but it was still his first bookmark, and when he clicked by one night, he was sucked in by Simone's taunting eyes and the lascivious way she licked her lips. Then she sealed the deal with ecstatic yelps and screams that penetrated so deep into his manhood that he signed up to pay an extra $19.99 a month just so Simone would be instantly on call at any moment, on his computer *or* his phone.

Mallory's description of Simone seemed to chasten Peter. Mallory was sure that man hadn't attracted the attention of any woman for decades. He had never seen a porno where a woman was matched with a man with a pointy white beard. But Peter's comment had interrupted his train of fantasy, and people seemed to have moved on to something else. The only thing he noticed during the remainder of the session was that Grace didn't say anything. He was surprised that she made a point of walking out with him.

"I didn't like the way Sebastian brushed off my problems with Thomas's parents," she began.

"Yeah. That really sucked." Mallory hadn't paid enough attention to notice.

"I don't know how I know this, but I know Thomas's parents don't like me."

"Maybe ... give them a chance. I think anybody who got to know you would like you." These words just came out by themselves.

"That's a nice thing to say. Thank you. But let me ask you something. The other night, when we went to Thomas's parents' house, you didn't mention anything about your new girlfriend, Simone."

"Oh. Uh." He really liked Grace. He thought she and Thomas were a perfect match. He decided that when he was with good people he liked, he would tell the truth. "Simone's not a real person, Grace. It was all bullshit. Don't believe everything you hear in therapy."

Chapter 34: Cancellation

Hi! This is Simone de Boudoir. Thank you for letting me share with you all my secret sexual fantasies! Dare to watch me on your screen as I explore the most sensitive peaks and the deepest valleys of my sensual needs. As I feel your eyes on me, we will surrender together to those waves of erotic pleasure that will wash away all our inhibitions.

If you wish to enhance your experience by signing up for my premium French Bliss Experience for a small additional charge of $39.99, please press 1 on your keyboard or touchpad.

If you would like to visit the boudoirs of my horny, lonely girlfriends, press 2.

If you are interested in gay men sex, press 3.

If you would like to change the credit card you use to access my site, press 4.

If you wish to pay by any other method than credit card, press 5.

If you can't reach the site even though your payment is up to date, press 6.

If you want to register a complaint about this website with the FCC, press 7.

If you are calling for any other reason, please hold, and our eager staff will be happy to assist you. Your waiting time at present is 187 minutes.

Mallory hung up in despair. He knew he couldn't afford the cost of even the standard Simone, but he had tried for two nights to cancel his subscription without success. He was pretty much locked into it. He hadn't planned on watching Simone forever. And he suspected Grace might think less of him if she knew Simone was a porn site. His new vow of telling the truth to his friends didn't go as far as telling the whole truth, all the time. He had at least told Grace that Simone was fictitious. He hadn't lied to Grace, just held back a little.

He waited on the landing that evening for Thomas to come home. He no longer believed he was doing Thomas a favor by befriending him. He now knew the opposite was true. Today, he was worried about what Grace had said in therapy. She thought Thomas's parents disapproved of her. Parental disapproval of this type was a totally new thing to Mallory. In the last several years, his mother had absolutely gushed over any woman who seemed to have the slightest inclination to go out with him. He had thought that's what all parents did. He didn't see how anybody could disapprove of Grace, who he thought was much prettier than Simone.

He was excited, as always, to finally see Thomas edge his way through the parking lot and bounce up the steps.

"Sit down. Sit down. Want some water? I still have some cognac in the fridge."

"No thanks, Mr. Mallory. I'm good." Thomas sat down next to him on the front step. "You still trying that cognac trick with the ladies?"

"No. You know that never worked." Mallory smiled, basking in Thomas's friendship. He was surprised to realize he liked having a friend, even a friend who wasn't doing him any immediate good. He had always thought this kind of friendship was a loser's game, and a poor substitute for a romance. But Thomas and Grace were now both his friends. They'd even taken him to a free meal. And, with Thomas and Grace now dating seriously, he felt a strange, vicarious pleasure in their own romance.

"Thanks for taking me to dinner at your parents' house." This was the first time he could remember ever thanking anyone for anything.

"It did me good, too. Gave me some protection." Thomas spread his fingers and held his hands out like claws. "My Mom and Dad, sometimes they can grab you and not let go."

Mallory laughed. "Your father wasn't buying your business plan. You really might have to sue him to get your own money." When Thomas didn't immediately respond, he added. "I mean, with a *real* lawyer."

"No. Listen. I found out there is an actual check, and it's made out to me. My father can't do anything with it without him forging my name. And he would never do that."

"That's great. Let's go get it, right now. Bang on the door. Hell, break the door down if we have to. It's your money, and they stole it."

"What?" Thomas had that wary look he got so often when hearing of Mallory's schemes. "That's a terrible idea. I love my Mom and Dad."

"How can you love them if they're doing this to you?"

Thomas pulled away and looked at Mallory like he was trying to get him in focus. "Man, you don't know anything about families, do you?"

*** ***

She told Zach she was leaving in a strong enough voice to hide her sorrow. "It's not fair to you, I know. We might not agree on everything, but who does?" Because she was the one who was leaving, she told him he should keep the apartment. "I do have a job. I should be able to get an apartment soon. I'll stay with Chub and Stephanie until then."

"Why?" Zach was making it hard for her by asking the hardest question.

"I think we're different kinds of people, Zach. I guess I don't really feel that connection with you anymore." She hated to be talking in generalities that meant, really, nothing. Why was she so worried about hurting him? Hadn't he run roughshod over her feelings?

"It's hard to stay connected when you sit out on the balcony every night until after I'm asleep."

His stupid, reflexive response energized her. "You told the whole world we were engaged when you promised me you wouldn't. I'm a private person, but you didn't respect that. At that engagement party, I felt like I was one of your, I don't know, *clients,* who had to be jollied and pushed along *in public* in order to make the sale."

"You never really wanted to get married."

"I thought I did."

"You think I'm halfway a criminal because I know how business is done."

"That's not true. There are some things you did that I didn't like, some things you said that still rub me the wrong way. I'm not going to give you a list. That would ruin what we had, which was a lovely thing for as long as it lasted."

"So. Now that you know me, I'm not good enough for you. Is that it?"

"I'm so sorry, Zach. I feel like I took something from you, and I didn't give anything back. I'm sorry."

He begged her to keep the apartment, but she was determined not to take that away from him, too. And she couldn't bear living there now. He helped her pack up her things, most of which she was putting in storage. She was encouraged that there was a little edge to him now, as if he were already starting to accept that his life would move beyond the here and now, would move beyond her. She took some comfort in the idea that her image might be already fading a little in his mind.

Chapter 35: Blackmail

Thomas had counseled Mallory that Manly Man's *Nuclear Family/War* website might not be the best place to find advice about dealing with family members. Spike, too, had criticized him for his narrow range of interests on the internet and encouraged him to broaden his knowledge base with information from other sources. Mallory hadn't done anything about this because he thought their advice was too vague, and he was terrified of all the words and images that flashed in front of his eyes whenever he strayed from his porn site or Manly Man. His experience in trying to cancel Simone de Boudoir had amplified his fears.

It was the tragedy that befell Spike that finally convinced Mallory that he might learn something on the internet about the forces that had kept him down all his life. Spike's real name was Spiro, but Mallory knew he was actually a real American because he played in a flag football league and two soccer leagues. He had told Mallory many times that his key to escape the world of the Dough and Go was a career in finance. Mallory vaguely remembered Spike saying he was taking a course at Community Tech over the summer that would complete all the requirements for his AA degree in business.

Spike got Mallory's attention by slamming his dinner on its thick ceramic plate down onto the tabletop in his booth. Mallory jumped back. He was terrified by any sort of violence. He searched the narrow restaurant for Spike's father. He found him on the other side of the counter, a dish towel in his hand. Their eyes met.

"Tell him," Spike's father commanded his son. "Tell him."

Spike ignored his father and went back toward the kitchen to get more plates. His father stood on alert until Spike returned. Spike seemed to have calmed down a little. His father didn't say anything else. Mallory was afraid to say anything until Spike, breathing a long sigh, told him he could order.

"Roast beef with mashed potatoes, three cinnamon buns. No,

make that two. I'm trying to cut down."

After serving his food, Spike surprised him by sitting down across from him in the booth. He glanced back as his father, who turned away. "He wants me to tell you something. First, you need to know I got over 5,000 followers on TikTok. You can almost call me an influencer. And I'm the second highest scorer on the school soccer team. And I got business savvy. And I got the ambition to go to the top. But I didn't get into the business program at State."

All Mallory knew about State was it had to be a good school because Lilly and Thomas went there. But he was under the impression that anybody could go to college. "Why not?"

"I'm the wrong color, and the wrong sex, and I'm not an illegal immigrant or gay or trans or non-binary, or in any government-protected group. Any of those people can get into any college, as long as they're WOKE or LGBTQ." Mallory had no idea what Spike was talking about. "And the government will pay for it, too."

"What?"

Spike explained in a low voice that there was a conspiracy between the universities, the government and the media to keep people like him from advancing. Mallory was shocked. He had thought it was just the Algonquin J. Tycoons of the world that were keeping ordinary people down. It was apparently a much bigger problem. Spike told him of several websites that were exposing this conspiracy. He recommended especially one called *The Real Honest God's Truth*. Mallory wondered why he hadn't ever heard of it before. Spike talked in almost a whisper, looking all the time over his shoulder to see if his father was listening.

"Why don't you want your father to hear?"

"He's old. He's set in his ways. The old ways. He blames everything on my C-plus average."

Mallory walked home and stayed up until after midnight researching the WOKE and LGBTQ and other even more frightening conspiracies. He found out from *The Real Honest God's Truth* that WOKE was a secret government agency whose goal was to replace all regular white people in jobs and colleges and government and the media with "people of color," whom Mallory assumed to be Mexicans, or with LGBTQ. He had no idea who LGBTQ was. He was shocked to find out these conspirators had already taken over much of the country. They were also in control of all the newspapers and news channels and all the online information sources. That part didn't bother Mallory too much, as he had never read a newspaper or listened to a newscast or followed anything online that didn't have to do with sex. But that night, he also learned from *The Real Honest God's Truth* that LGBTQ was trying to outlaw even talking about regular men and women. By the time he finished reading about the secret WOKE agency and LGBTQ's rulings, he wasn't sure he would even be allowed to marry a white woman – or a woman at all.

For the first time in his life, he understood why he was at the bottom of the totem pole. It wasn't his fault at all. The conspirators who ran the government had planned all along to force him to live in a low-grade apartment with a low-grade job and no car and no wife and no girlfriend, and not even any pet. And now they were doing away with women, the last source of comfort left to ordinary, manly men like himself and Spike.

"This explains everything," he was murmuring to himself as he groggily stumbled his way toward the spot where he met Kathie's car each morning. But he decided not to tell Kathie. Kathie was an ordinary person, he knew. She wasn't part of any conspiracy. It was enough that he had this special knowledge of how the world really worked. He wouldn't tell Thomas either, or Lilly, or Chub, or Selby. None of them were part of the conspiracy. It was enough that he knew.

*** ***

Lilly was too exhausted to check her email before she arrived at

Roofs the next morning. Chub had slept on the sofa so she could use his bed. Stephanie had crawled in with her in the morning, asking why she was there, and why she was crying. She hugged her niece and said they were happy tears, and it was halfway true. When she arrived at work, Mary jumped out of her seat and hugged her and made such a fuss that half the staff on the second floor came and hugged and congratulated her until they got her crying again. Not a soul seemed sorry McFadden was gone. She walked into the director's office, now her office, and sank down into the comfy swivel chair with a giant sigh of relief. She honestly thought she could do a better job than McFadden, and the staff seemed to be on her side. But she was exhausted. Then she read the email from McFadden at the top of her incoming messages.

Well played. If my wife ever finds out about Gwendolyn in Miami, I will bring criminal charges against you for your blackmail. I never want to speak with you again.

*** ***

"How's it going, Thomas? How's that nice little piece you're dating?"

"She's no *piece*."

"Sorry." He truly was sorry. "She's a nice kid."

"She's not a piece. She's not like all these drunk college girls. She's helping me get together my NIL plans. She likes my business idea. She's solved some internet problems I didn't even know I had. She'd be my business partner even if she wasn't …."

"… a piece."

Thomas did laugh. "Okay. She's hot, too." But Mallory noticed he didn't seem happy. He thought he had made great strides in therapy if he could tell the mood of a Black person. They had all been blank screens to him before. Then again, so had pretty much everybody else in the world.

"I got a problem with my parents," Thomas admitted.

"The $100,000? It's yours. We can go get it."

"No. Not that." They were sitting on the steps, as usual. Thomas was staring out at the parking lot. His face looked creased with worry. This was a look Mallory had never seen on him before. "I … uh …. Look, you're my friend, right?"

"Right."

"Not just my *white* friend?"

"I'm your friend."

"Well, I'm gonna tell you something. My mother and father, they're nice and all to Grace. They say they like her. But they want me to drop her."

"Why? You just told me she's so great."

"They say that, too. But they want me to drop her."

"But why?"

"I don't tell this to nobody but you. They won't say why. Oh, maybe they do, but it's in code, you know. But I know their code. They think she's too white."

*** ***

Mallory was shocked to see Chub standing at the entrance to his cubicle, wringing his hands, but even more surprised to see Lilly standing next to him. They didn't waste time with greetings. "We have to talk outside."

"Outside? It's 95 degrees outside."

"Outside."

Mallory sighed and grumbled as he followed them through the lobby and outside until they were standing in the parking lot under the merciless August sun. Lilly's white blouse was wrinkled, and he could see semicircles of dampness at her armpits. He knew he had looked the same way when Kathie had picked him up that morning. Chub was pushing his combover back from falling in his face. He stood to the side and a little behind Lilly, with his head down as if his little sister had just chastized him.

"What's this all about?"

Lilly looked like a disheveled but angry schoolteacher. "You have committed a crime, Mr. Mallory."

It wasn't the first time he had been accused of that. This was the point where he usually punched back hard at his accuser. But he felt weak now because Lilly, his friend, was the accuser – and also because he didn't know what she was talking about. "What crime?"

"Okay, I know your intentions were good, yours and Chub's." Chub seemed to study his shoes as she went on. "You were trying to help me. And it was pretty good detective work to find out that McFadden was cheating on his wife in that hotel in Miami. I still don't understand how you did that." Chub, still looking at the ground, shook his head like he also didn't understand how they did that. "McFadden has resigned, and basically given me his job."

"Oh, that's great!"

"It's not great that you blackmailed him, threatened to tell his wife. That's a crime. I got his job because of your crime."

"Oh." Mallory hadn't considered that what he did was a crime. He hadn't committed any crime on purpose, except for pretending to be Attorney Ramsteel. "I guess he deserved what he got. And he's gone. And you got his job. And his wife's none the wiser. It's a win-win-win for everybody. Right?"

Lilly batted her palm against her forehead several times, the frustrated teacher again. "Okay. Okay. We all lucked out. But I want you to say here, right in front of me and Chub, that Chub and I had nothing whatsoever to do with blackmailing McFadden."

"You and Chub had nothing whatsoever to do with blackmailing McFadden. I did it all myself." The conversation came to a halt. But Mallory felt that wasn't the whole story. He wanted to finish it. "And do you want to know why I did it?"

Lilly bit her lip.

"Because I love you. Chub and I, we both love you."

Chapter 36: Love is What?

Mallory preferred not to think about exactly how he had saved Lilly's job. It was enough that she knew he had saved her. Of course, he didn't want his heroics to go entirely unnoticed. When Kathie picked him up the next morning, he told her he had intervened at Roofs and kept Lilly from being fired.

"Oh, sure." Kathie didn't seem like she believed it one bit.

"Ask Chub."

She came to his cubicle mid-morning. "I'm taking you out to lunch."

"They don't have cinnamon buns in the break room anymore."

"Not the break room. I'm taking you out. Name a place you'd like to go."

Spike was not on duty at the Dough and Go, so his father waited on them. He smiled a hello to Mallory and didn't even leer at Kathie's glorious crown of blonde curls like Spike would have done. Mallory felt a sort of relief that he didn't have to explain their relationship to anyone. They were just there to eat. And, of course, he was there to eat up Kathy's praise.

"You have some kind of weird talent," she said now. "You saved Chub's job twice. Now you've saved his sister's job." He really liked the way she was looking at him.

"I don't know what it is," he admitted. "I don't know what I'm doing half the time."

"I used to think you were just a blowhard. But you convinced me to fake Chub's job for two weeks, and it really worked. And I felt good about helping, too."

Mallory had forgotten that Kathie played a part in saving Chub from being fired. She too had talent, he realized. And he thought he should probably thank her for picking him up and taking him to work every day.

"I don't mind, if somebody's in trouble. Do you have any chance of getting a car somehow?"

He decided not to lie. "Not really. Not unless I get a raise or something."

"Well, it's nice for me to have someone to talk to in the morning."

"You're the only person at work who talks to me now, except Chub. Nell hates me now. She thinks I turned you against her."

She cast her eyes down. "I know. I feel so guilty about her."

"You shouldn't. She got you stone drunk that night."

She jerked her head from the road to face him. "How do you know about that night?"

"I was there, remember? Cat sitting? You came in the house plastered."

"But you left before …. I don't want to talk about that night."

Other than his platonic talks with Lilly or Grace, which didn't count, or his hateful bickering with Nell, which was even more worthless, Mallory had not had such a long conversation with a woman in months. Kathie looked him in the eyes like he was a real person, not some ogre to be avoided. He wished he had worn his suit.

"I wonder if I can get a better job, if I try." Of course, according to *The Real Honest God's Truth*, he was the wrong color and the wrong sexual orientation and carried the wrong immigration status to ever get a decent job. But *The Real Honest God's Truth* seemed to fade into the background when he was talking to Kathie.

"No! Do not get another job. We need you at UniCast. You're the only one who can keep management straight."

He thought she might be flattering him. He started allowing himself to imagine those thick, blonde curls crushed against his pillow. But she was too independent and self-assured to be tricked into bed by his usual methods. Not to mention that she was three inches taller than he was. He thought he was having just another pathetic fantasy. Until she asked him to meet her for dinner.

Of course, she had to pick him up. They had burgers at a little bistro that got noisier as the evening progressed. When she offered to buy him a beer, he tried to defer.

"What? Beer not good enough for you? Oh, that's right. I hear you're a cognac man," she smirked.

He grabbed the bottle off the table and took a gulp. "Nell's told you everything?"

"She told me you were always pushing cognac on her."

"Yeah. Wasting it." Just the thought of Nell was ruining his mood. "She's trying to get me fired. But I have the fourth-highest customer satisfaction rating in the Customer Service Department."

"I know," she said. "Sixty-one percent." She met his eyes and held them. "And it will be sixty-eight percent next month."

He stared back at her in bewilderment. "*Next month*? How could you possibly …?"

"Who do you think does the statistics?"

Kathie's apartment was spacious but sparsely decorated. It did have a view of the lake, as Nell had told him long ago, but you had to strain your neck to see it. She sat on the sofa across from him and offered him just a soda. He had no idea what she had in mind.

"Kevin, I want to apologize to you. All that time you were cat sitting for Nell and I – I had no idea she was leading you on."

"I was kind of lost, I admit."

"I hope I didn't make it too much worse for you."

He didn't try to take advantage of her guilt. He sympathized with her own misery and regret over the whole Nell affair. It must have been bad for her, too. Strangely, he didn't mind that their date had morphed into such a somber discussion. He was interested in learning how she rode out these unpredictable storms that now seemed to affect almost everybody. It might take a long time to figure her out. He could tell by her attitude he wasn't getting in her bed that night, but he didn't mind. Maybe that would happen another night. He thought he could suppress for a while his urge to find out if she was a screamer.

*** ***

When Lilly had confronted him about blackmailing McFadden, Mallory had taken the blame for that illegal act. He thought it was worth suffering Lilly's wrath if he at least got credit for saving her job. But a few days after being reamed out by Lilly in the parking lot, Attorney Ramsteel visited a financial firm downtown. He asked for one of their top salesmen by name. He was told he had to wait for Mr. Prescott. Zach Prescott. An office assistant led him to an office with thick, soundproofed walls, heavy wooden doors, heavy wooden chairs, and a pretty good view of the city. There were apparently no cubicles in Zach's world.

He was testing out one of the chairs when Zach appeared. "Mr. Mallory? What are you doing here? I was told there was an Attorney Ramsteel here to meet me."

"One and the same."

"What's going on, Mr. Mallory?"

"Acting as Attorney Ramsteel, I tried to get information out of Roofs to save Lilly's job."

"Lilly told me you blackmailed McFadden." Zach's face curved into a wary half-smile. "More power to you."

"You know I didn't do it. I'm not that smart."

"What are you saying?"

"Somebody a lot smarter, somebody who has access to an IT department, and all kinds of computer geniuses at his workplace, got a whole lot more information than I did, including the name of McFadden's mistress – all probably illegally."

"Why are you here?" Zach's voice suddenly lost its tone of breezy natural assurance.

"I want to know what kind of man you are, Zach."

"Are you blackmailing me? So, fuck it! I'll tell you right now, I'm not sorry for what I did. People like Lilly need somebody like me to protect them."

"But she threw you over."

"Then she needed my protection even more."

Mallory was totally shocked. "So, what do you get out of it? Really, I don't get it."

Zach put his head in his hands. "I don't know. I don't know." His words seemed to leak out slowly and sink onto the table. "I just couldn't bear to watch her lose everything she's worked so hard for."

*** ***

Lilly found an apartment within a week. It was much smaller than her previous one, had no balcony, and some of the appliances were old. At least it was on the tenth floor and full of sunlight. And it was still better than almost all of Roofs' 125 apartments. She signed a one-year lease. She couldn't fit all her stuff in, so she just left the rest of it in storage. She knew it was not the financially wise thing to do. She had constantly advised clients never to pay for rental storage space for stuff they would likely never use again. But she was too tired to argue with herself.

She missed Zach, but she was sure she would never go back. She was afraid even to think about Selby. It had been exciting, but sad, to be living with a man she had doubts about while dallying with an attractive stranger. She worried that any stranger she might have met in that situation would have seemed like the cure. Selby had seemed like the cure, but now she was literally in a different place, and she had a different job, and she had a niece she hadn't paid enough attention to. She didn't want to deal with Selby until she knew who she really was.

She didn't have any trouble occupying her mind with other thoughts. The staff at Roofs seemed intent on flooding her with their joy that McFadden was gone. She felt almost the same relief, but she knew she couldn't show it. Mary was the only one she sometimes shared a secret smile with. She worked late most nights, as she always had, but she was learning how to delegate some of her duties to her competent staff. She used her new authority to change her schedule so she could share a few afternoon hours a week with Stephanie. She socialized with her and Chub on weekends.

Selby called her exactly a month after she moved out. She thought she'd be nervous, but it was just the opposite. He seemed exactly the same, which gave her confidence that she was the same person, too. She seemed to remember everything they had ever said to each other. She smiled to remember every part of that gorgeous afternoon on the river when they had lain lazily sprawled across his boat, rocking gently in the soft swell, their heads two feet above the water, watching the jellyfish jelly their way to nowhere. She remembered him falling asleep then. Their phone conversation seemed to flow on that same current still. She feared that she liked him so much she wouldn't have room in her heart for everything else she loved. But she decided she'd take a chance on that.

Tom Keech has written eight novels – about state politics, teenagers entangled in suburban corruption, college romance, the medical board's prosecution of a predatory physician, the political dystopian series, The Red State/Blue State Confessions, and now the Kevin Mallory series.

His previous life included careers as a juvenile counselor, a legal aid attorney, an administrative law judge and an Assistant Attorney General for the State of Maryland. He is currently a member of the Ethics Review Panel of his local school board and a founding member of the Willing Writers of Annapolis.

CPSIA information can be obtained
at www.ICGtesting.com
Printed in the USA
LVHW050721200423
744813LV00010B/26